BAD KITTY

Camp Daze

NICK BRUEL

A NEAL PORTER BOOK
ROARING BROOK PRESS
NEW YORK

For Jim, Catherine, Zoe, and Astrid

Library of Congress Control Number: 201794447

ISBN: 978-1-62672-885-1

Our books may be purchased in bulk for promotional, educational, or business use. Please contact your local bookseller or the Macmillan Corporate and Premium Sales Department at (800) 221-7945 ext. 5442 or by e-mail at MacmillanSpecialMarkets@macmillan.com.

First edition 2018
Printed in the United States of America by LSC Communications, Harrisonburg, Virginia
1 3 5 7 9 10 8 6 4 2

• CONTENTS •

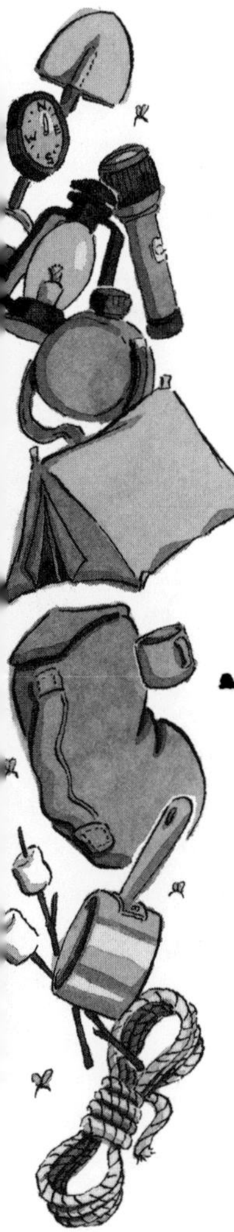

•CHAPTER ONE•

ONE FINE AFTERNOON

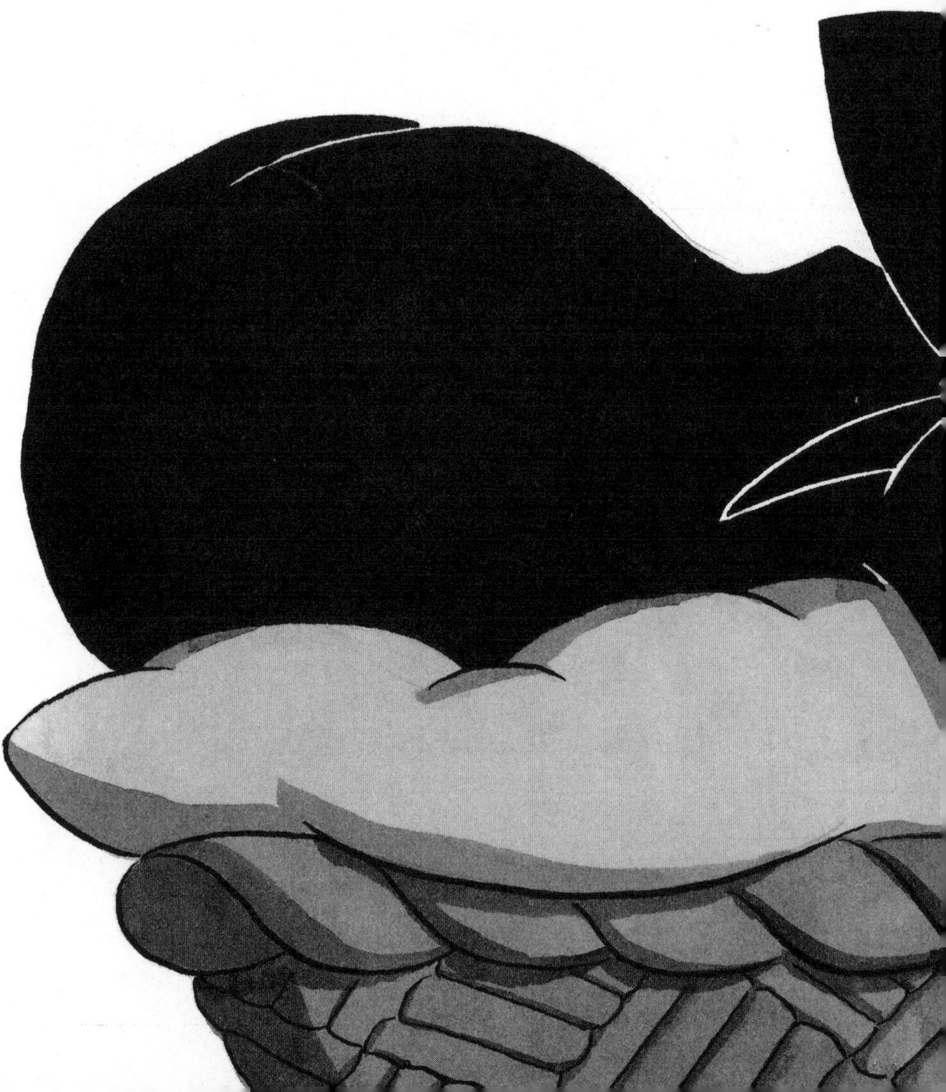

Good morning, Kitty!

Or perhaps I should say, "Good afternoon," seeing as it's 3:00 pm and morning ended hours ago.

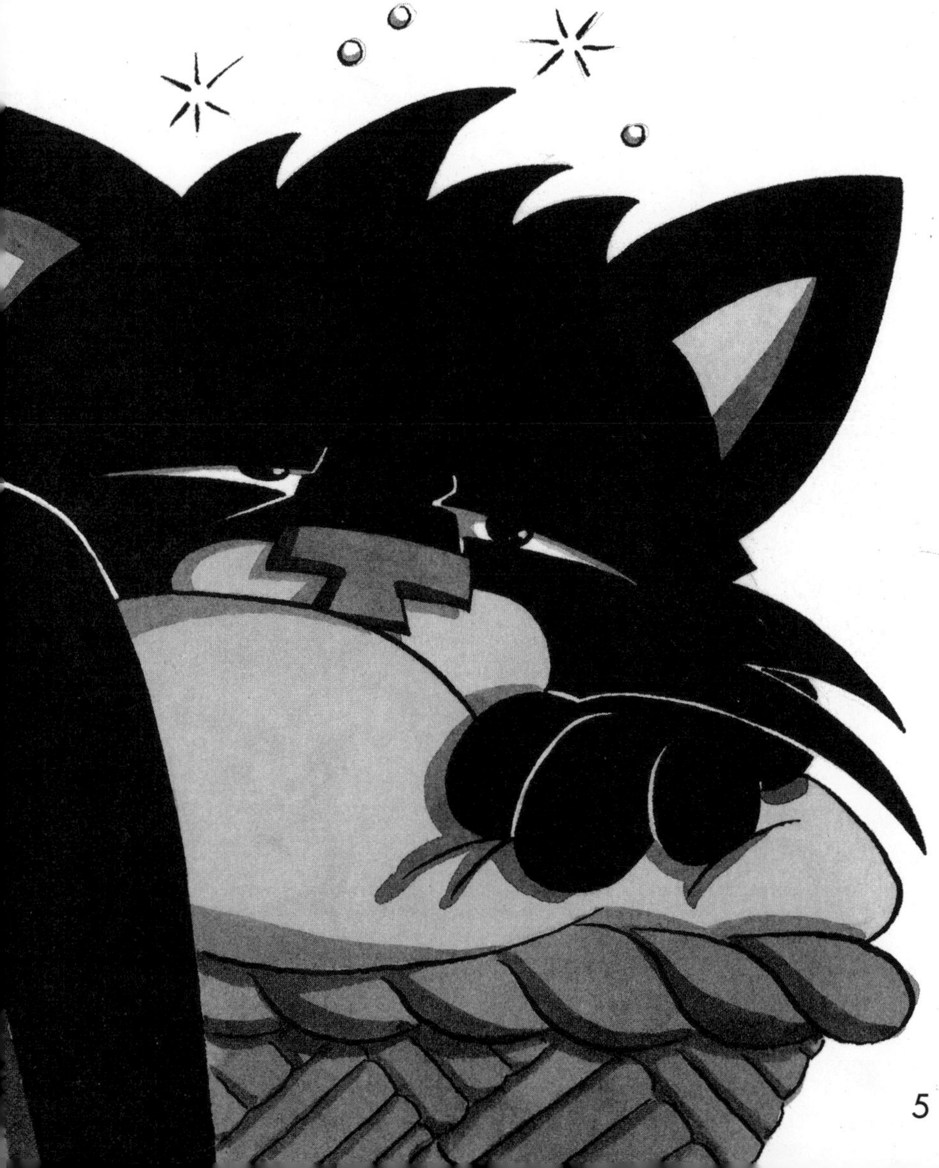

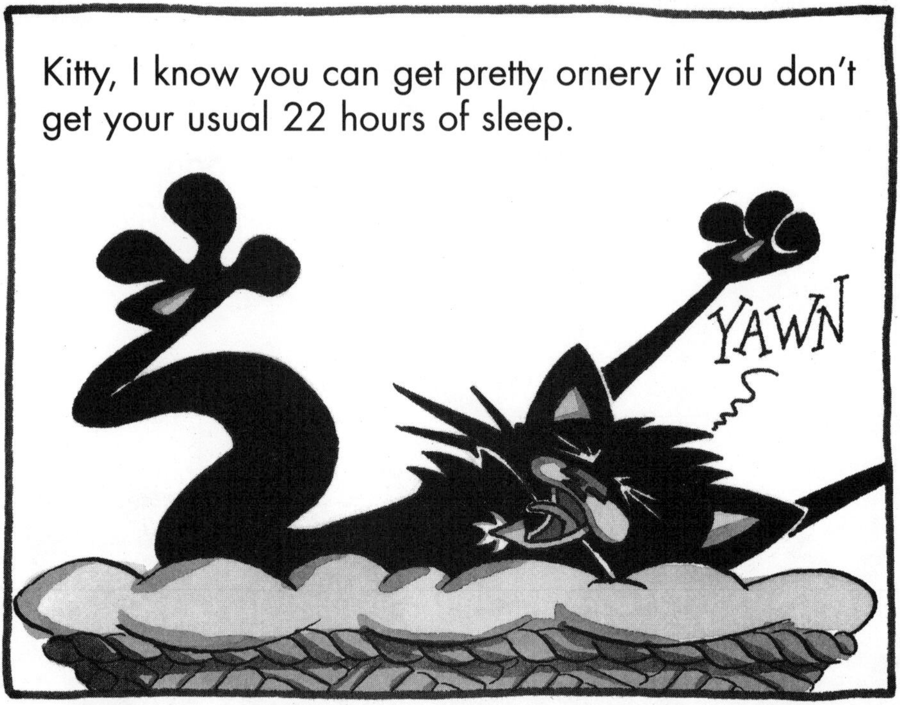
Kitty, I know you can get pretty ornery if you don't get your usual 22 hours of sleep.
YAWN

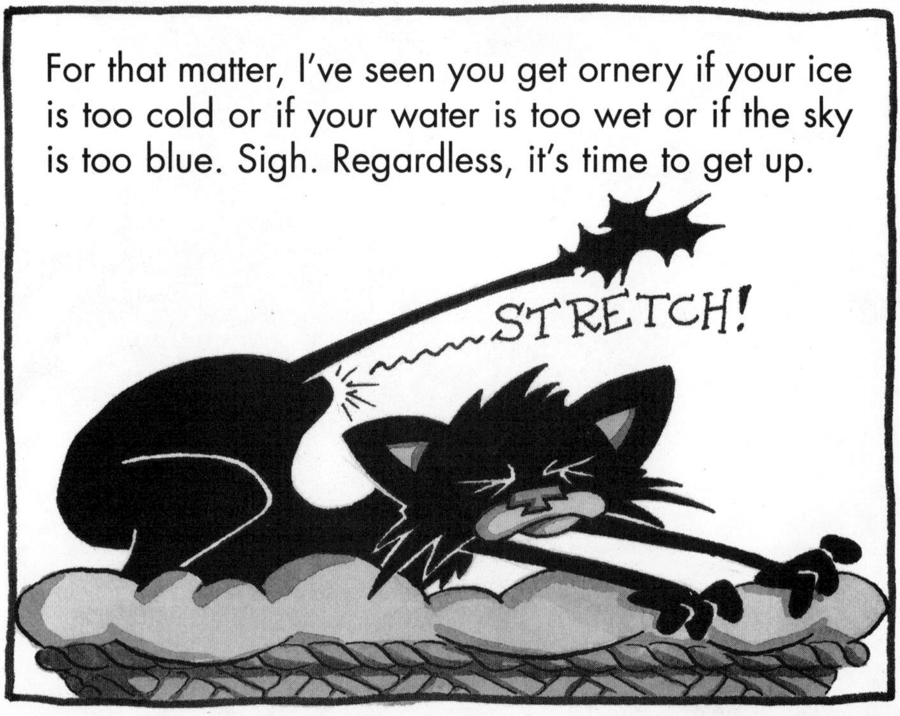
For that matter, I've seen you get ornery if your ice is too cold or if your water is too wet or if the sky is too blue. Sigh. Regardless, it's time to get up.
STRETCH!

Besides, your breakfast is ready, and I have a really, really, really BIG surprise for you today!

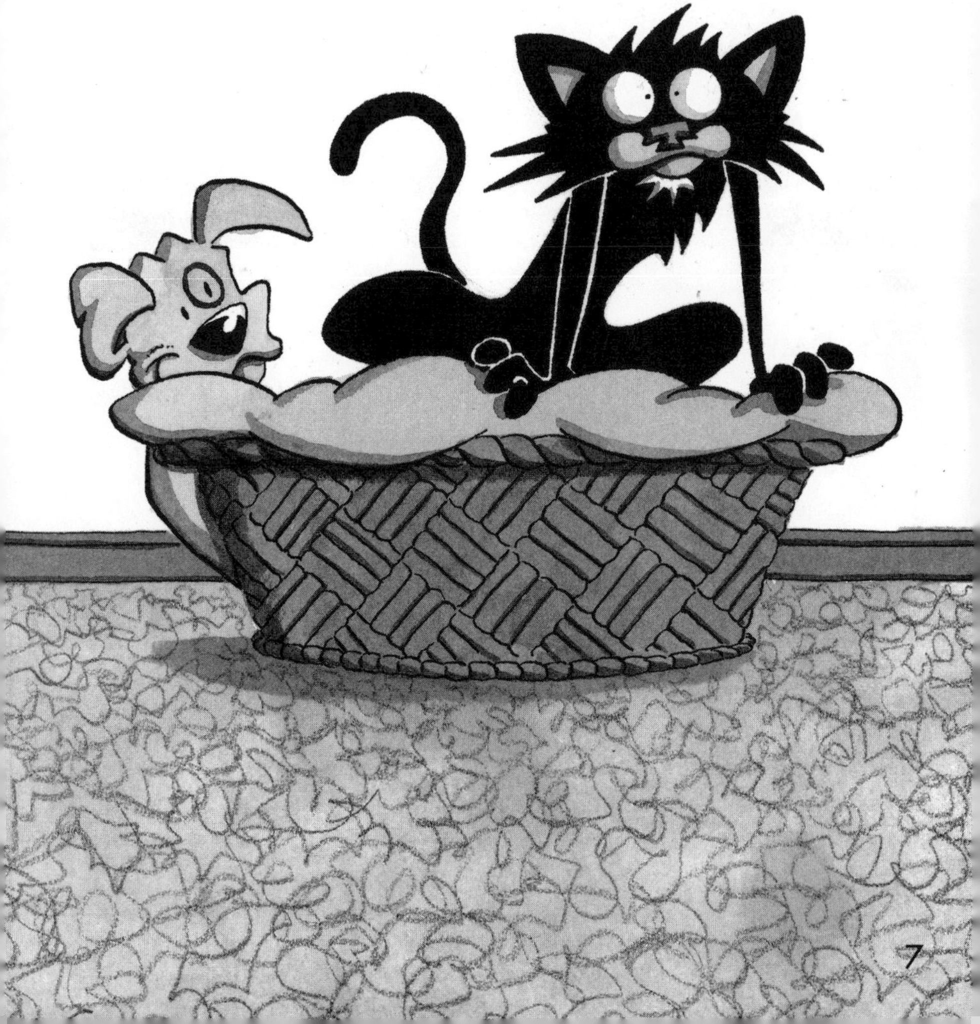

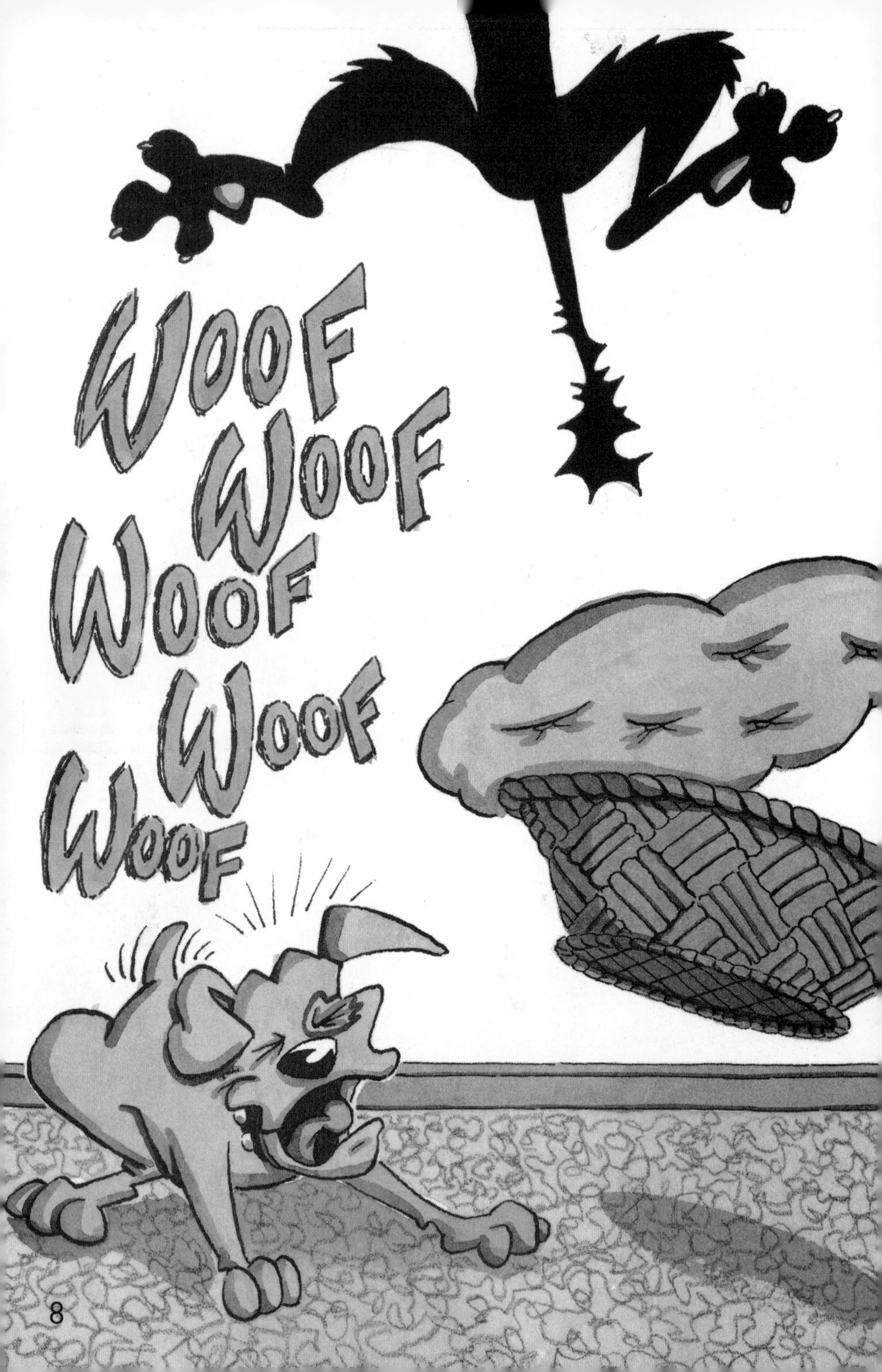
WOOF
WOOF
WOOF
WOOF
WOOF

Sorry, Kitty. That wasn't the surprise. Are you okay? Puppy has been waiting patiently all day to play with you, and I guess he got a little excited when he saw you were finally up. The really, really, really BIG surprise is . . .

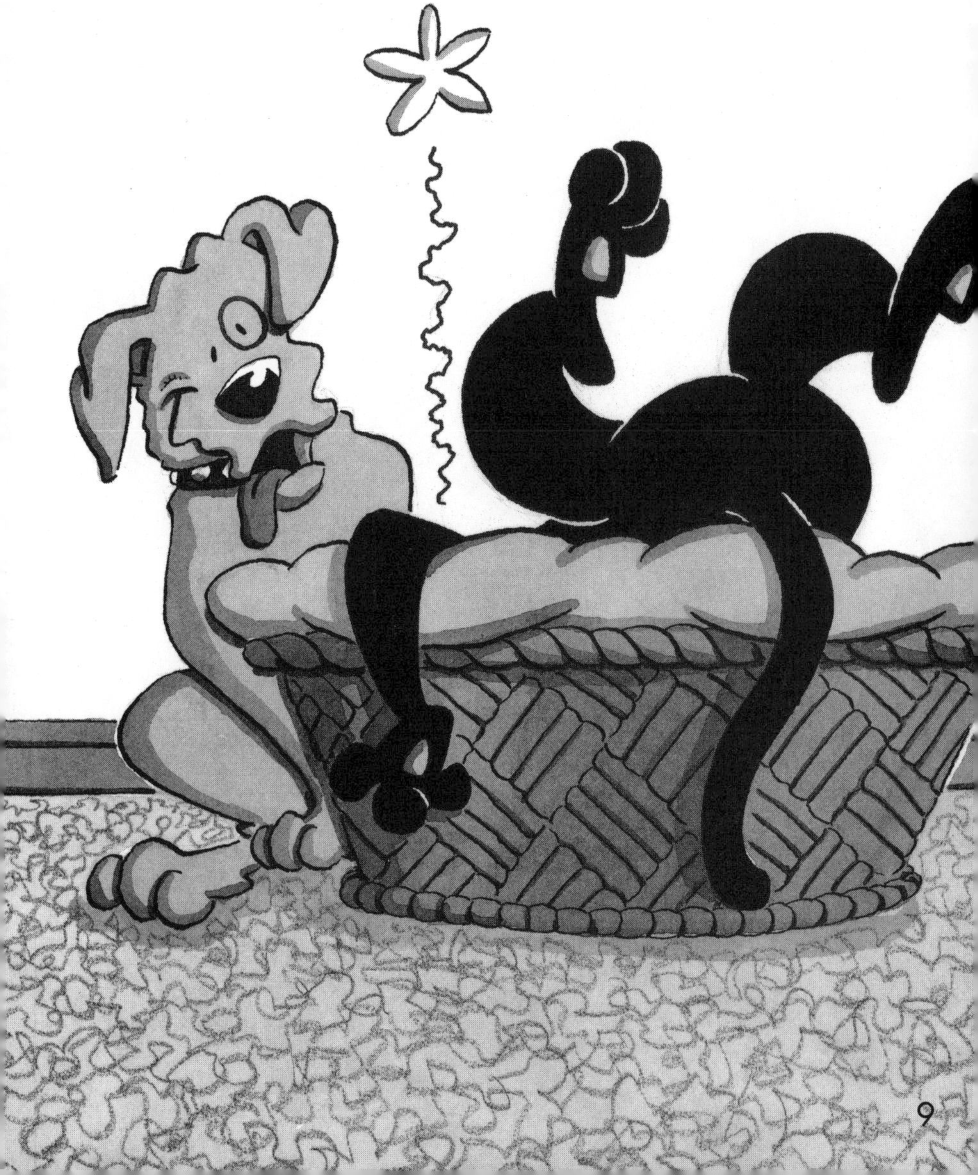

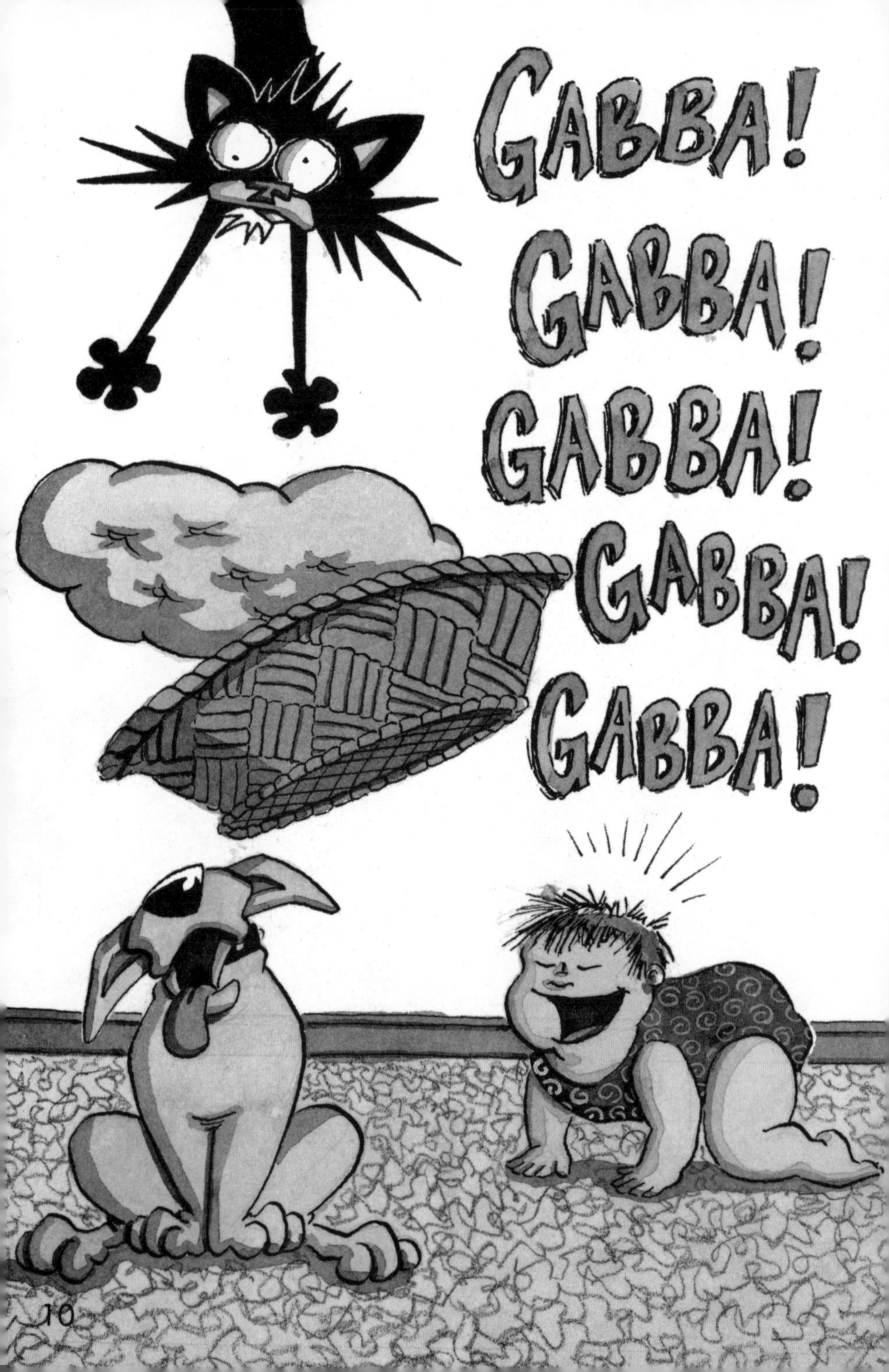
GABBA!
GABBA!
GABBA!
GABBA!
GABBA!

Sorry again, Kitty. That wasn't the surprise either. Baby has been waiting patiently all day to play with you, too.

Are you sure you're okay? That's twice now that you've landed on your head.

Anyway, the really, really, really BIG surprise is . . .

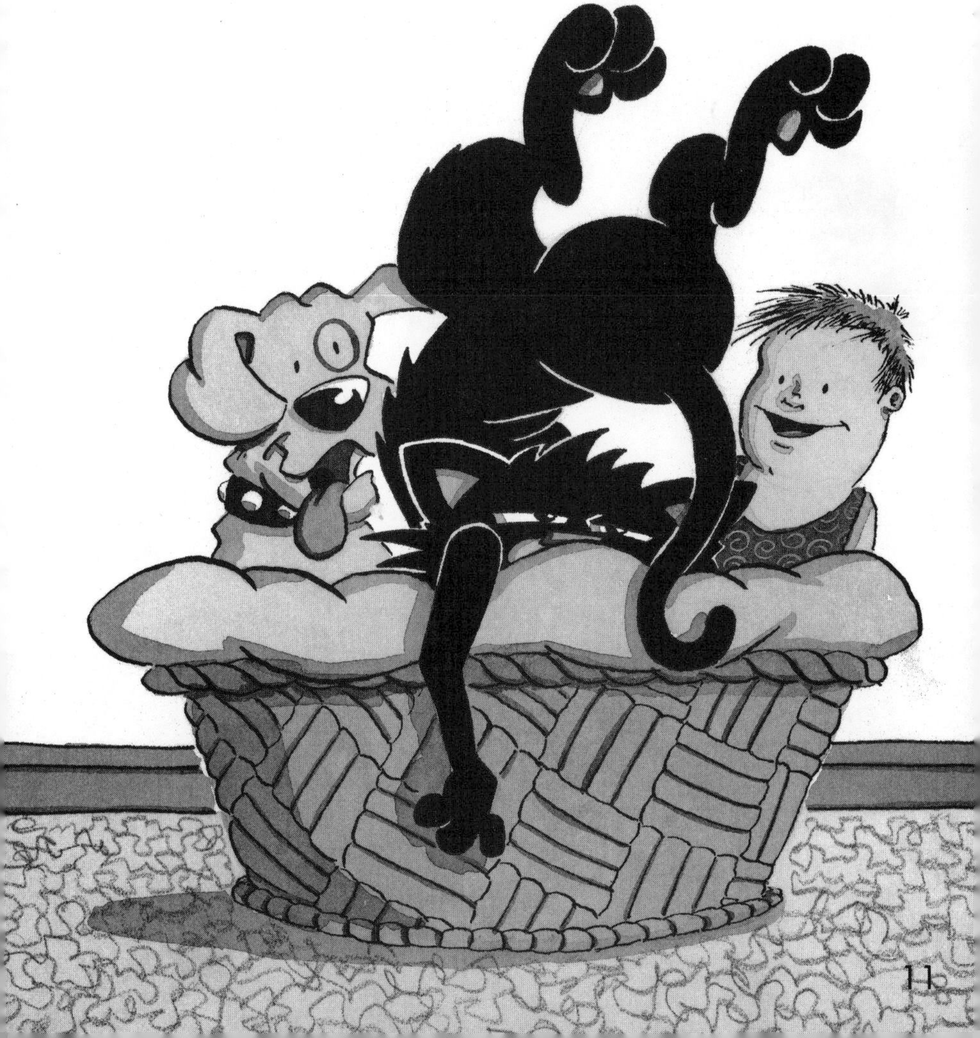

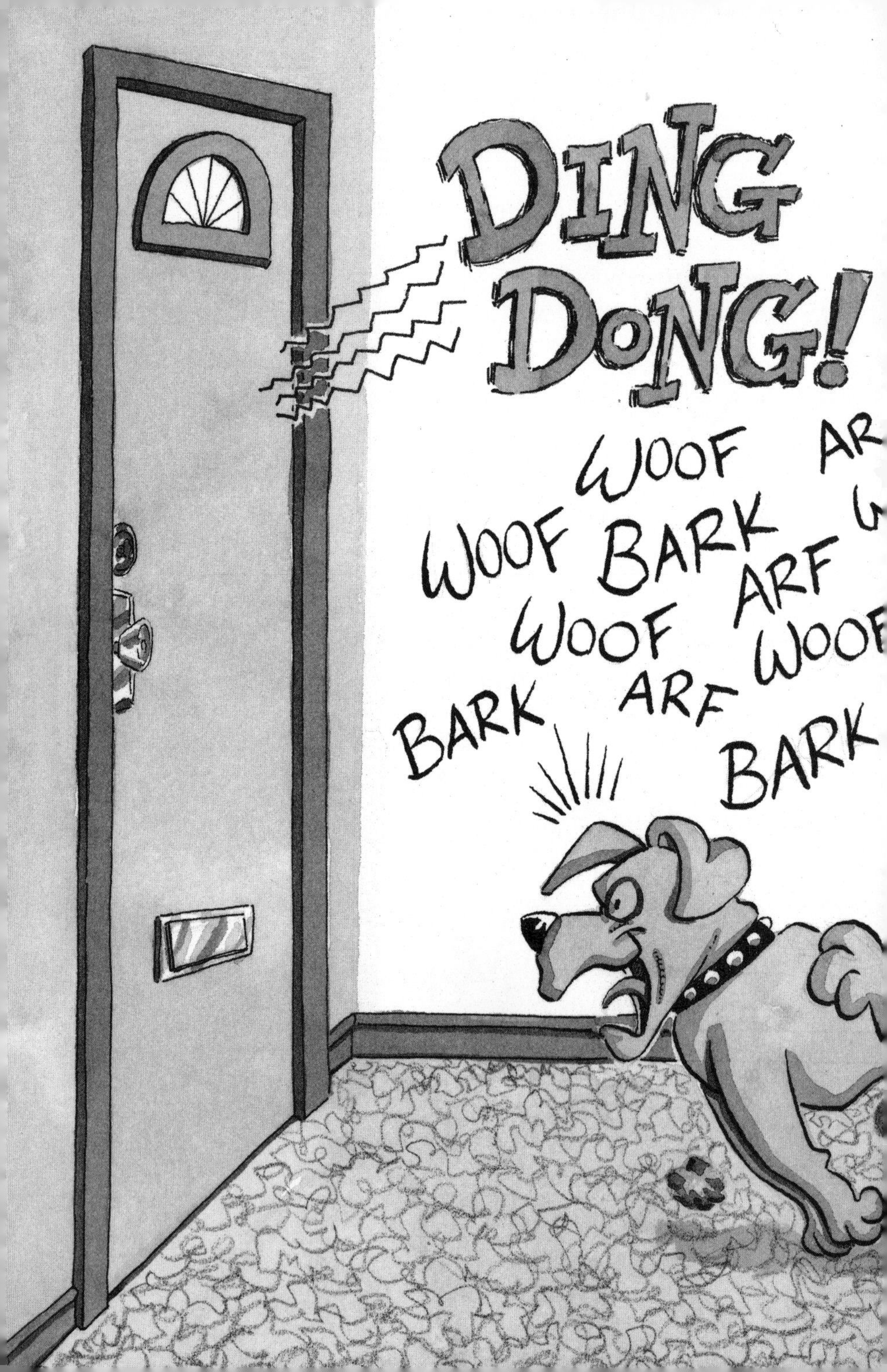
DING DONG!
WOOF
WOOF BARK
WOOF ARF
BARK ARF
BARK

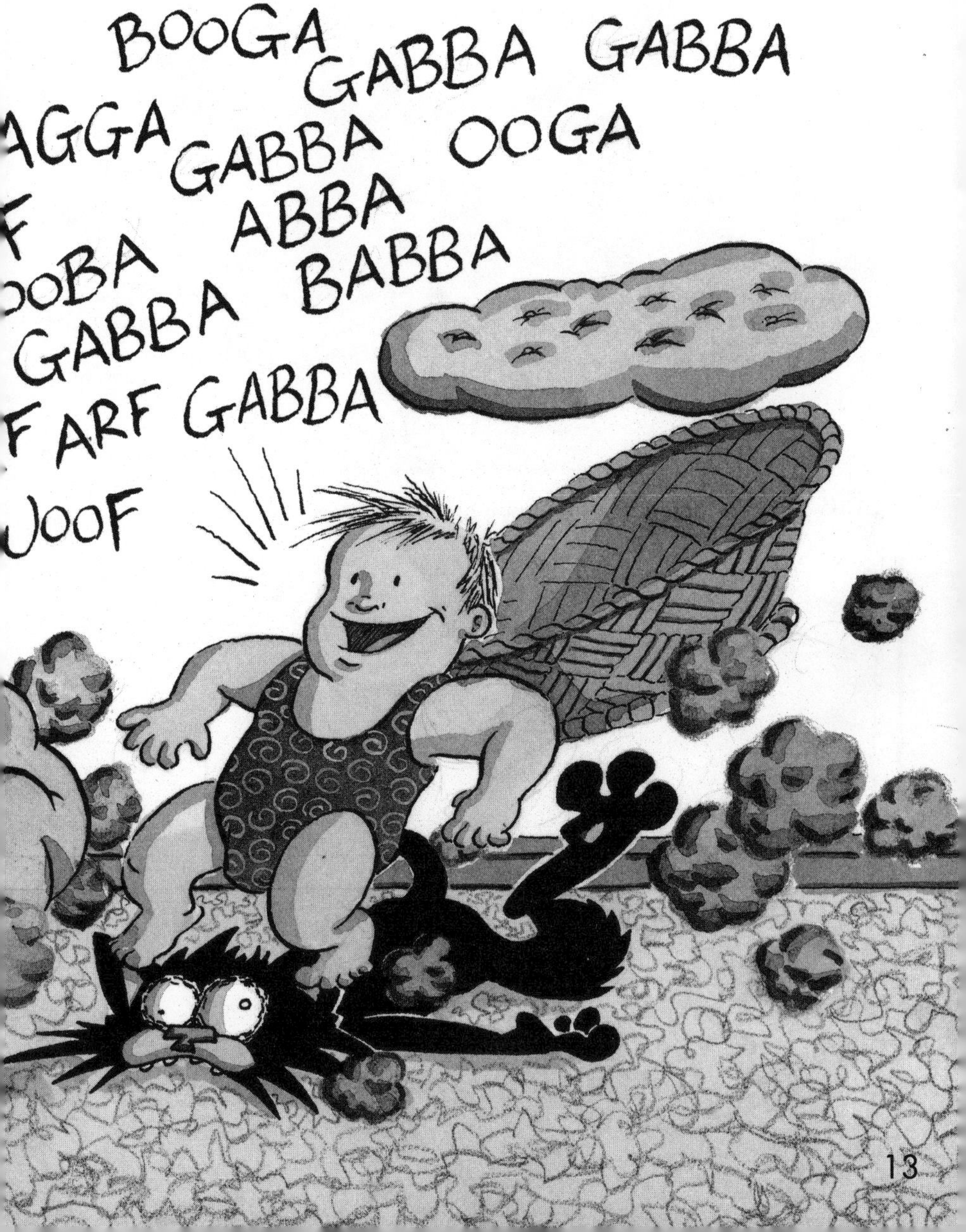
BOOGA
GABBA GABBA
AGGA
GABBA OOGA
F
ABBA
OOBA
BABBA
GABBA
FARF GABBA
JOOF

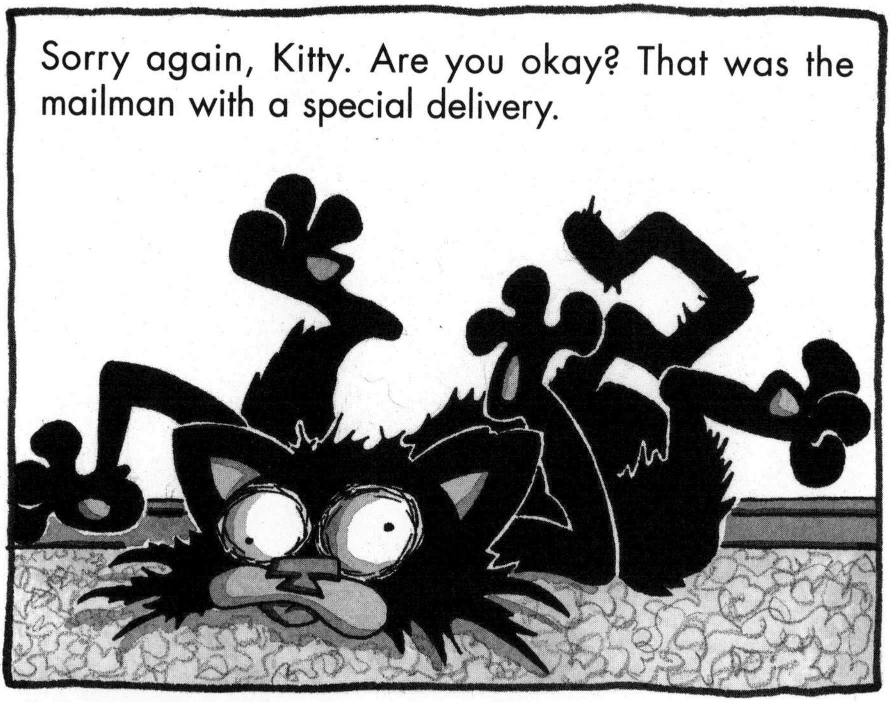
Sorry again, Kitty. Are you okay? That was the mailman with a special delivery.

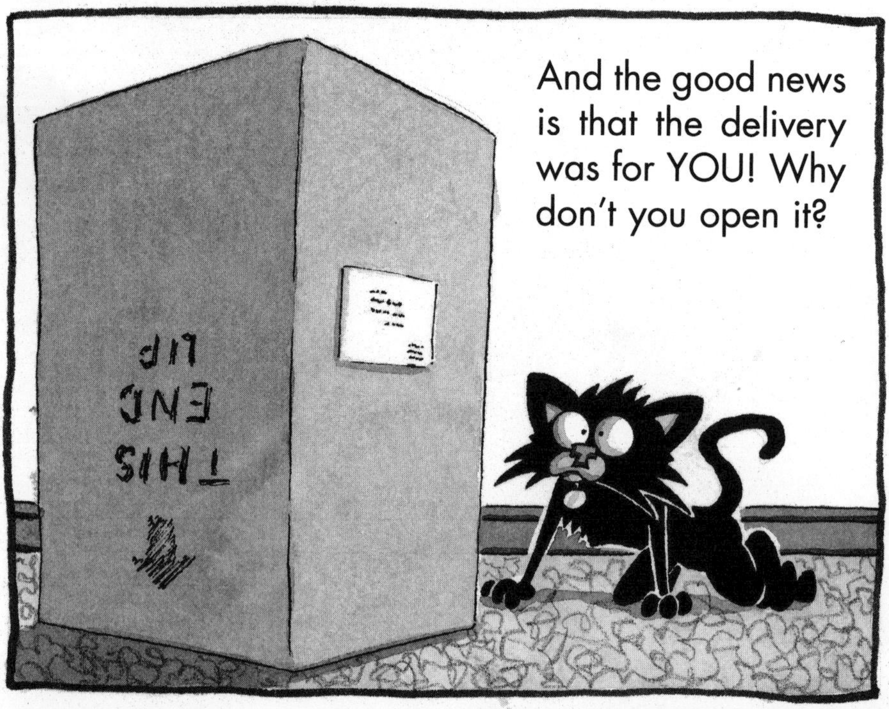
And the good news is that the delivery was for YOU! Why don't you open it?

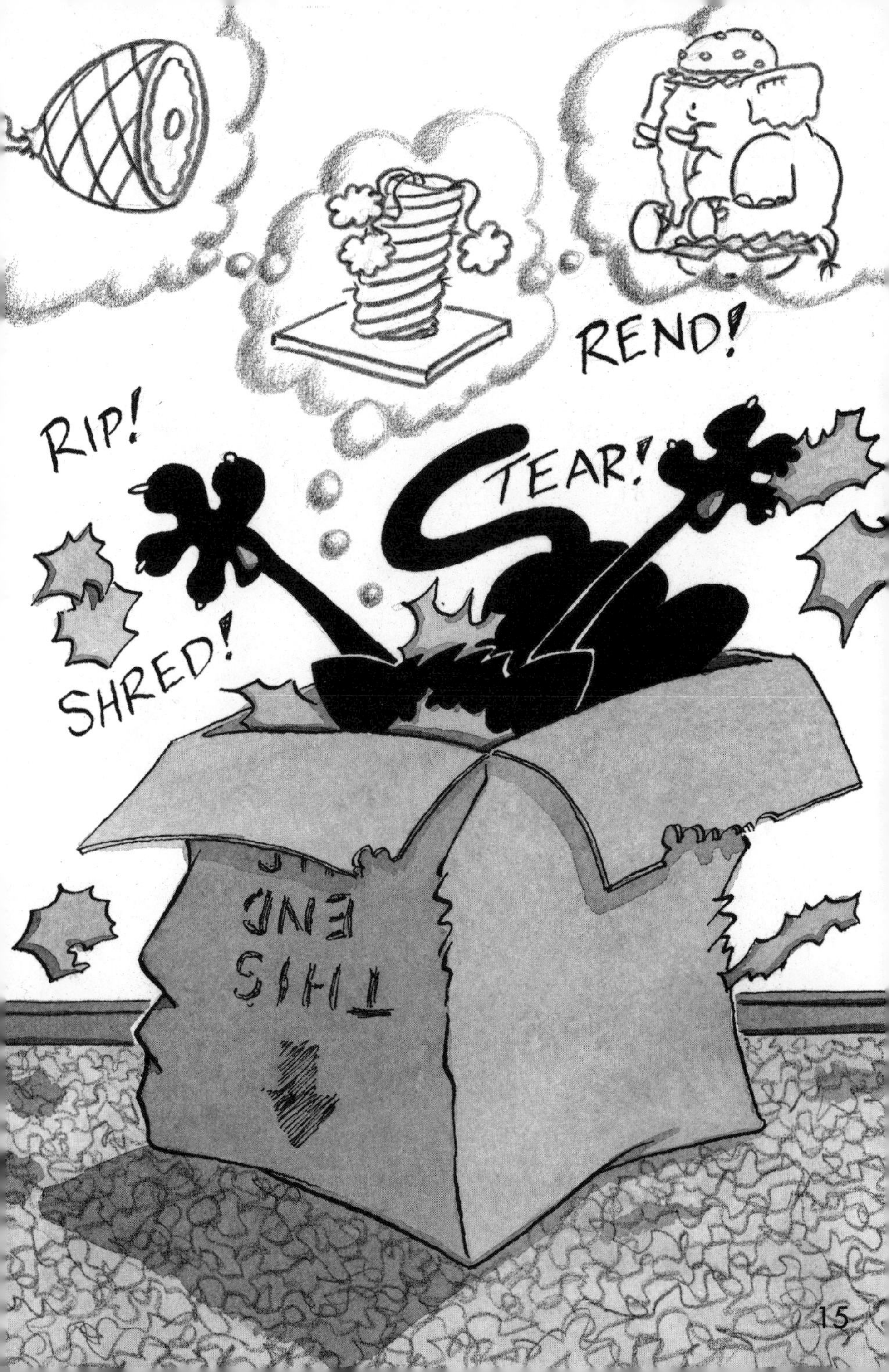
REND!
RIP!
TEAR!
SHRED!
THIS END

It's a BRAND-NEW collar with a cool tag that has YOUR name on it! Isn't it COOL?! Isn't it AWESOME?! This will help if you ever get lost. All of the really cool cats are wearing them nowadays. That's what the salesman told me. All of your cat friends are going to be super-crazy jealous!

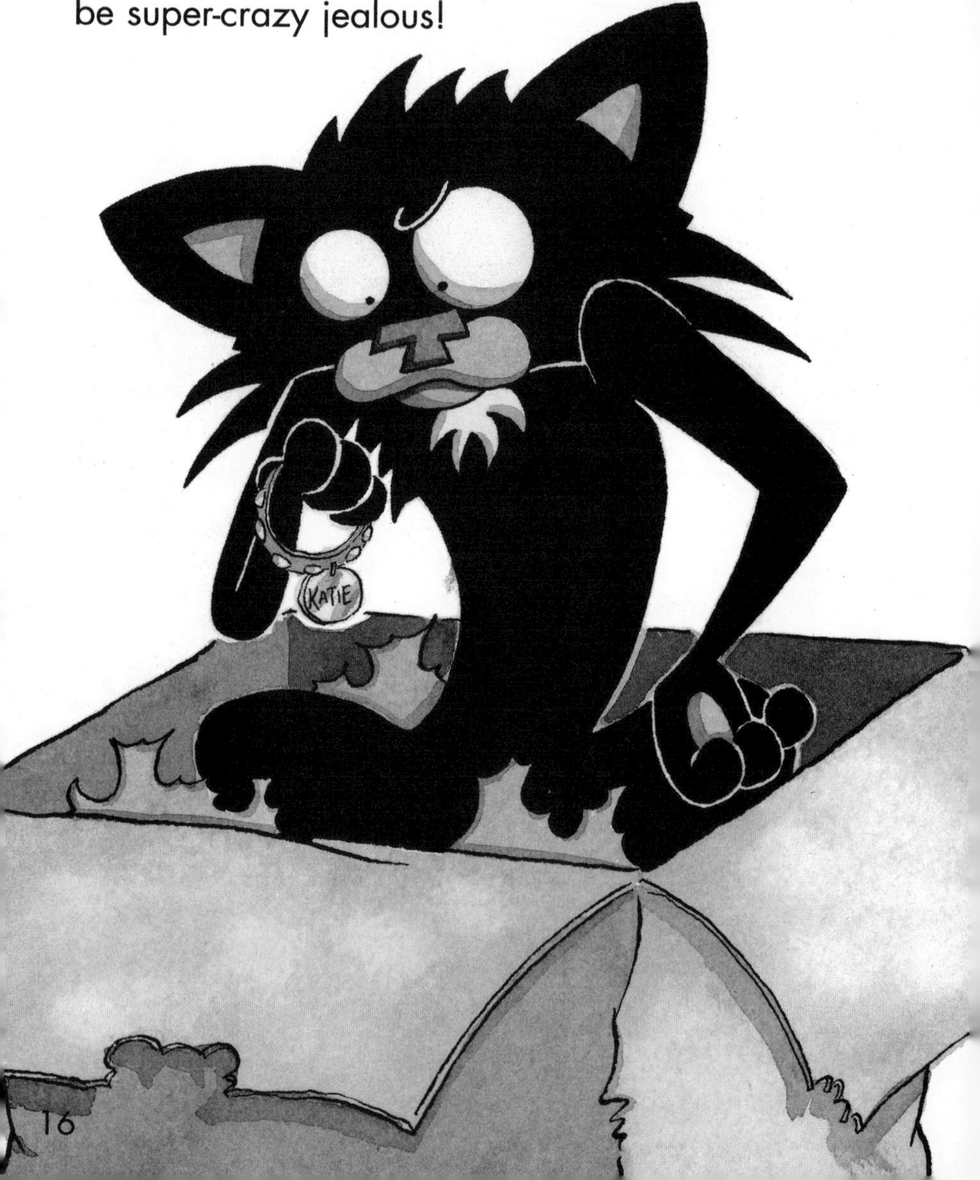
KATIE

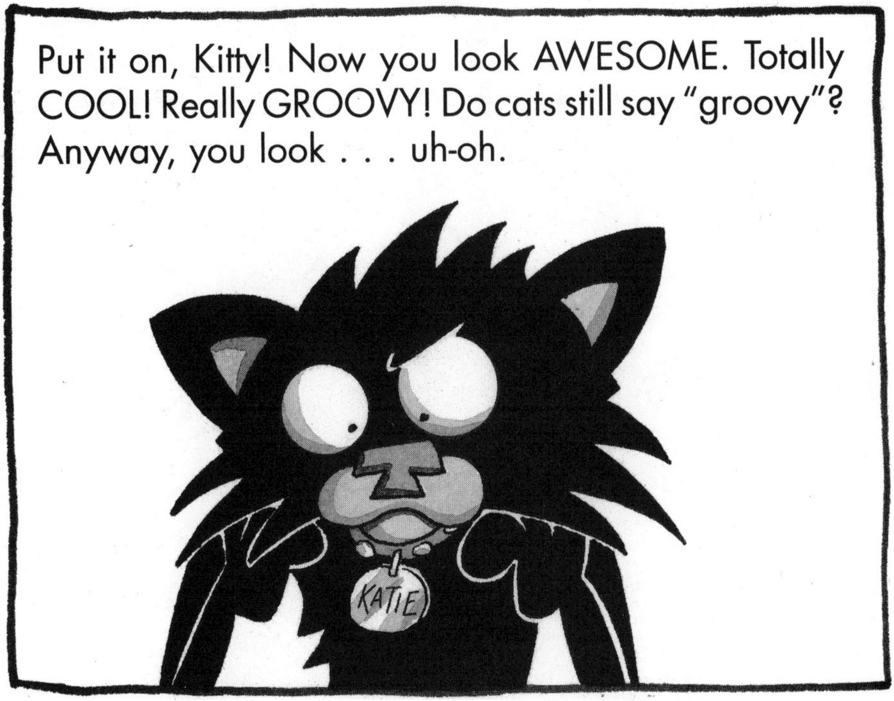
Put it on, Kitty! Now you look AWESOME. Totally COOL! Really GROOVY! Do cats still say "groovy"? Anyway, you look . . . uh-oh.
KATIE

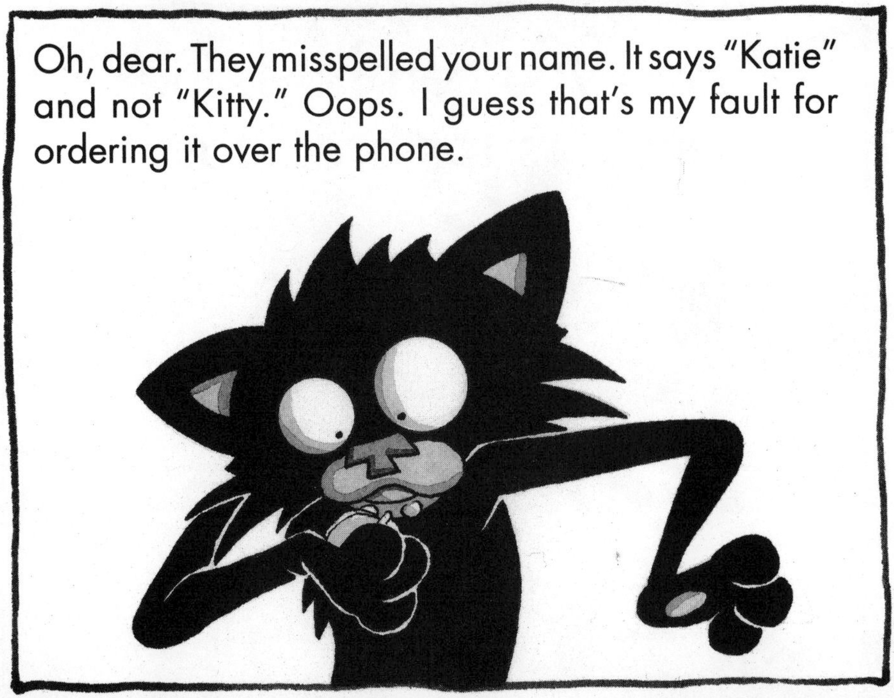
Oh, dear. They misspelled your name. It says "Katie" and not "Kitty." Oops. I guess that's my fault for ordering it over the phone.

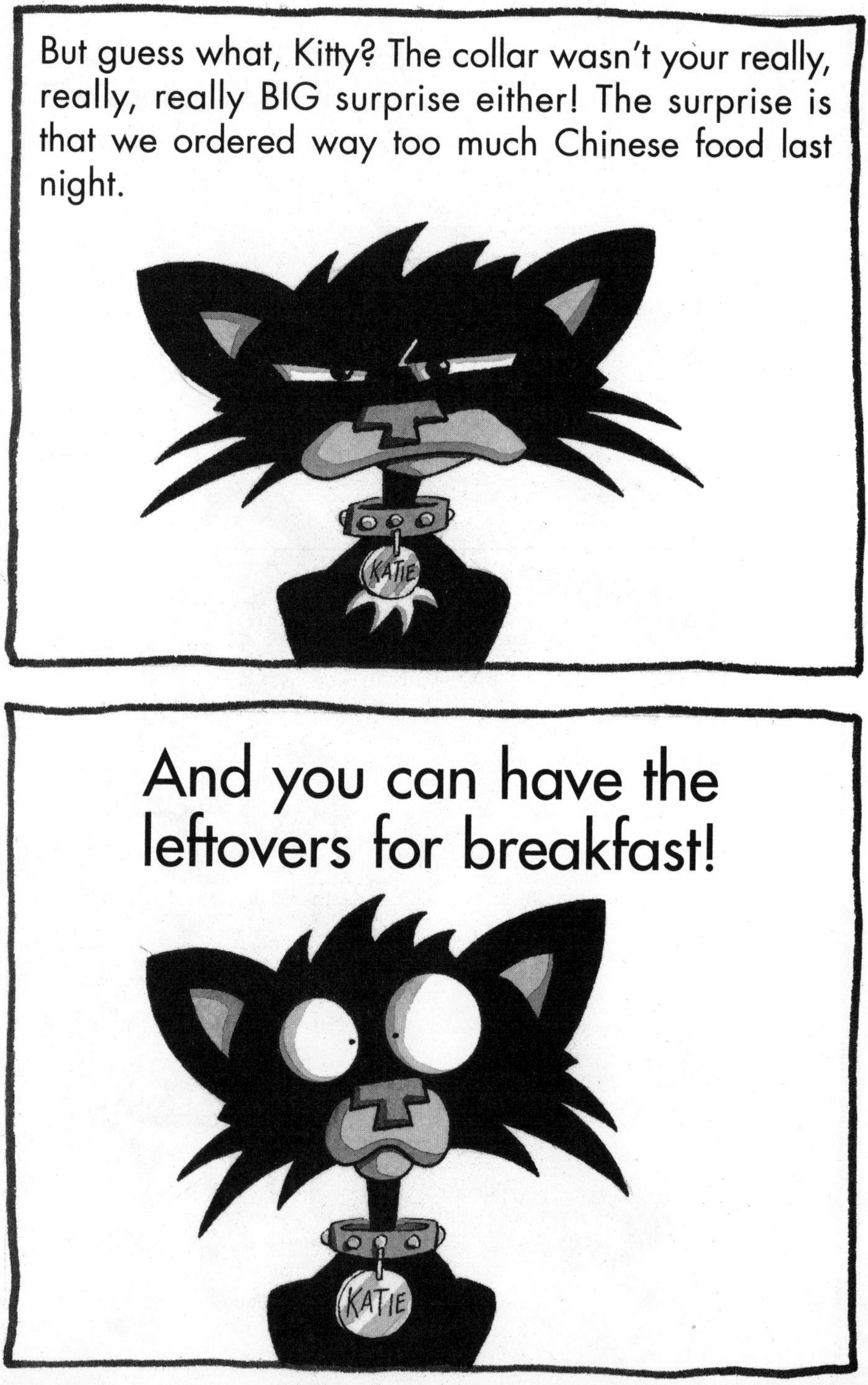
But guess what, Kitty? The collar wasn't your really, really, really BIG surprise either! The surprise is that we ordered way too much Chinese food last night.
KATIE
And you can have the leftovers for breakfast!
KATIE

There's chicken fried rice and beef lo mein and duck chow fun and shrimp with broccoli and scallops with mixed vegetables and fried dumplings and steamed dumplings and Shanghai dumplings and egg rolls and spring rolls and . . . and . . .

AND IT'S ALL YOURS, KITTY!

Bon appétit!

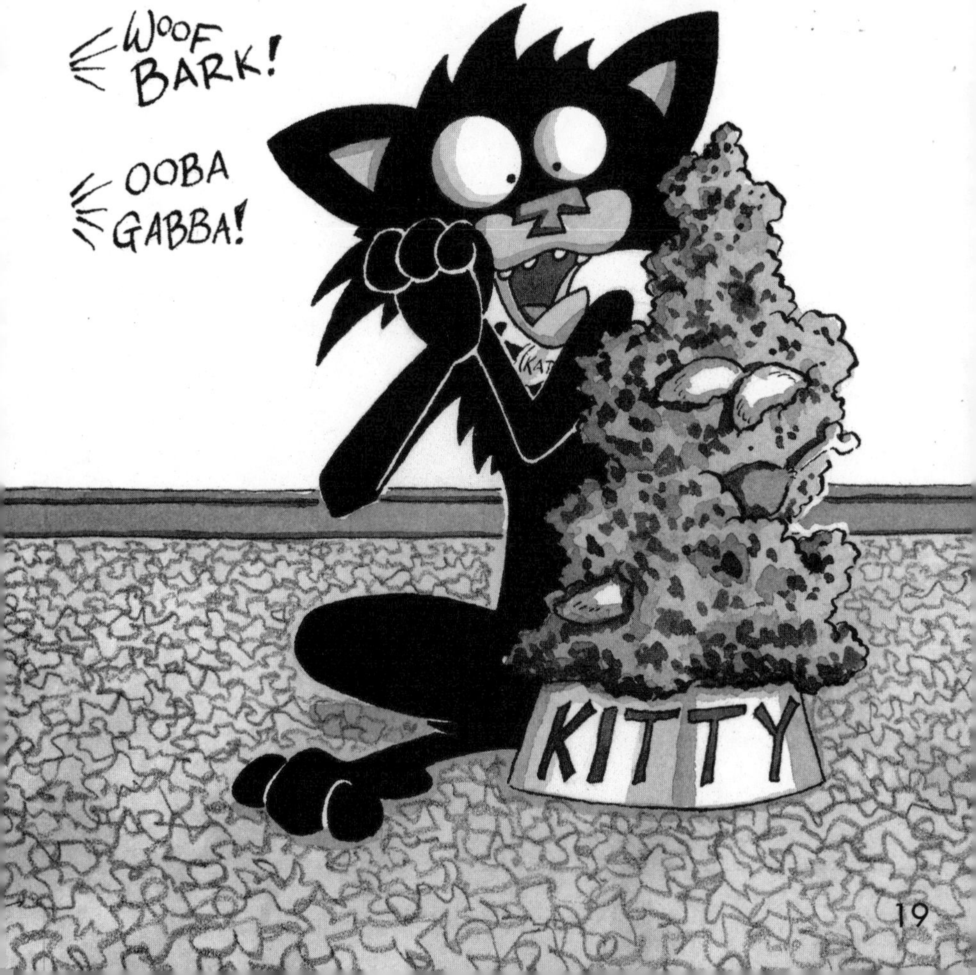
WOOF
BARK!
OOBA
GABBA!
KITTY

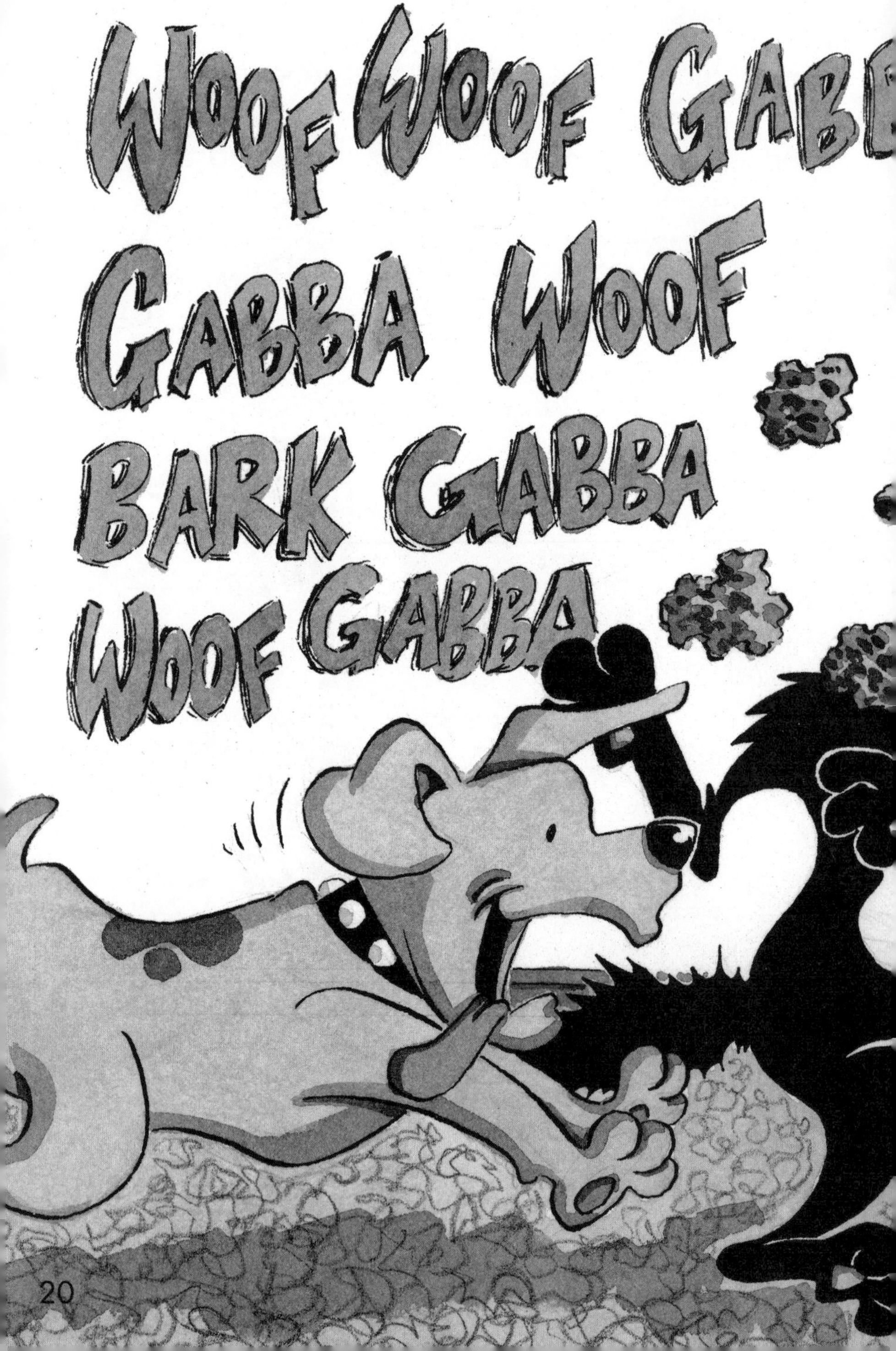
WOOF WOOF GABB
GABBA WOOF
BARK GABBA
WOOF GABBA

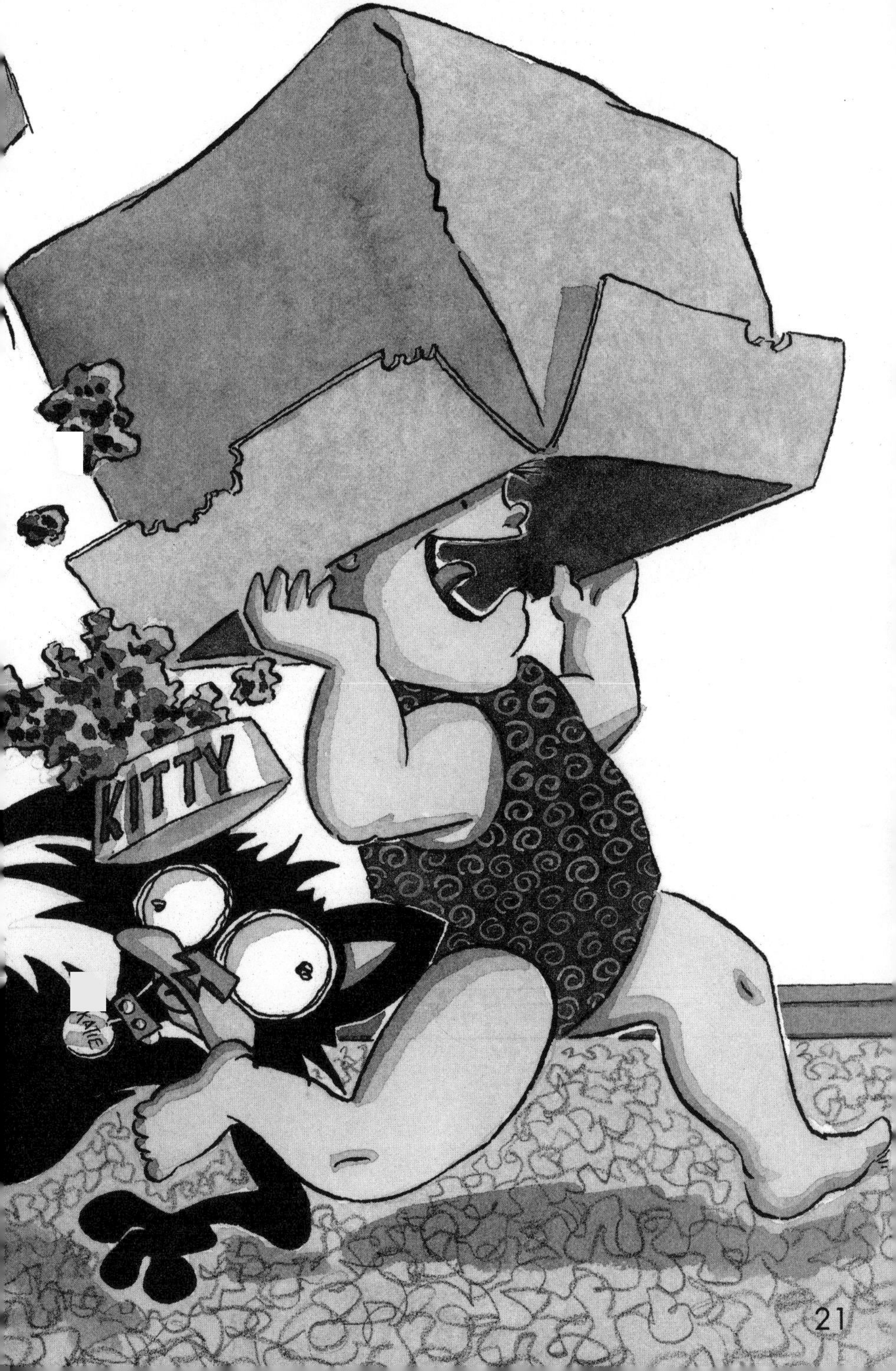
KITTY
KATIE

Oh dear.

What a mess.

Sorry about that, Kitty. I'll clean this up and get your usual breakfast: a can of gray chicken-flavored paste with green bits.

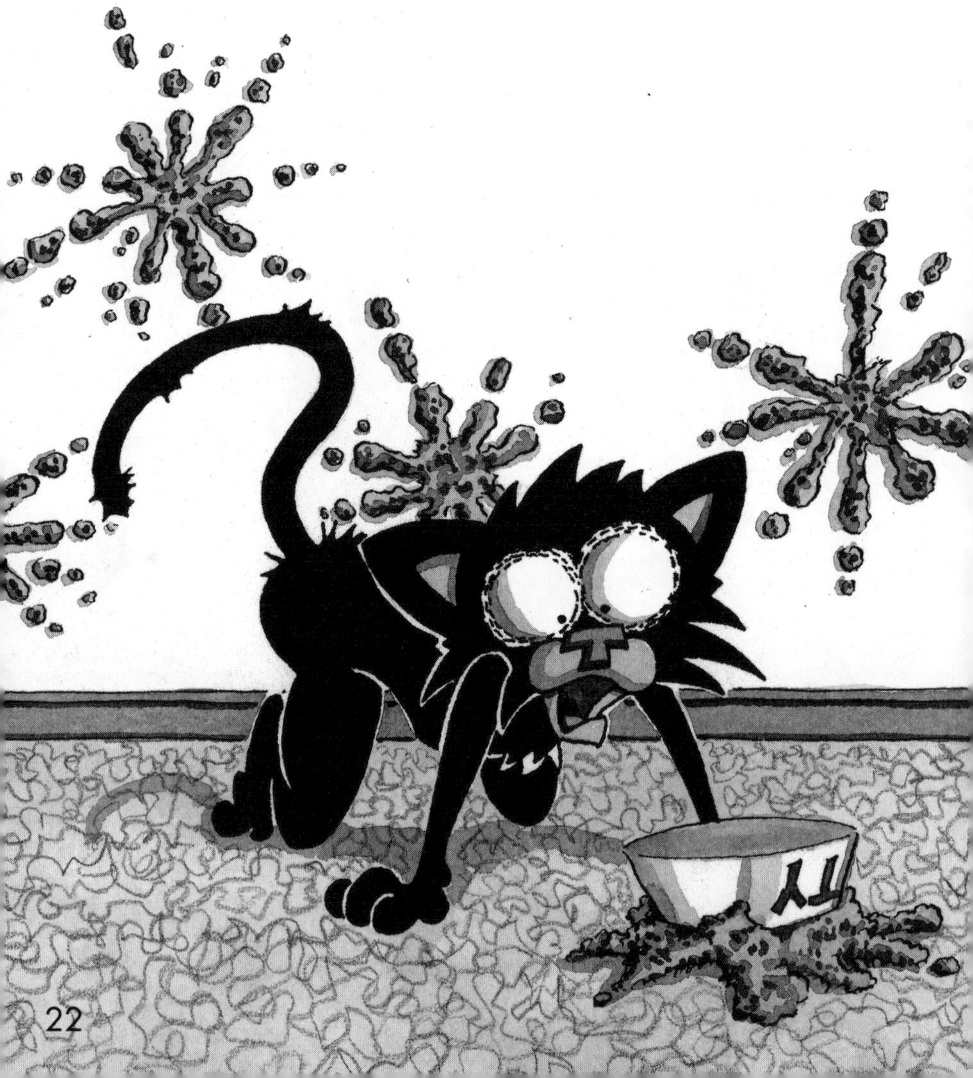

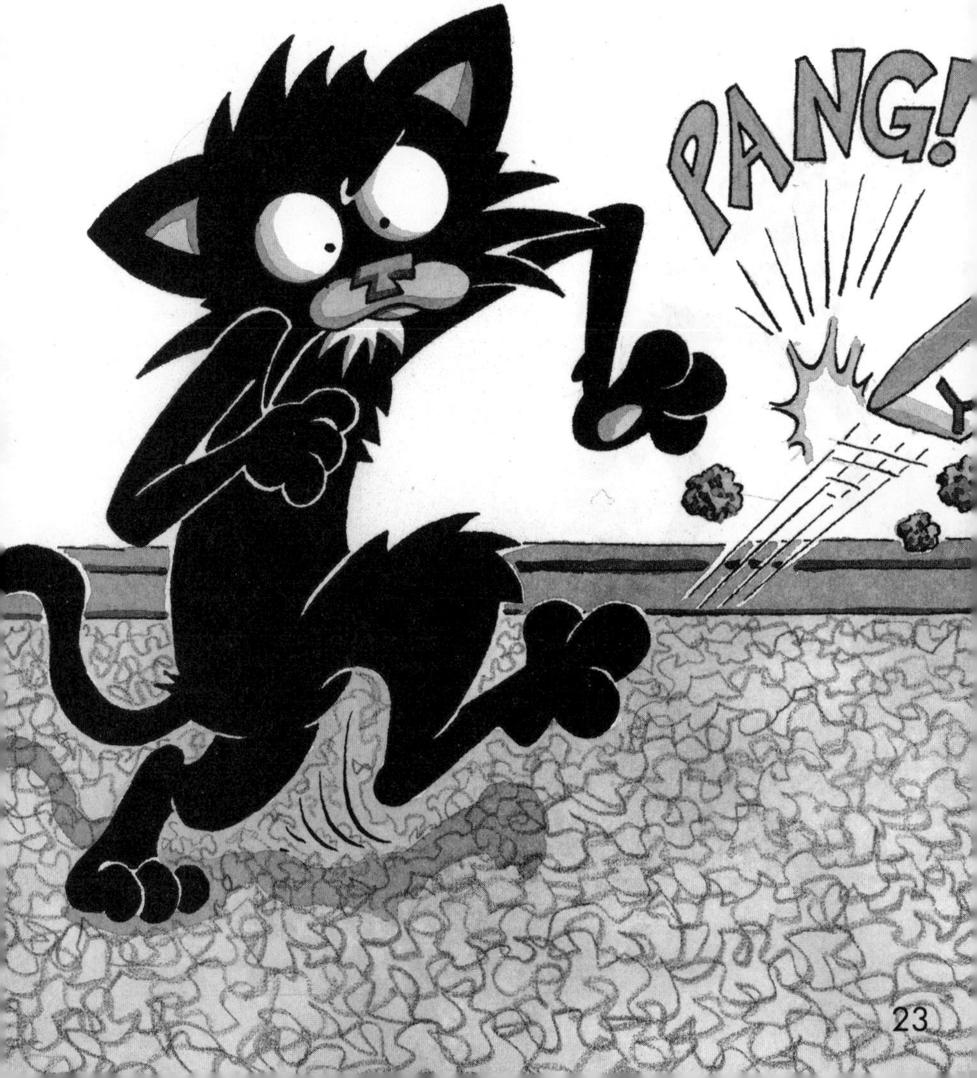
PANG!

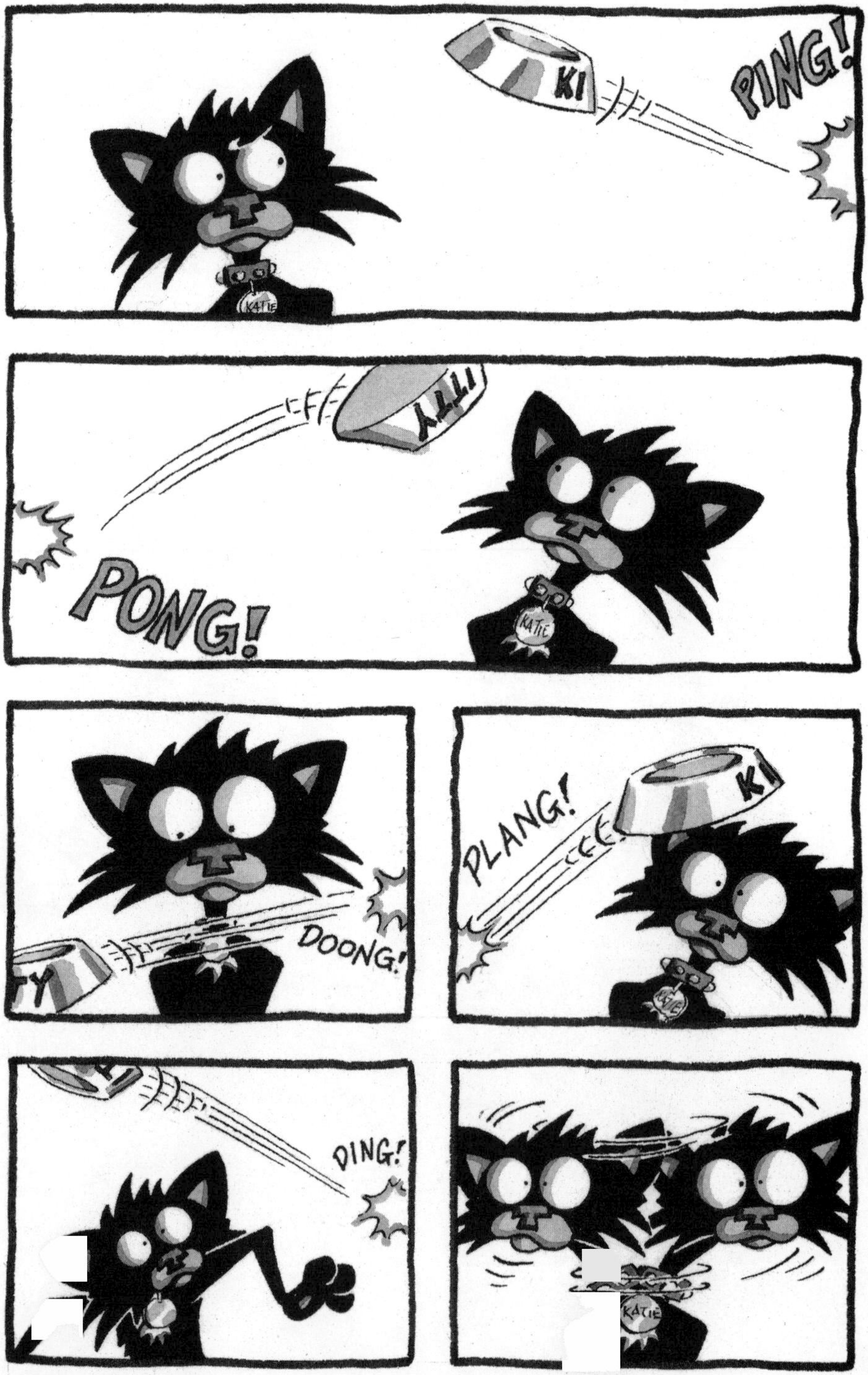
KI
PING!
TTY
PONG!
KATIE
TY
DOONG!
PLANG!
KI
DING!
KATIE

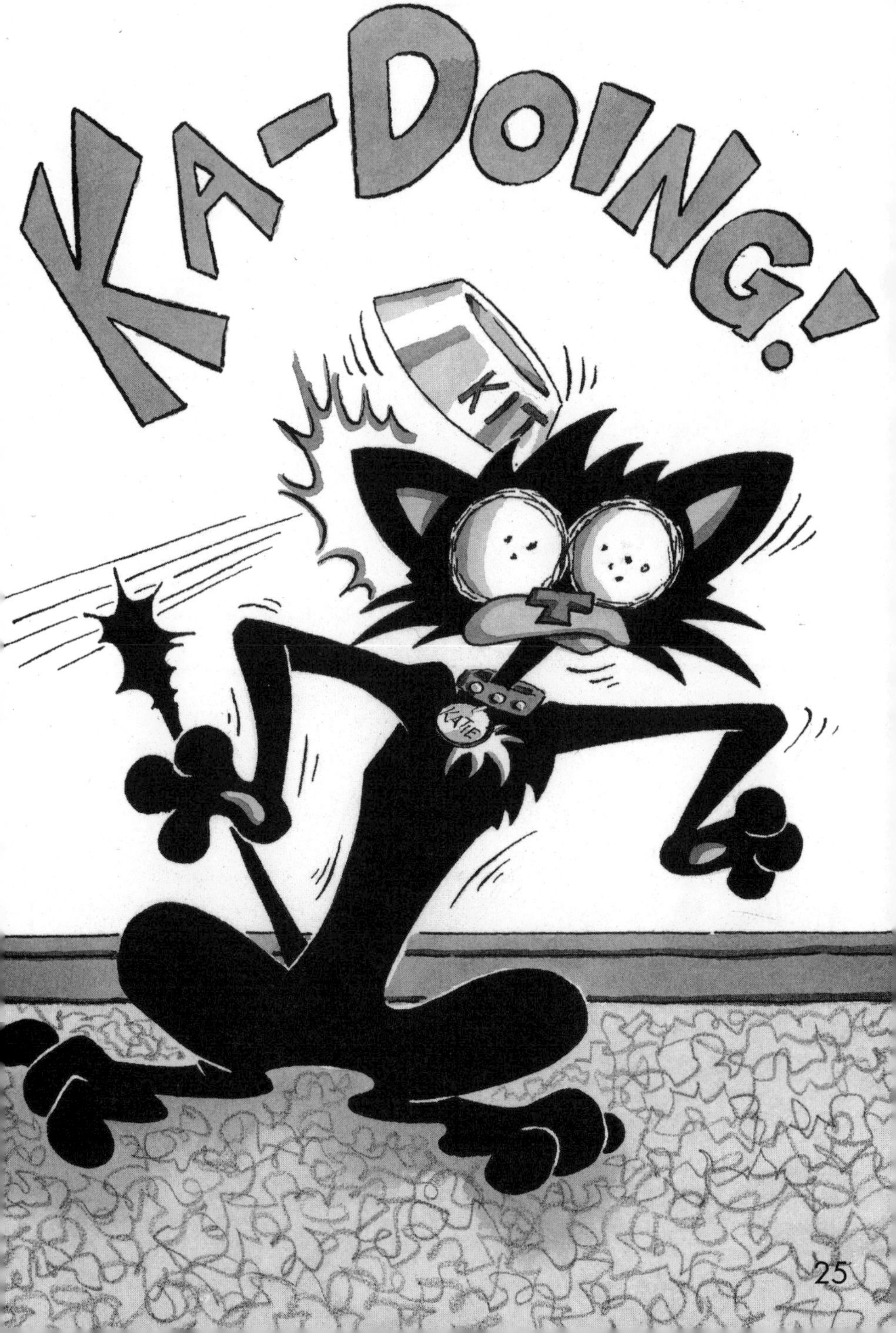
KA-DOING!
KIT
KATIE

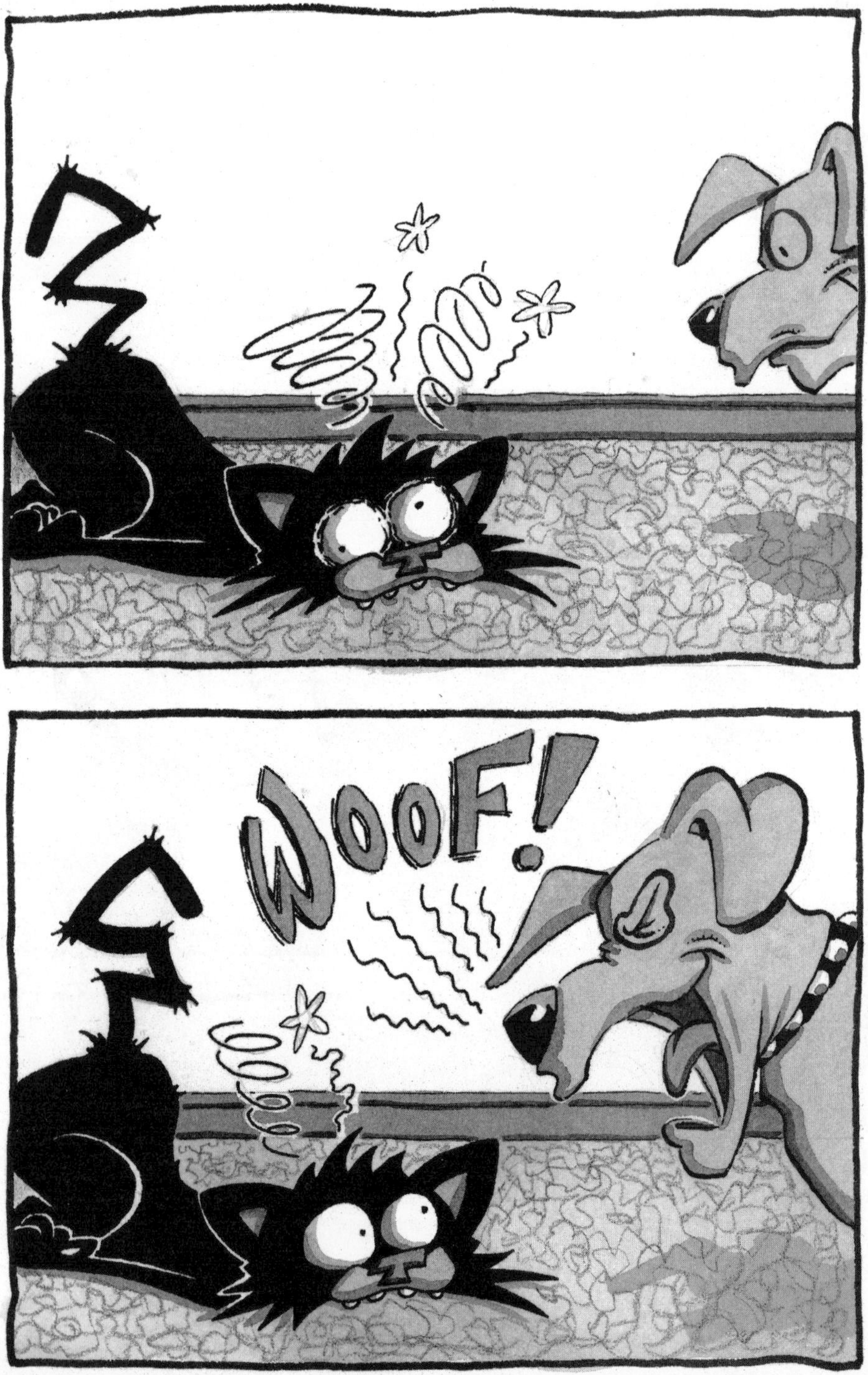
WOOF!

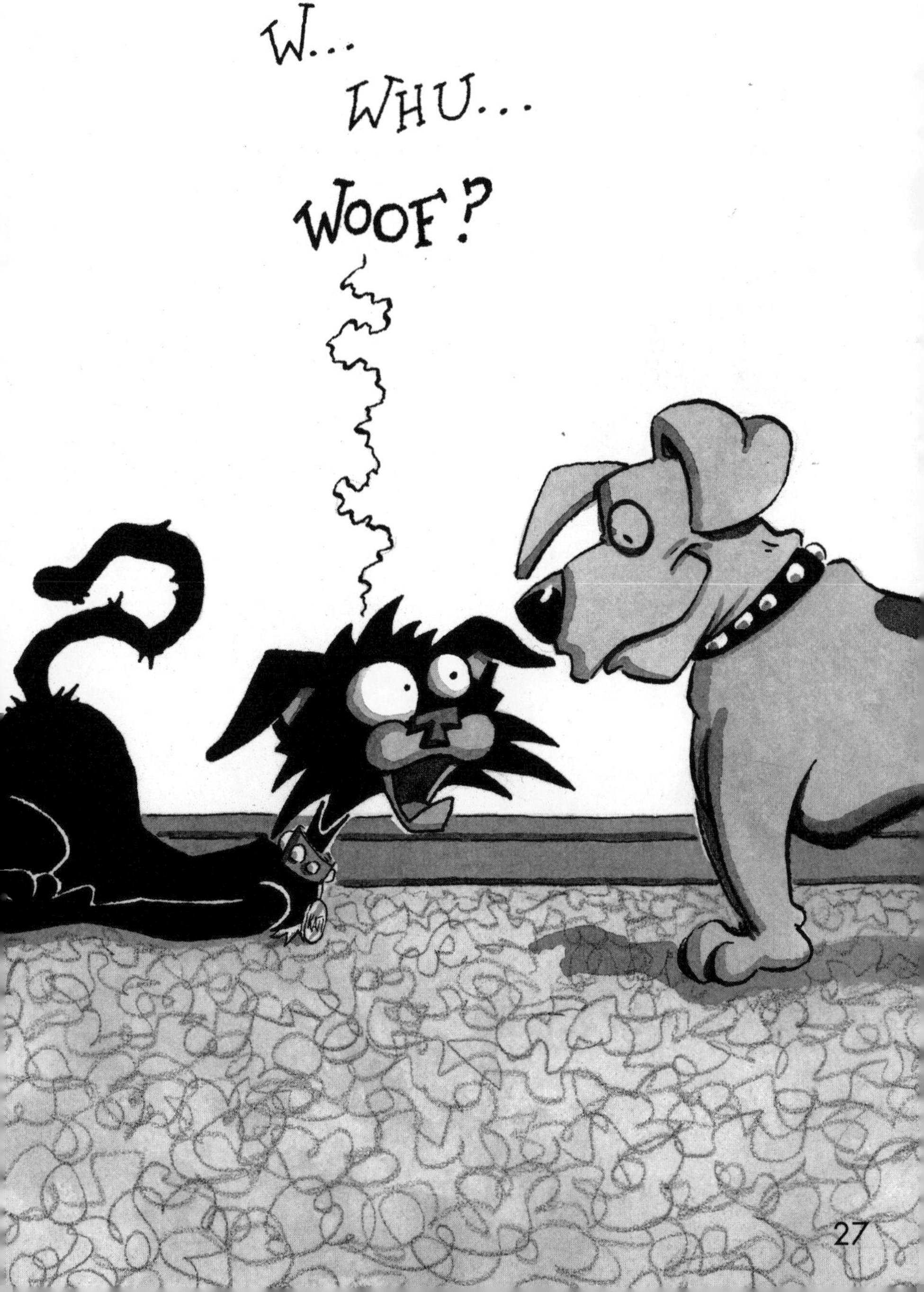
W...
WHU...
WOOF?

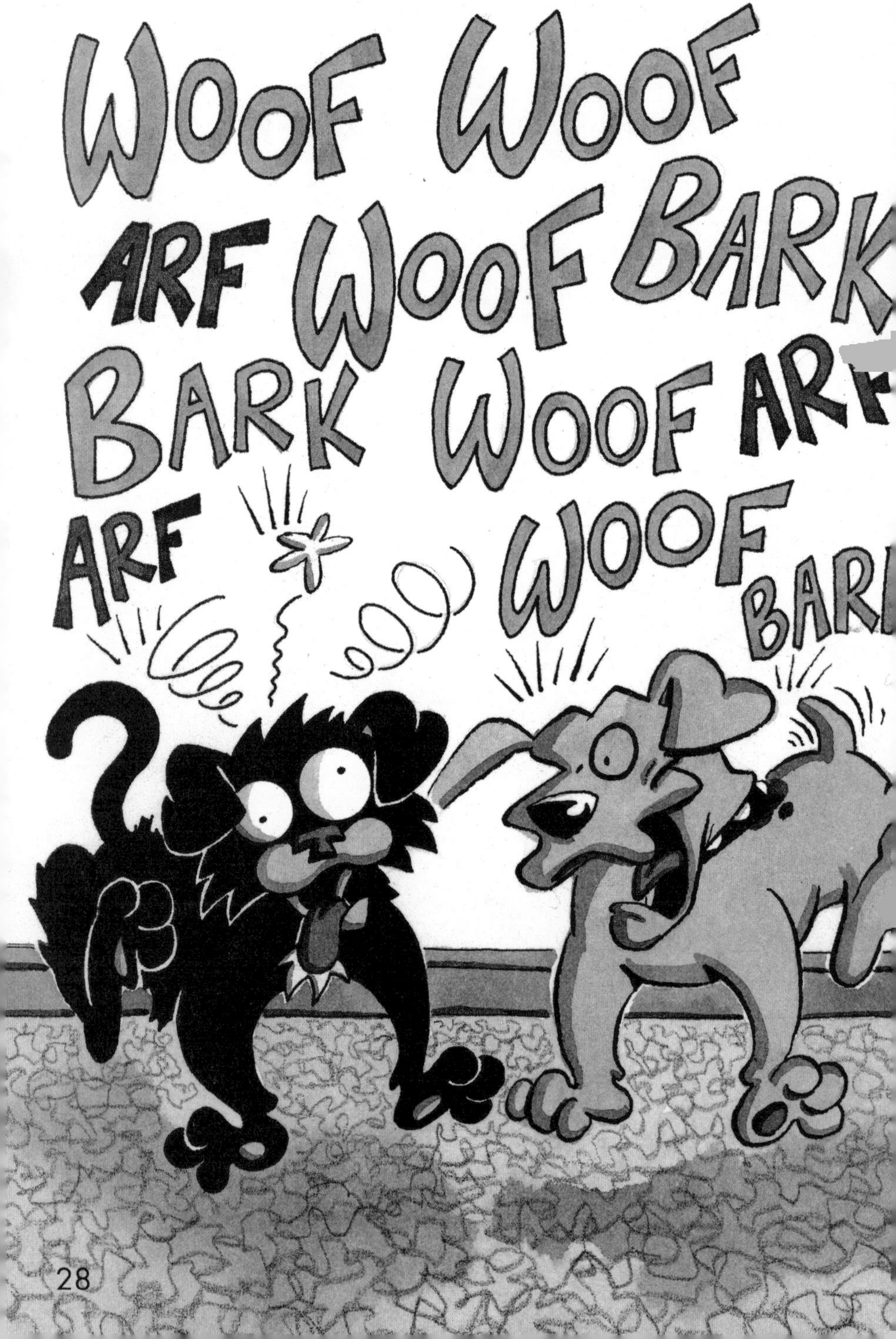
WOOF WOOF
ARF WOOF BARK
BARK WOOF
ARF
WOOF

•CHAPTER TWO•

ONE WEEK LATER

Hi, Puppy. You've been playing with Kitty a lot these past few days. But now you look exhausted. Why don't you lie down and take a nice, long nap?

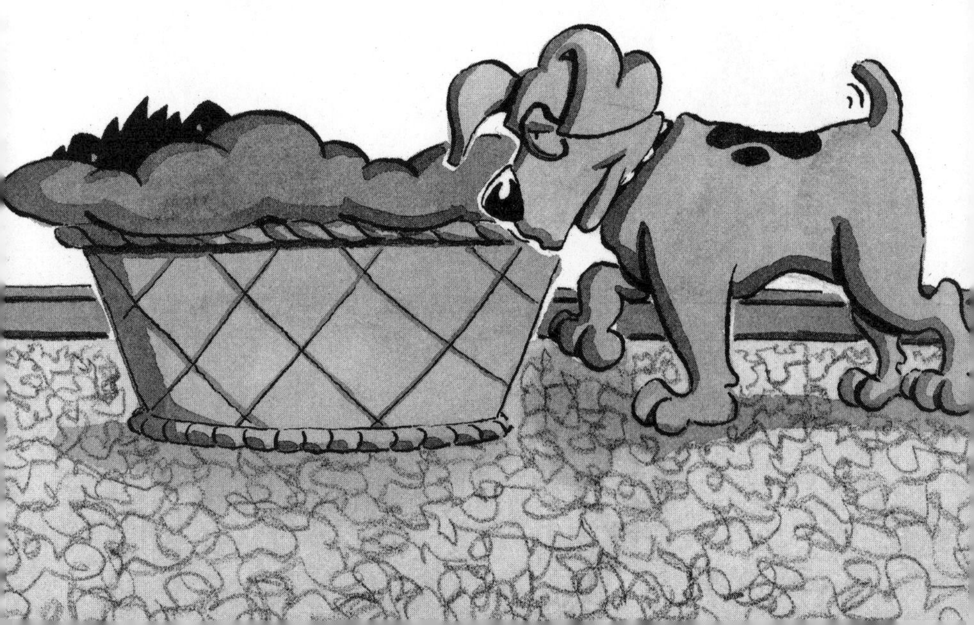

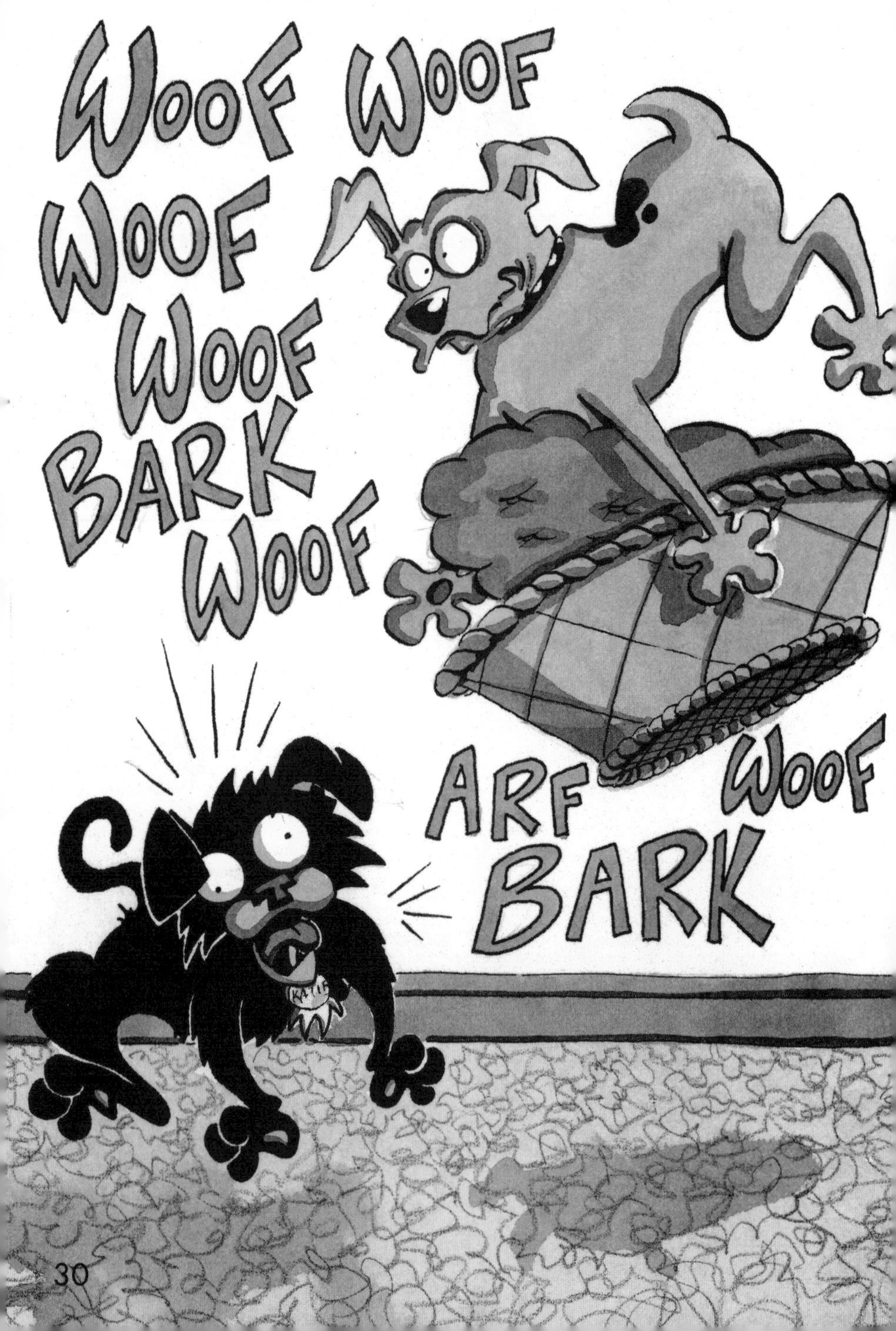
WOOF WOOF
WOOF
WOOF
BARK
WOOF
ARF
WOOF
BARK
KATIE

KITTY! STOP THAT!

I'm thrilled that you and Puppy are suddenly getting along so well, but you've been playing with him nonstop for about a week now. He's turning into a nervous wreck. Just leave him alone for a little while and let him rest.

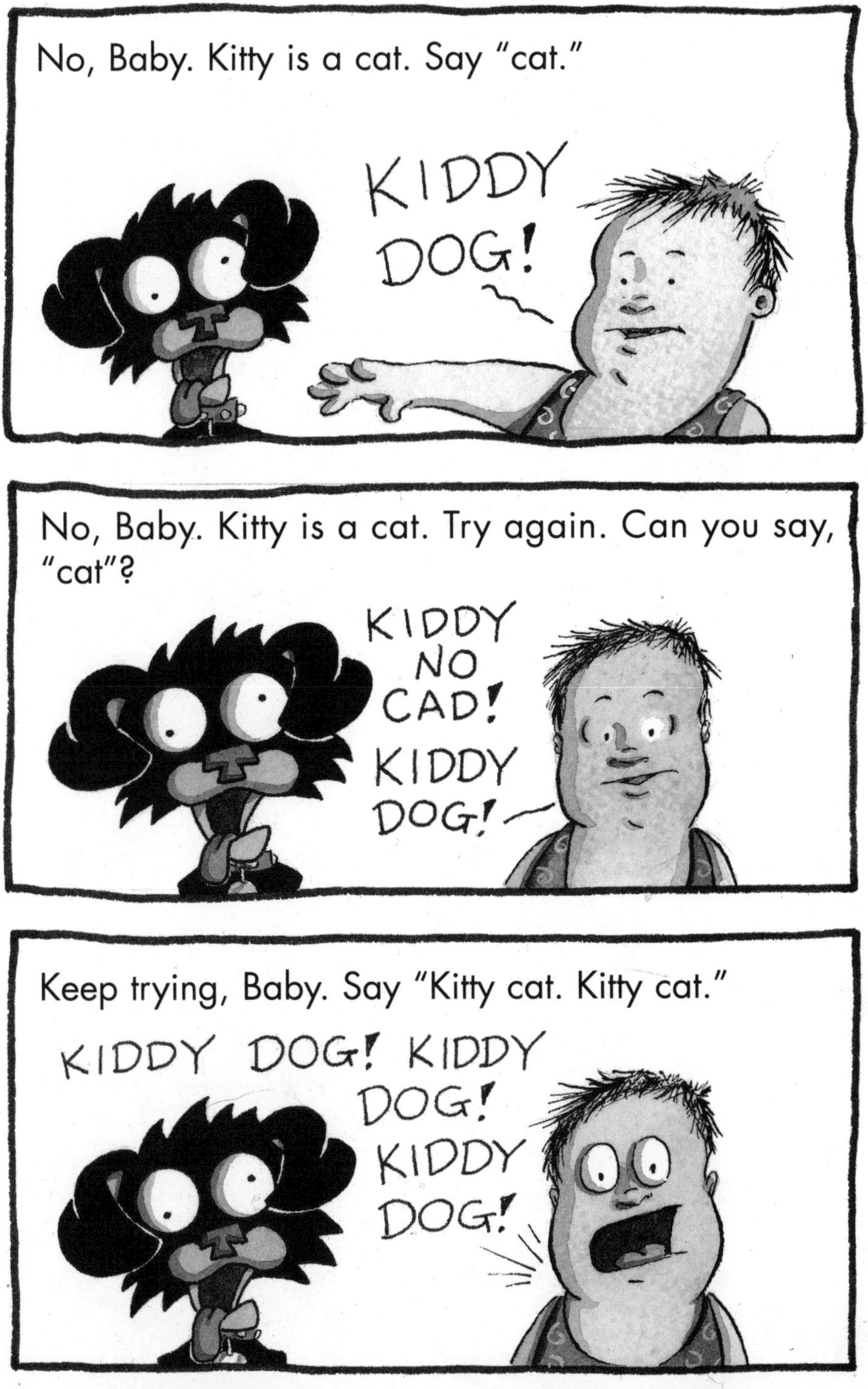
No, Baby. Kitty is a cat. Say "cat."
KIDDY DOG!
No, Baby. Kitty is a cat. Try again. Can you say, "cat"?
KIDDY NO CAD! KIDDY DOG!
Keep trying, Baby. Say "Kitty cat. Kitty cat."
KIDDY DOG! KIDDY DOG! KIDDY DOG!

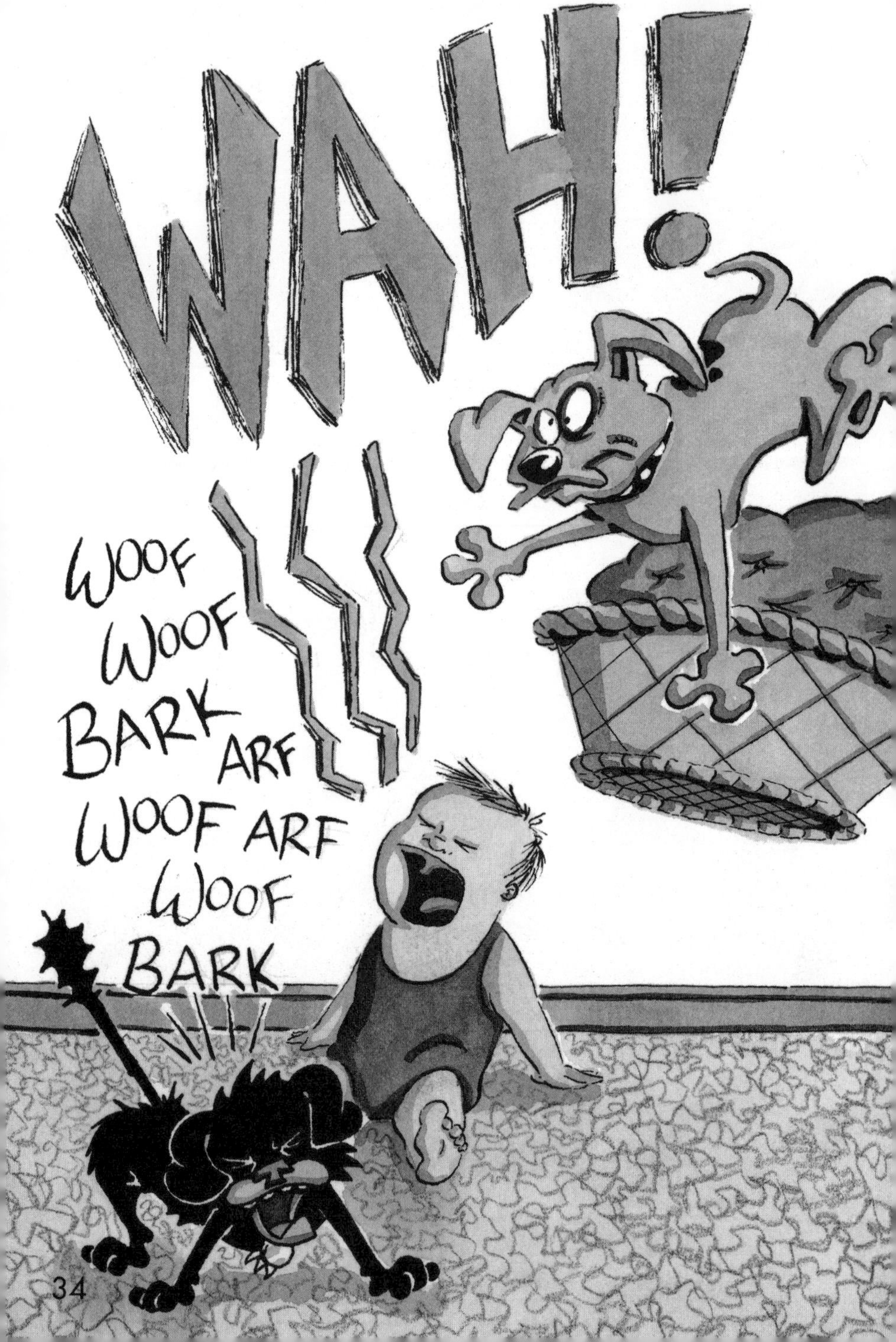
WAH!
WOOF
WOOF
BARK
ARF
WOOF ARF
WOOF
BARK

Wow, Puppy. You look pretty stressed out. Maybe you need a vacation. I think you need to go somewhere to relax and just be a dog.

But where? Hmmmmmmm . . .

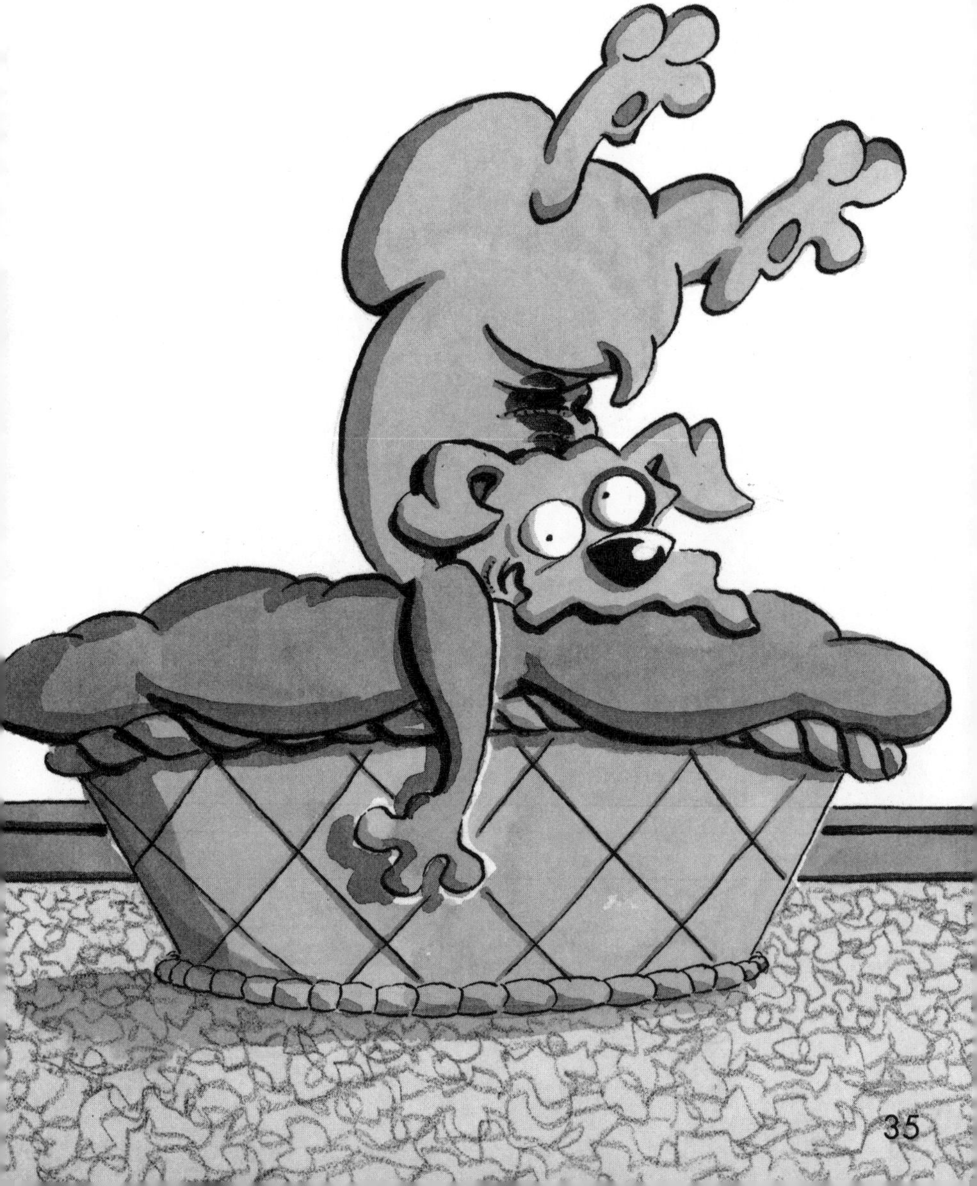

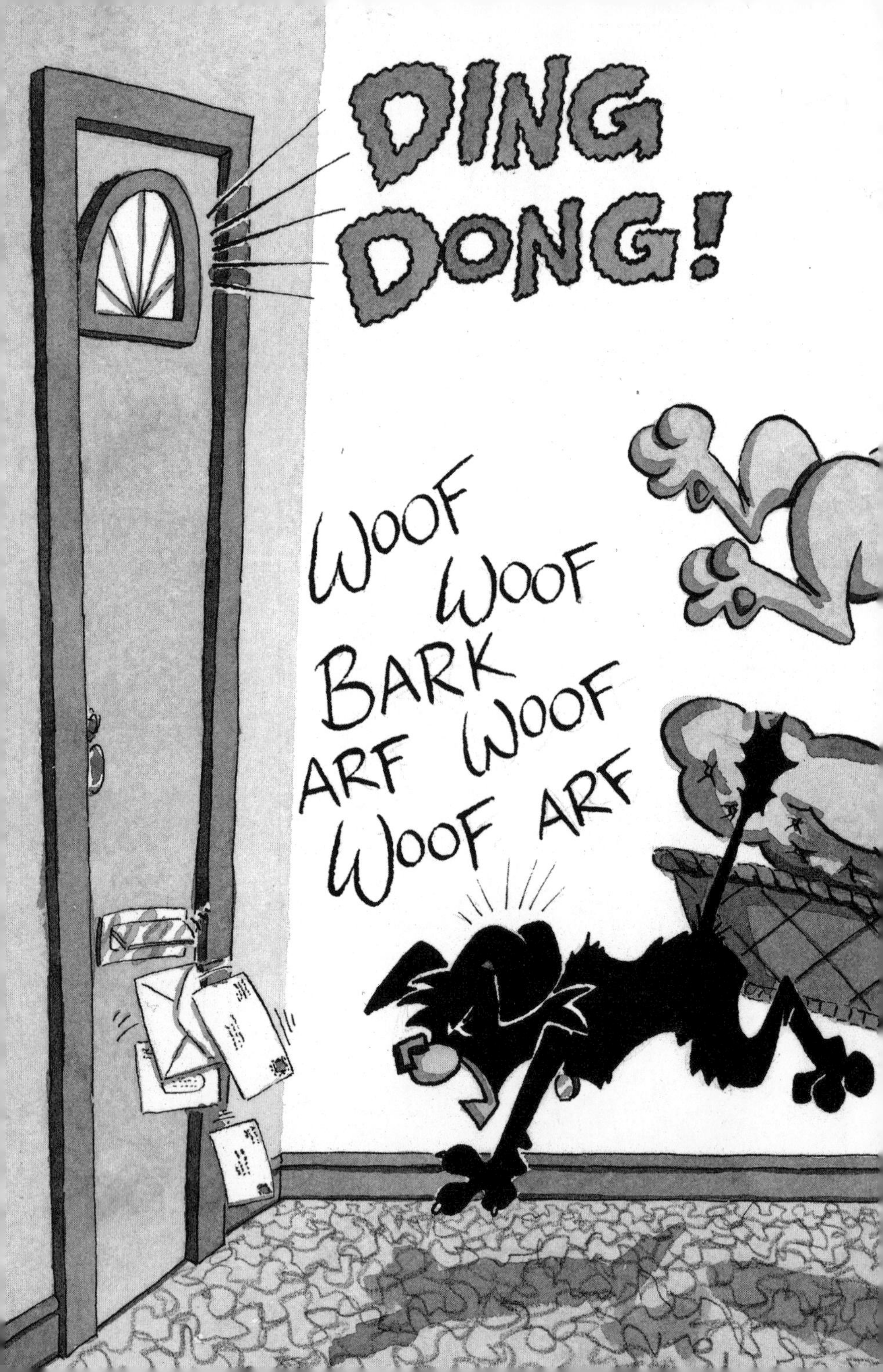
DING DONG!
WOOF WOOF BARK ARF WOOF WOOF ARF

Hey! Check it out! This could be the answer to your problems, Puppy! It's an advertisement for a new dog camp—a place where dogs can go for the weekend and get rid of their stress.

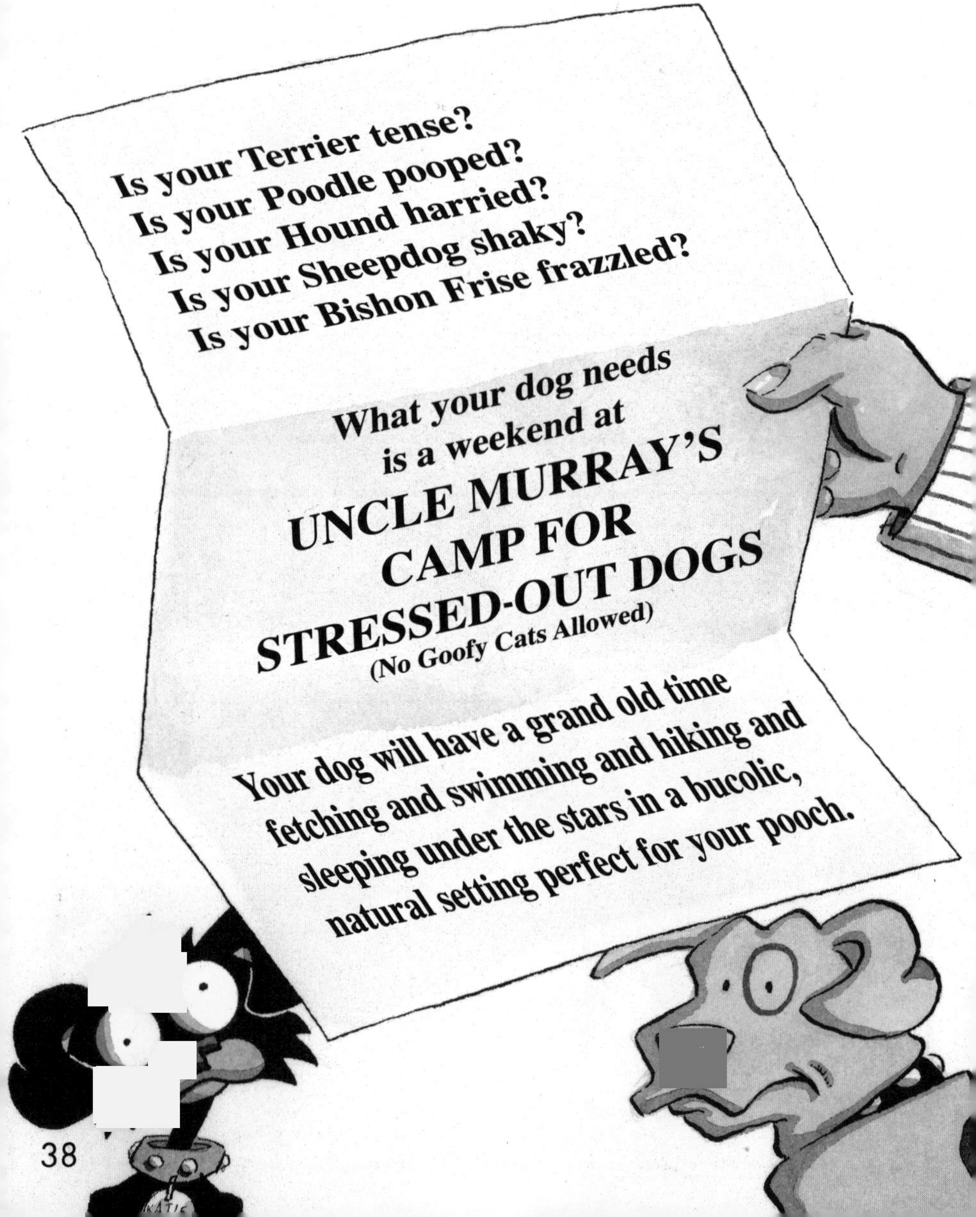

Is your Terrier tense?
Is your Poodle pooped?
Is your Hound harried?
Is your Sheepdog shaky?
Is your Bishon Frise frazzled?
What your dog needs
is a weekend at
UNCLE MURRAY'S
CAMP FOR
STRESSED-OUT DOGS
(No Goofy Cats Allowed)
Your dog will have a grand old time
fetching and swimming and hiking and
sleeping under the stars in a bucolic,
natural setting perfect for your pooch.

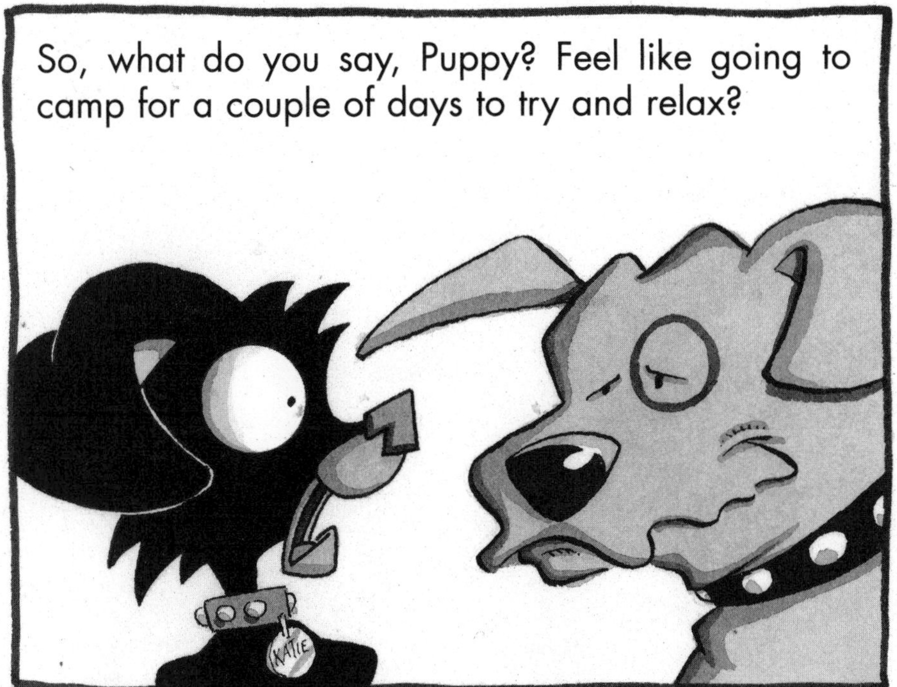
So, what do you say, Puppy? Feel like going to camp for a couple of days to try and relax?
KATIE

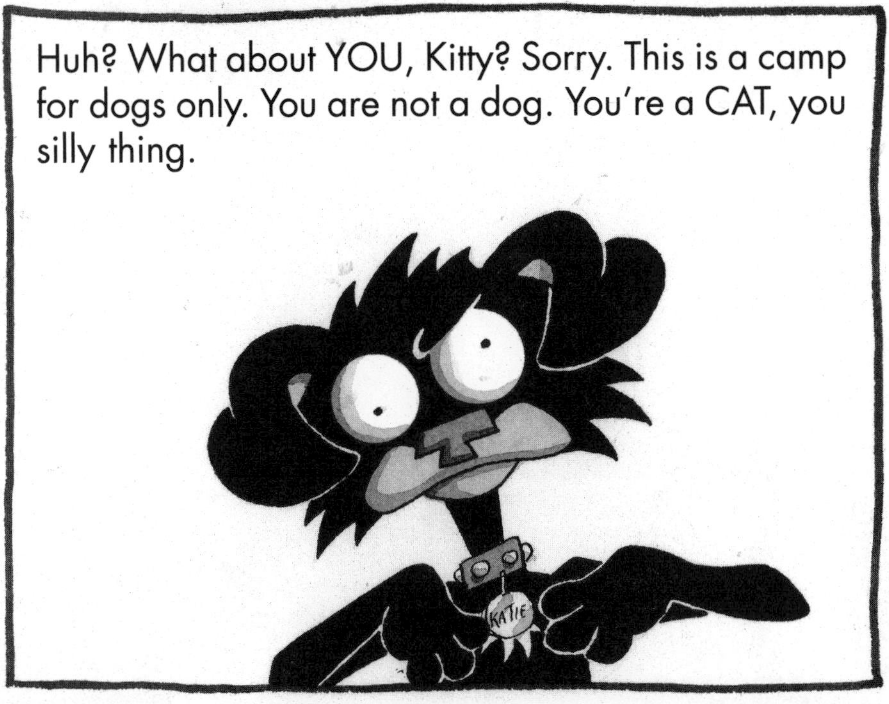
Huh? What about YOU, Kitty? Sorry. This is a camp for dogs only. You are not a dog. You're a CAT, you silly thing.
KATIE

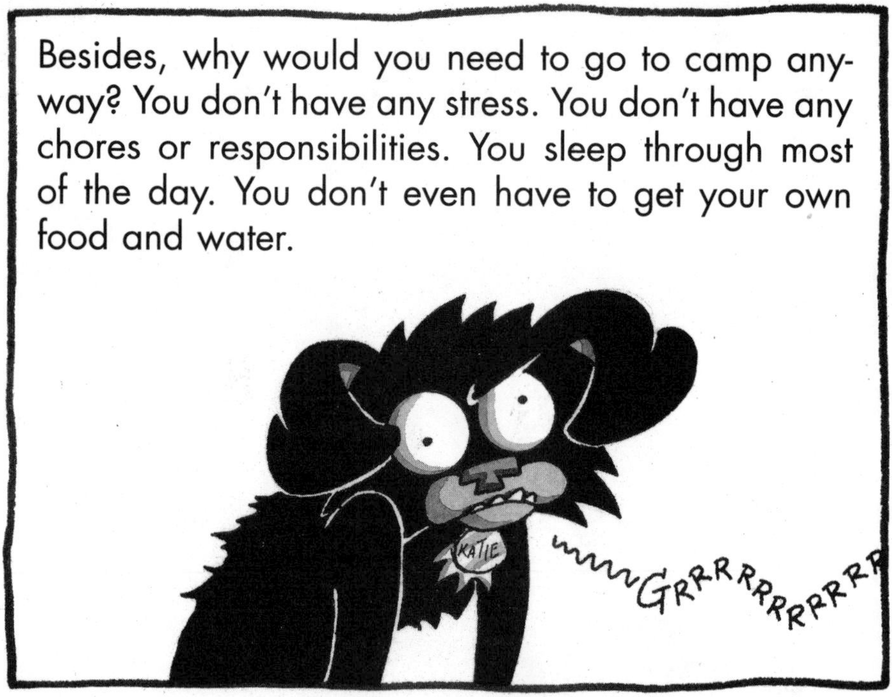
Besides, why would you need to go to camp anyway? You don't have any stress. You don't have any chores or responsibilities. You sleep through most of the day. You don't even have to get your own food and water.
KATIE
GRRRRRRRRRRRR

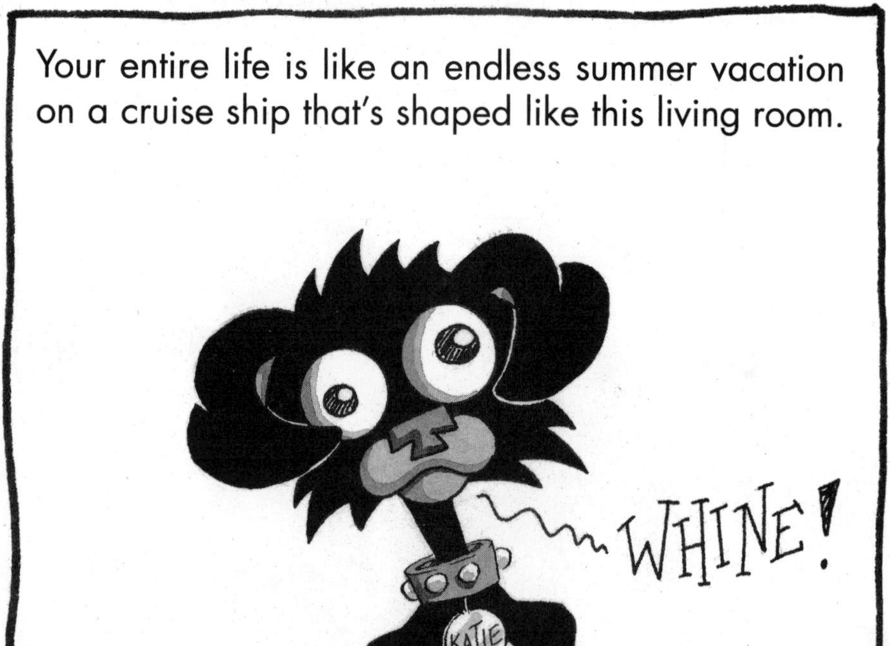
Your entire life is like an endless summer vacation on a cruise ship that's shaped like this living room.
WHINE!
KATIE

Let's go, Puppy. I'll help you pack.

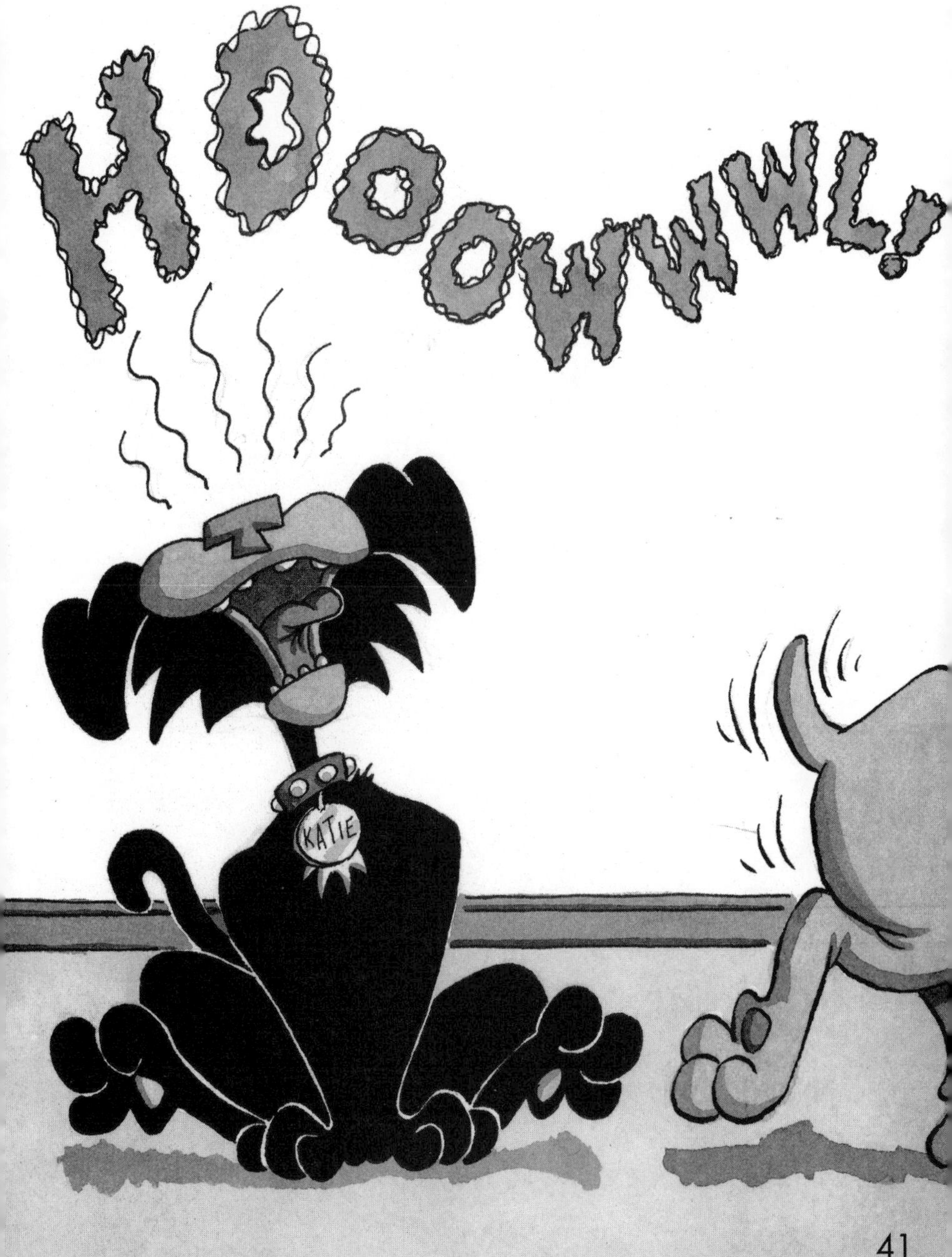
HOOOWWWL!
KATIE

•CHAPTER THREE•

CAMP!

Here we are, Puppy! I hope you're ready for two days of fun, rest, and relaxation.

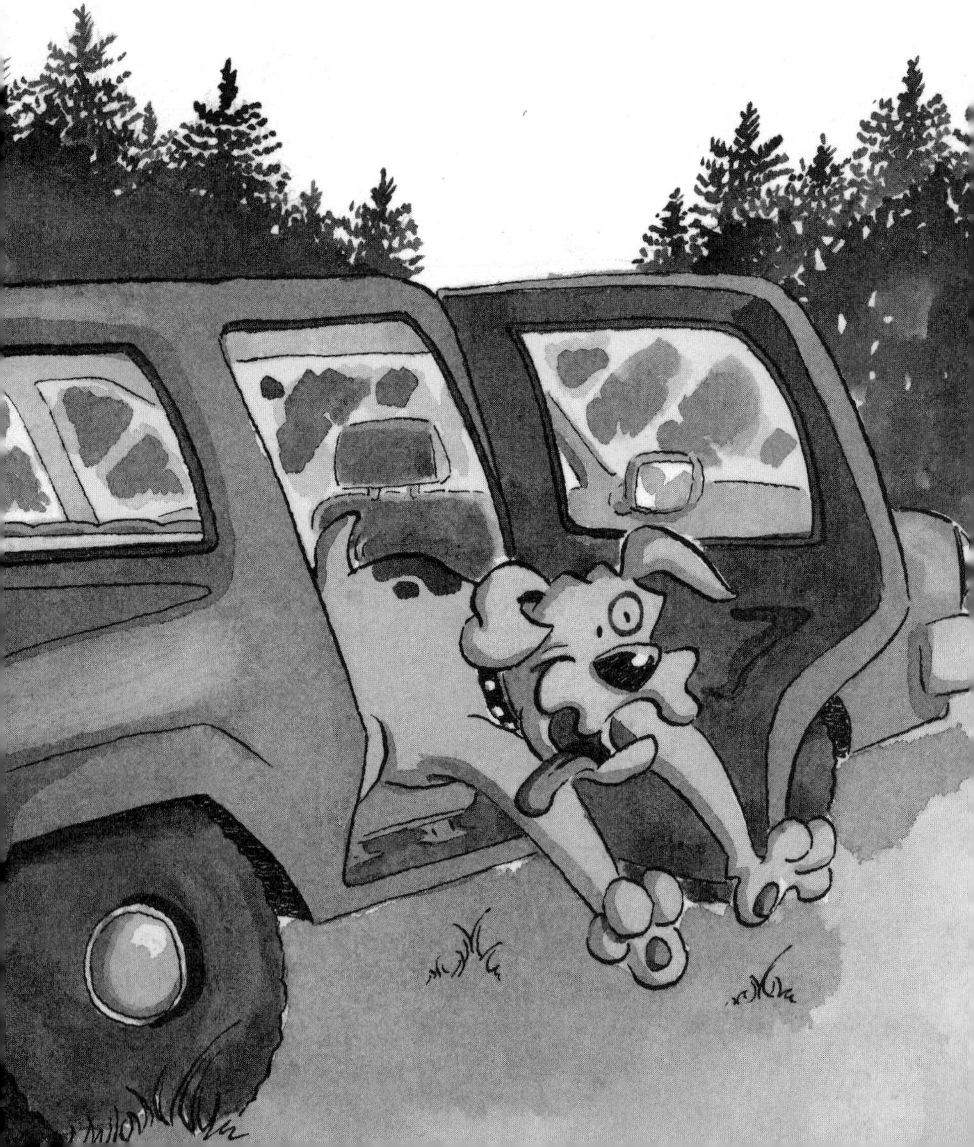

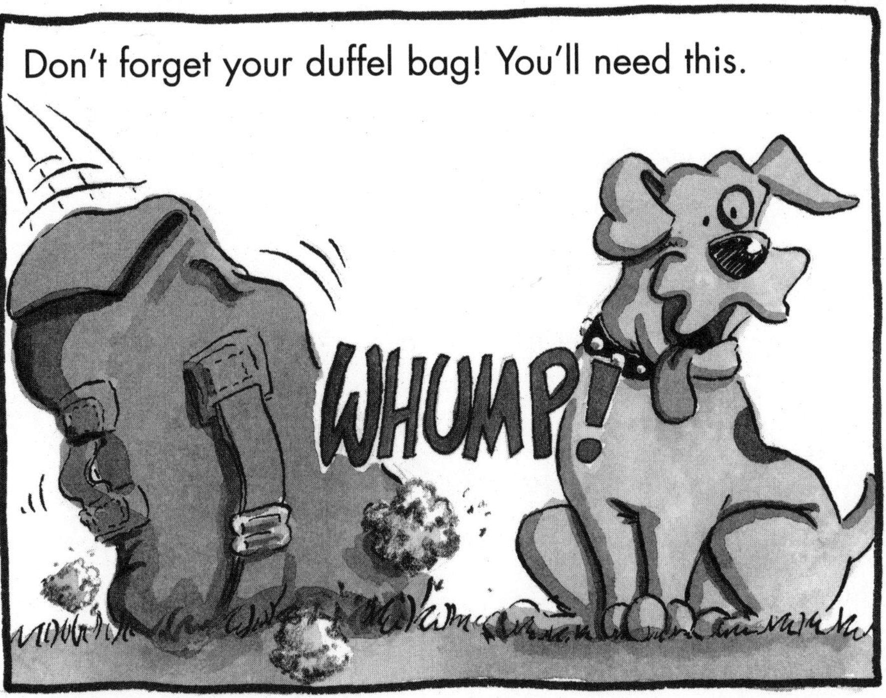
Don't forget your duffel bag! You'll need this.
WHUMP!

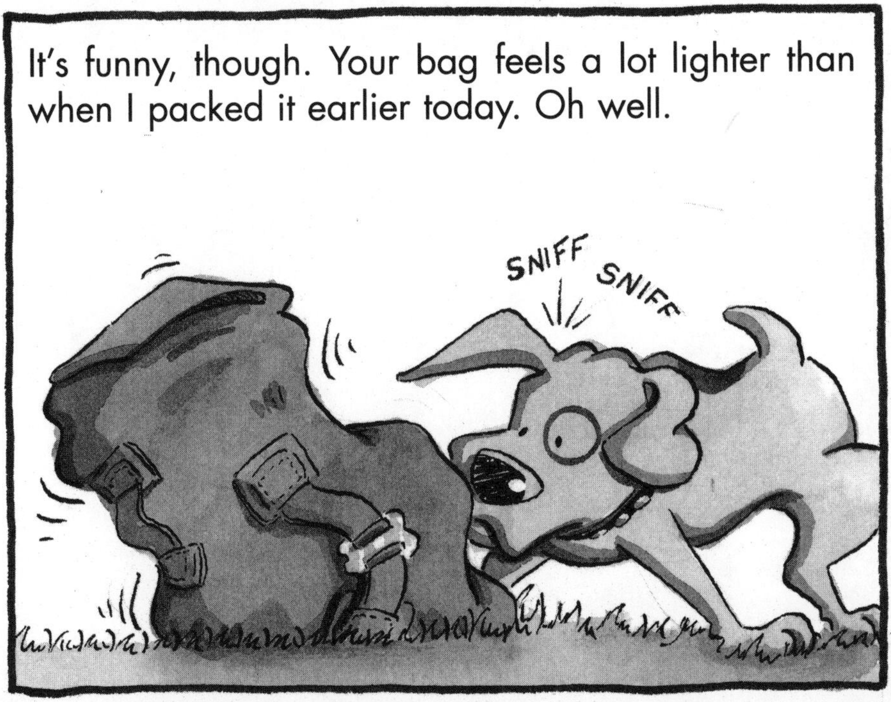
It's funny, though. Your bag feels a lot lighter than when I packed it earlier today. Oh well.
SNIFF
SNIFF

Have fun, Puppy! See you in a couple of days!

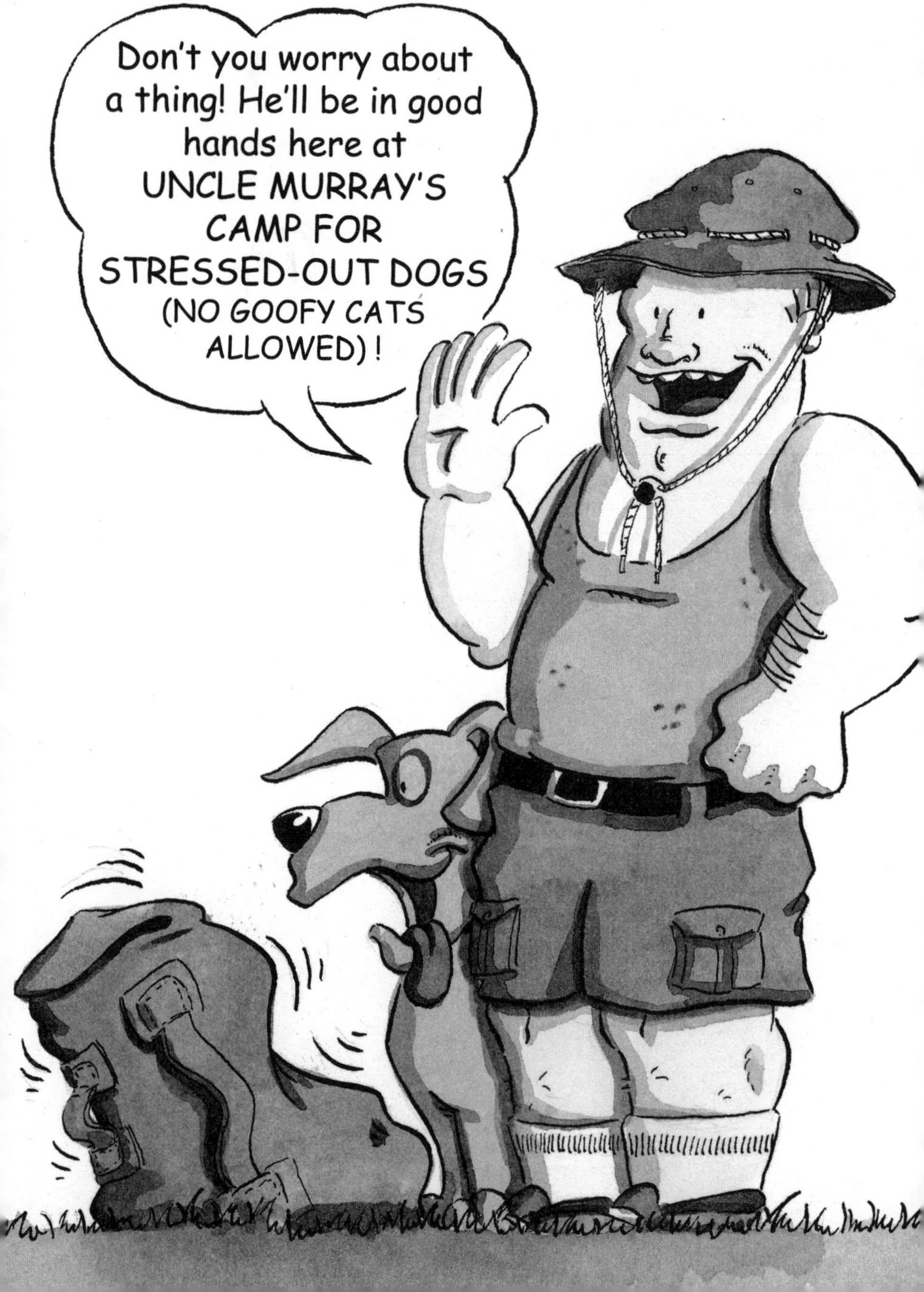
Don't you worry about a thing! He'll be in good hands here at UNCLE MURRAY'S CAMP FOR STRESSED-OUT DOGS (NO GOOFY CATS ALLOWED)!

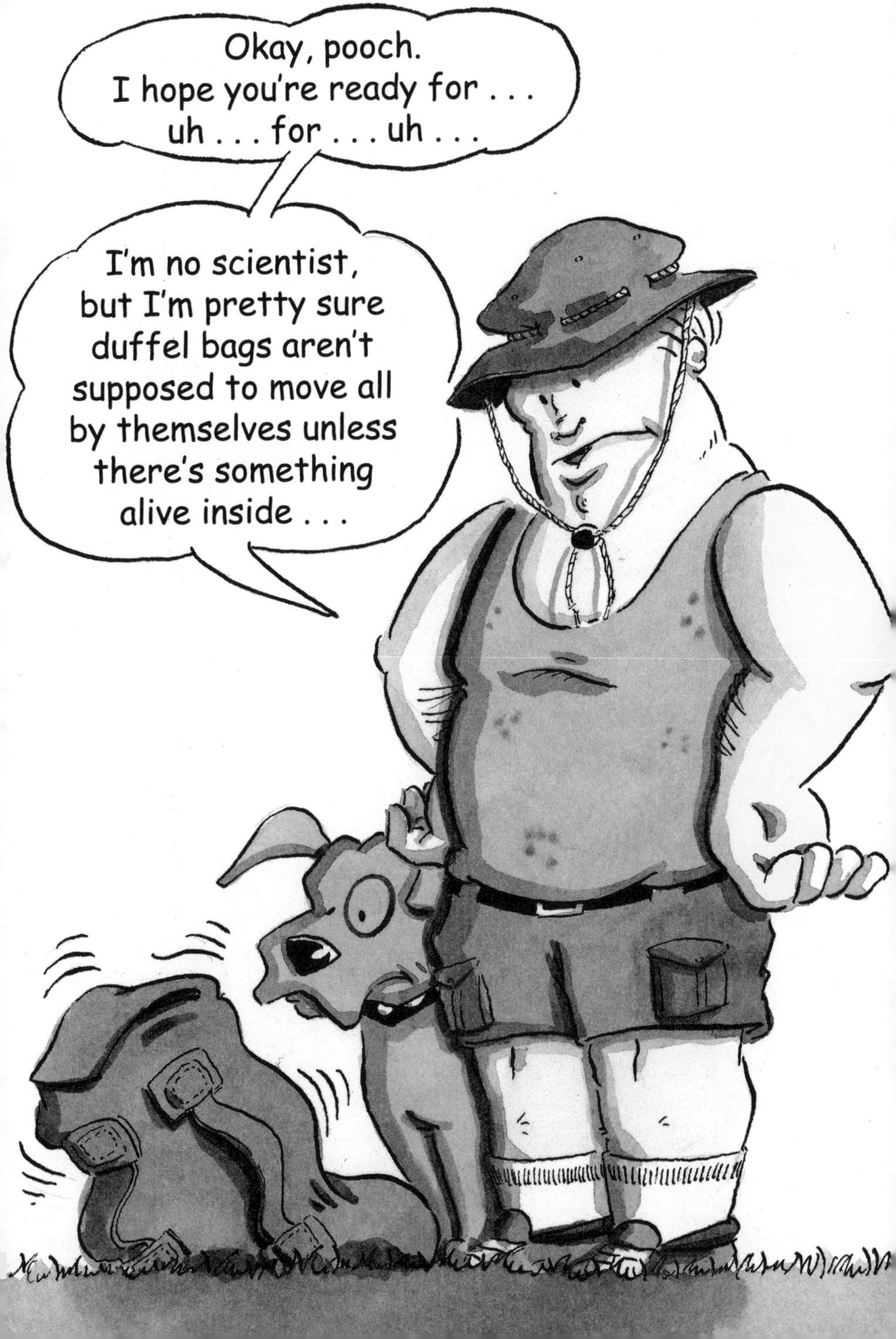
Okay, pooch. I hope you're ready for . . . uh . . . for . . . uh . . .
I'm no scientist, but I'm pretty sure duffel bags aren't supposed to move all by themselves unless there's something alive inside . . .

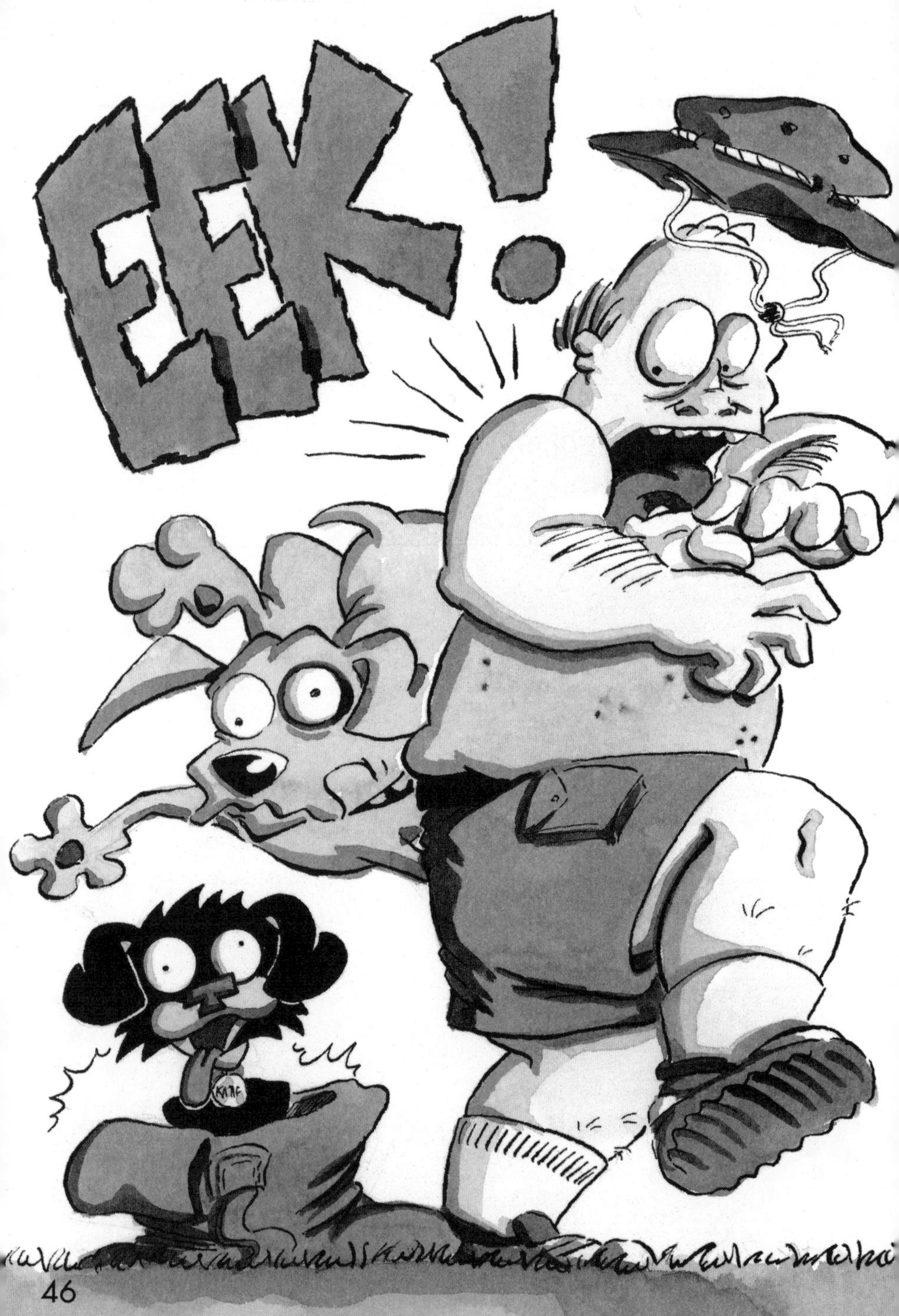
EEEK!

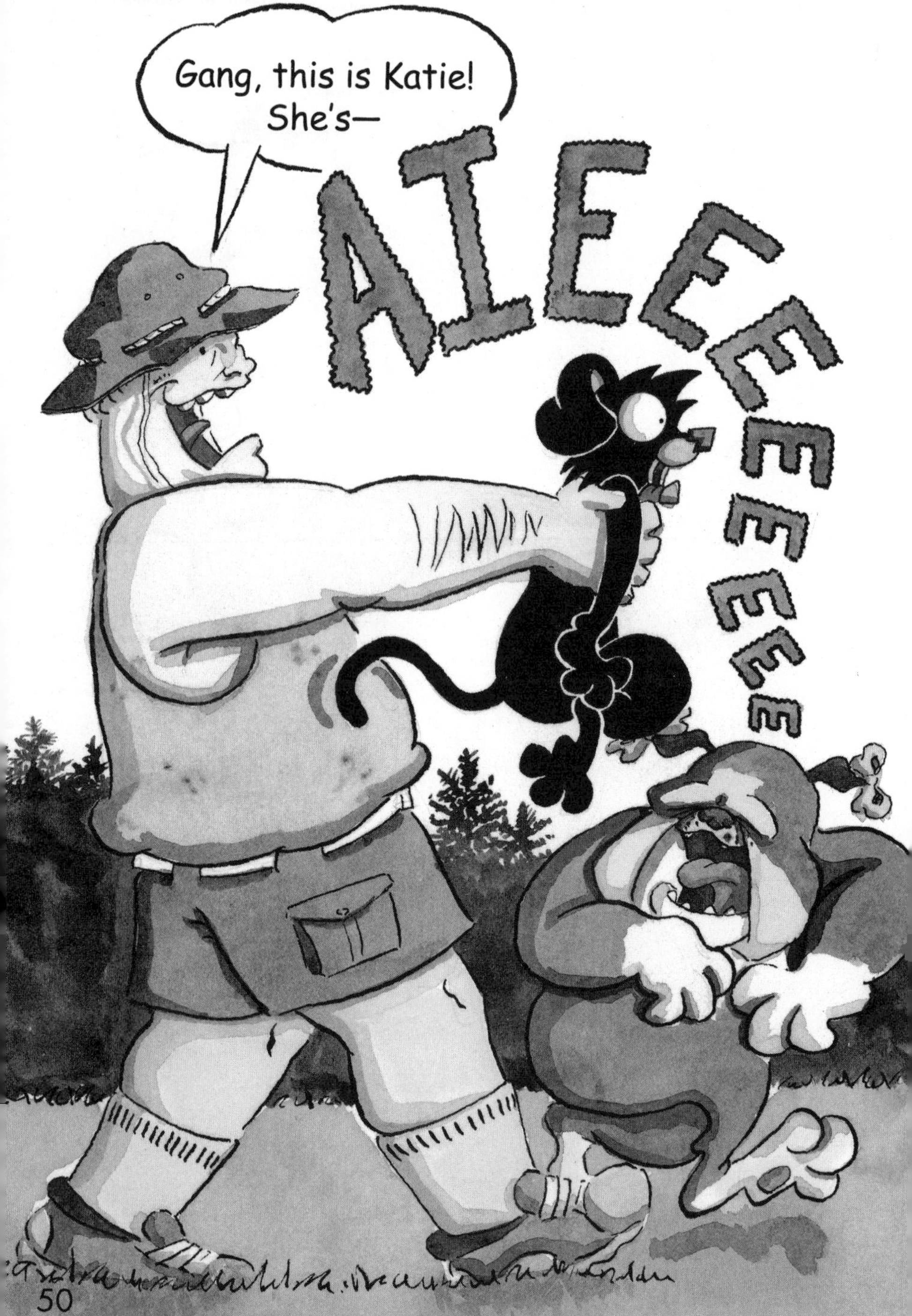
Gang, this is Katie! She's—
AIEEEEEEEEE

52

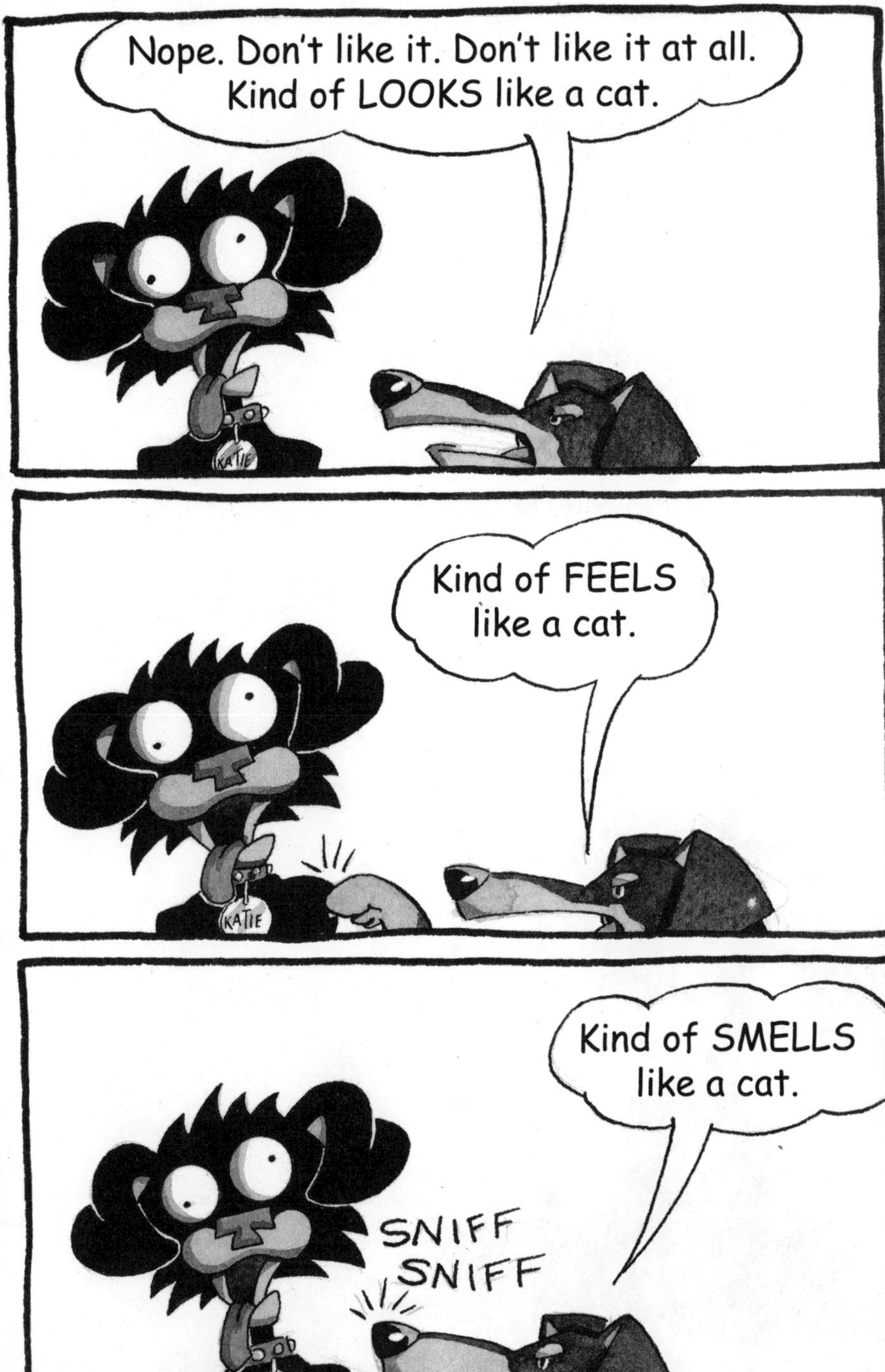

Nope. Don't like it. Don't like it at all. Kind of LOOKS like a cat.
KATIE
Kind of FEELS like a cat.
KATIE
Kind of SMELLS like a cat.
SNIFF SNIFF
KATIE

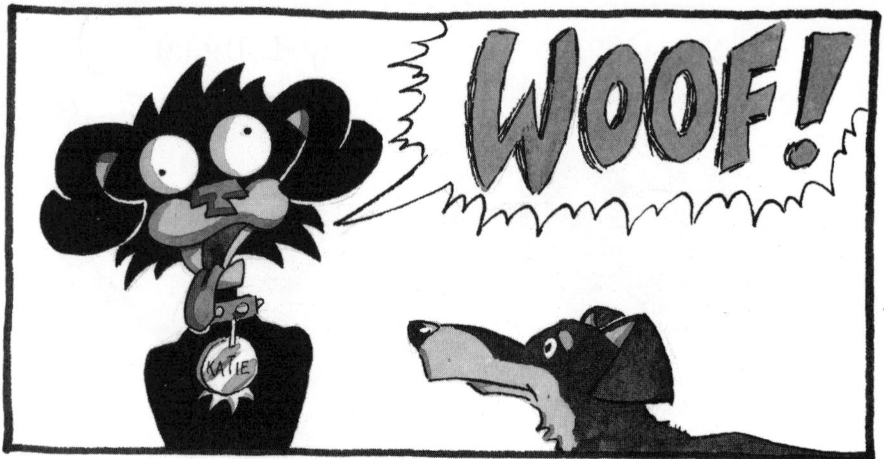
WOOF!

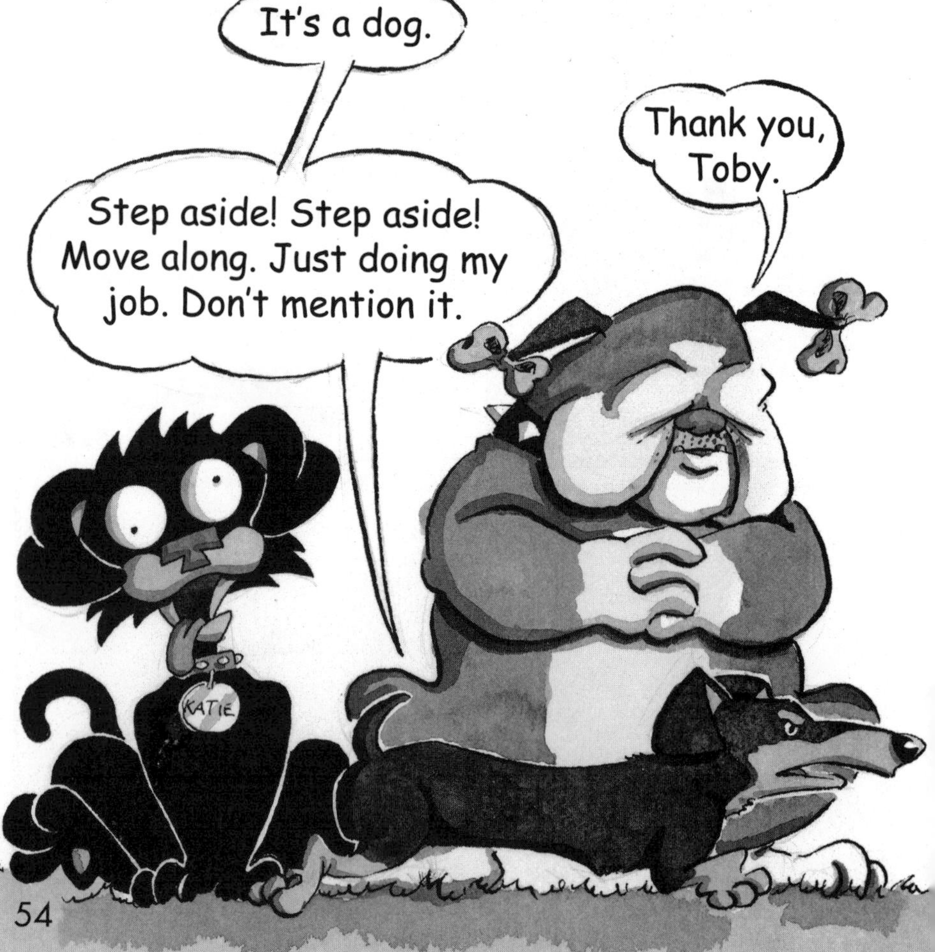
It's a dog.
Step aside! Step aside! Move along. Just doing my job. Don't mention it.
Thank you, Toby.
KATIE

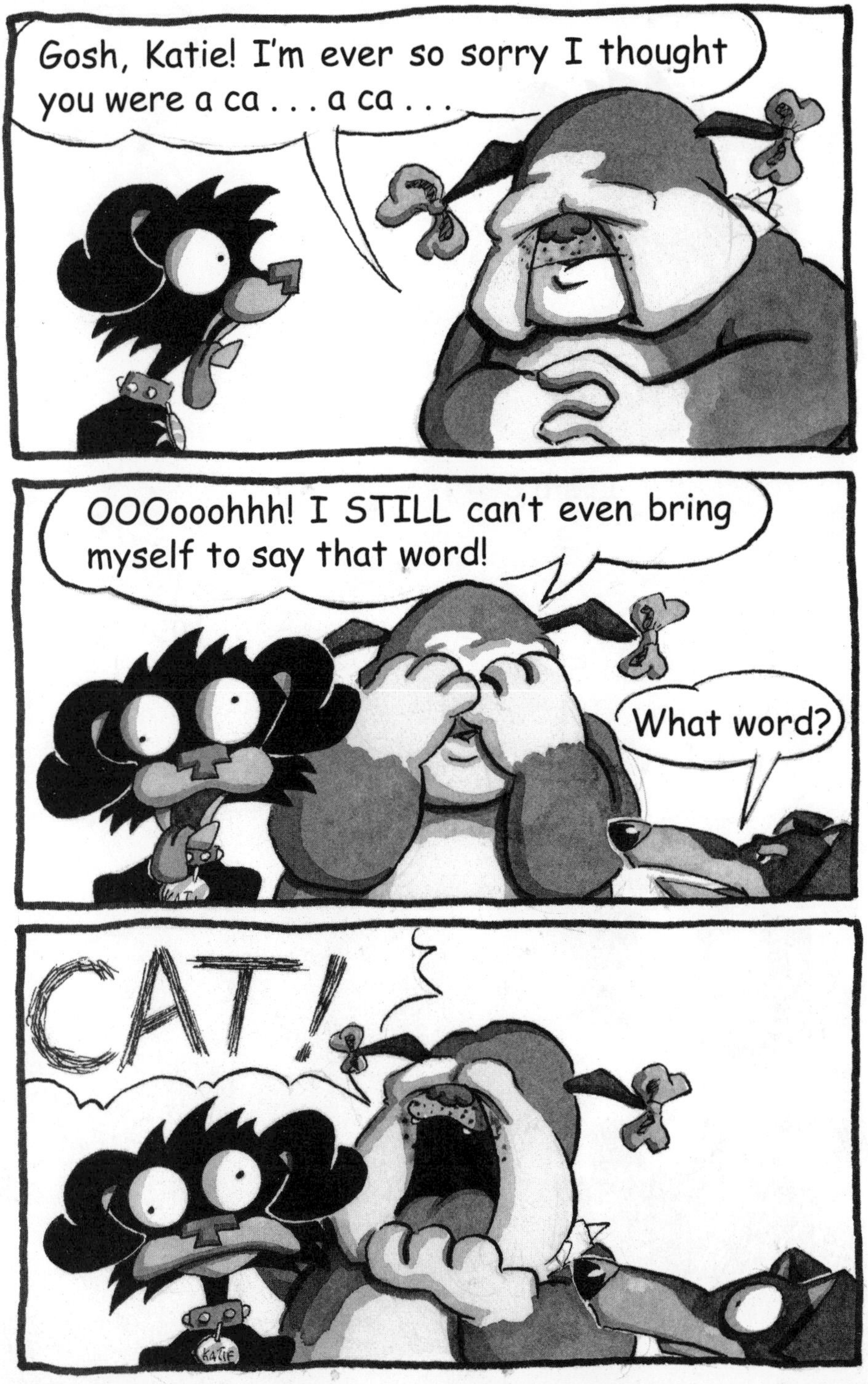

Gosh, Katie! I'm ever so sorry I thought you were a ca . . . a ca . . .
OOOooohhh! I STILL can't even bring myself to say that word!
What word?
CAT!
KATIE

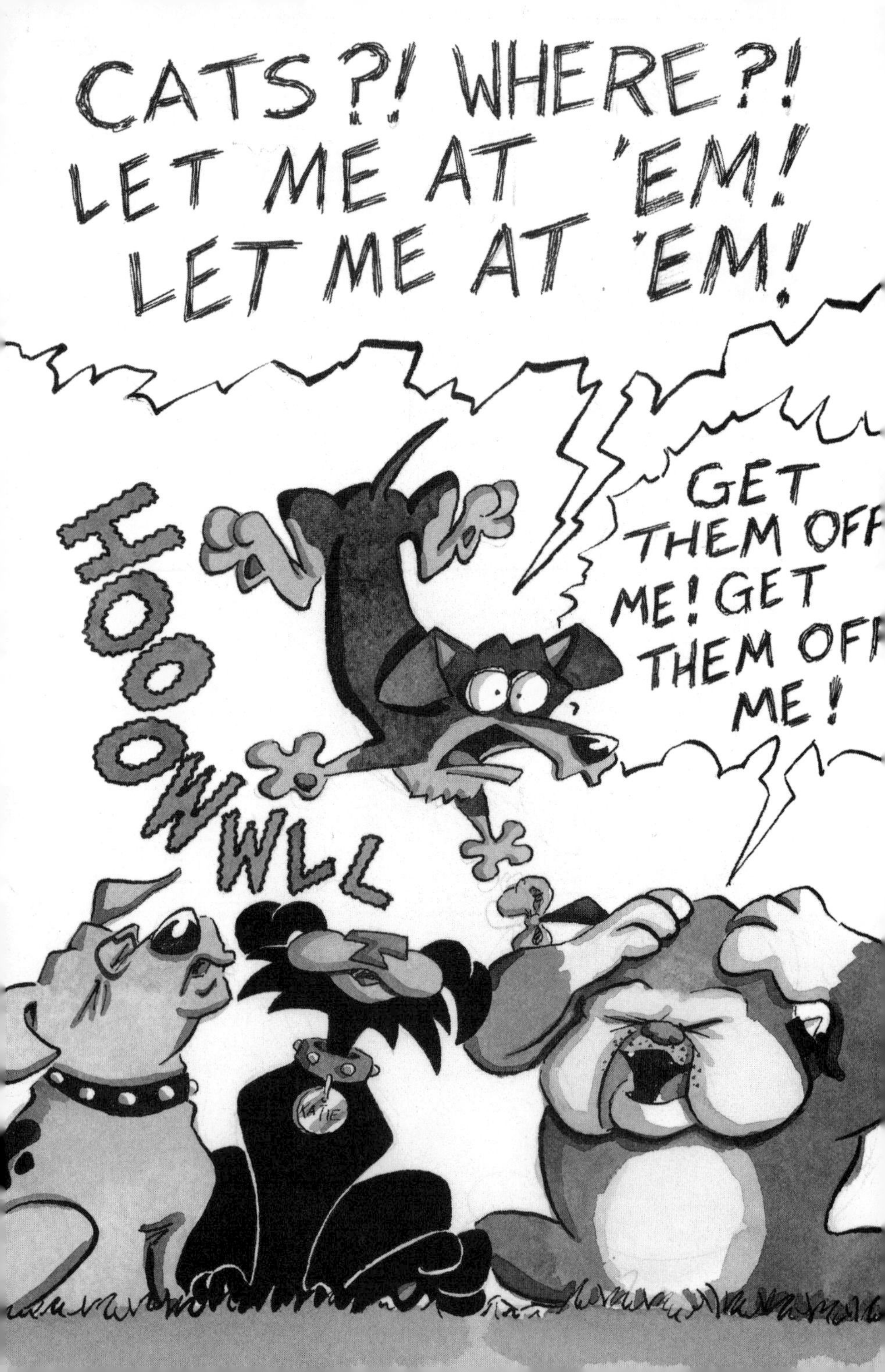
CATS?! WHERE?! LET ME AT 'EM! LET ME AT 'EM!
HOOOOWWLL
GET THEM OFF ME! GET THEM OFF ME!

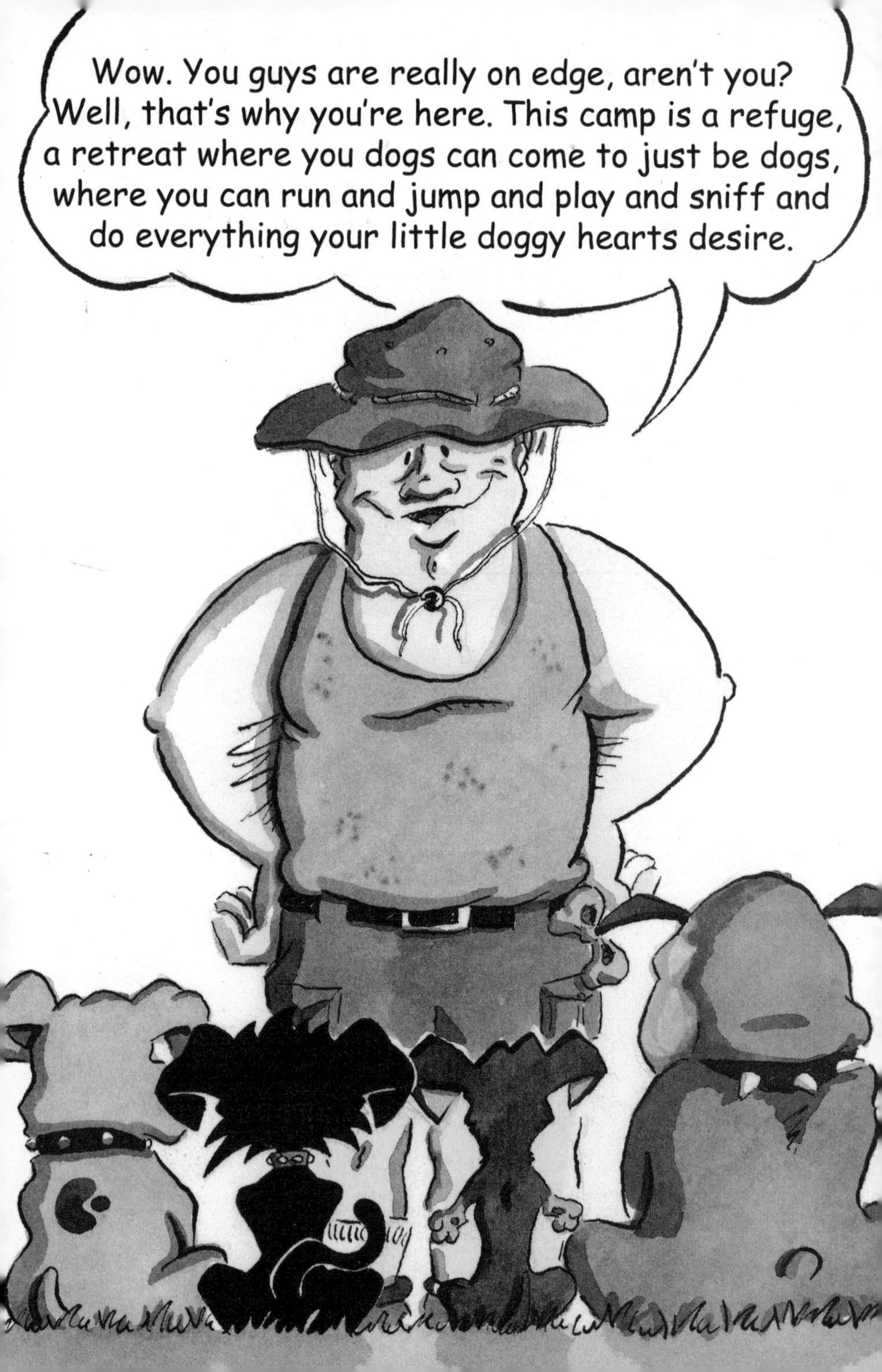
Wow. You guys are really on edge, aren't you? Well, that's why you're here. This camp is a refuge, a retreat where you dogs can come to just be dogs, where you can run and jump and play and sniff and do everything your little doggy hearts desire.

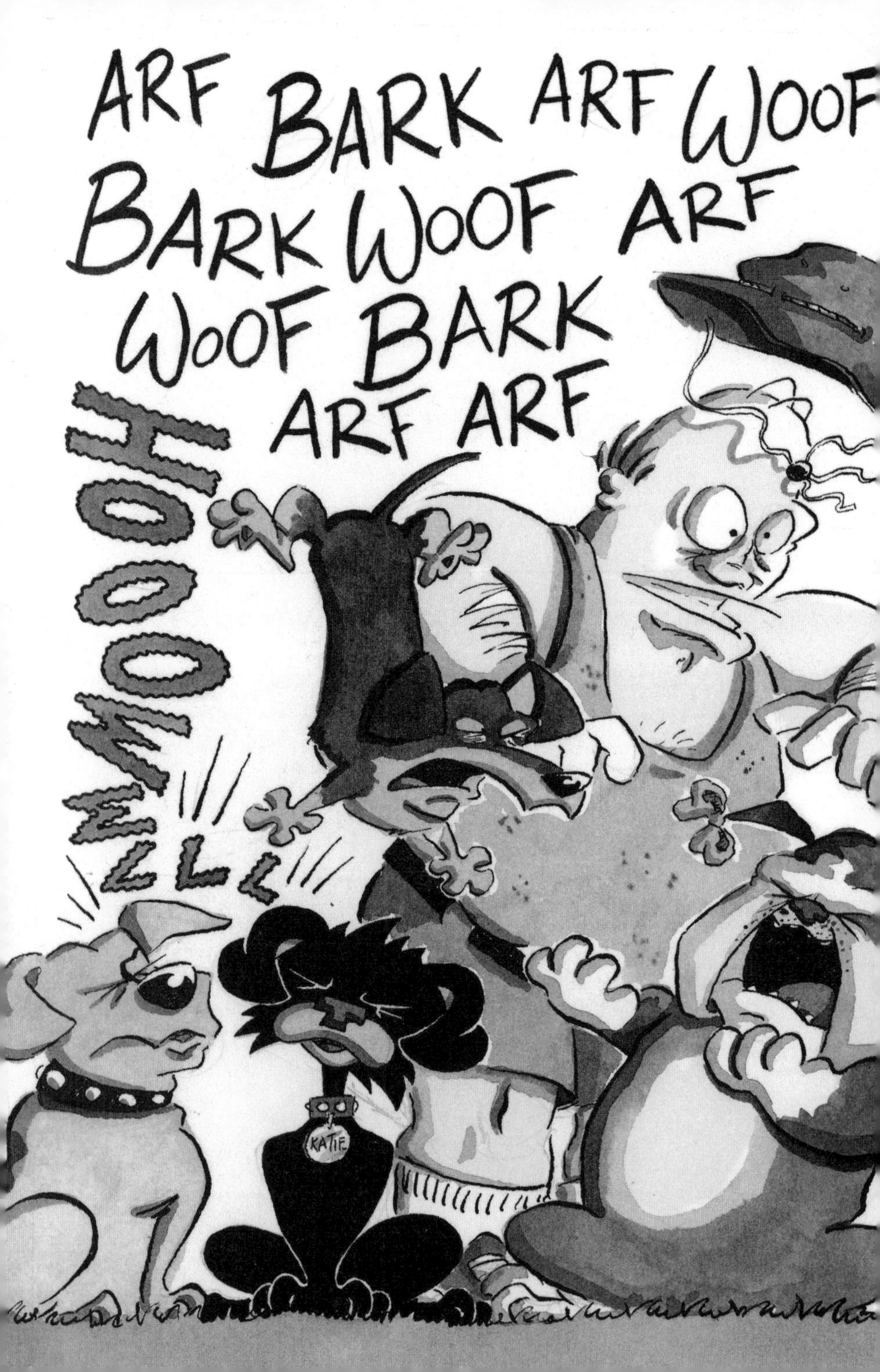
ARF BARK ARF WOOF
BARK WOOF ARF
WOOF BARK
ARF ARF
HOOOWWLLL
KATIE

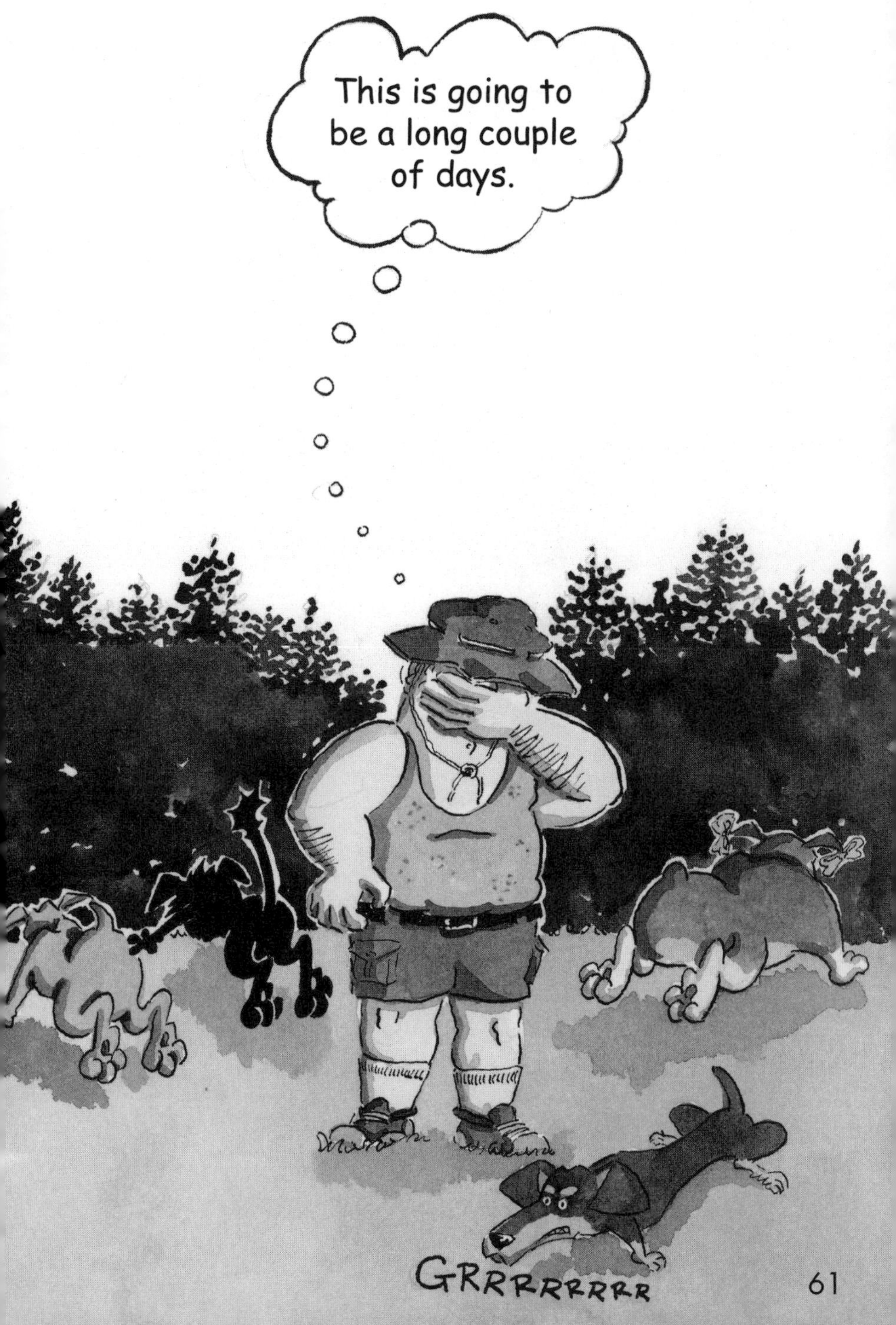
This is going to be a long couple of days.
GRRRRRRRR

•CHAPTER FOUR•

FETCH

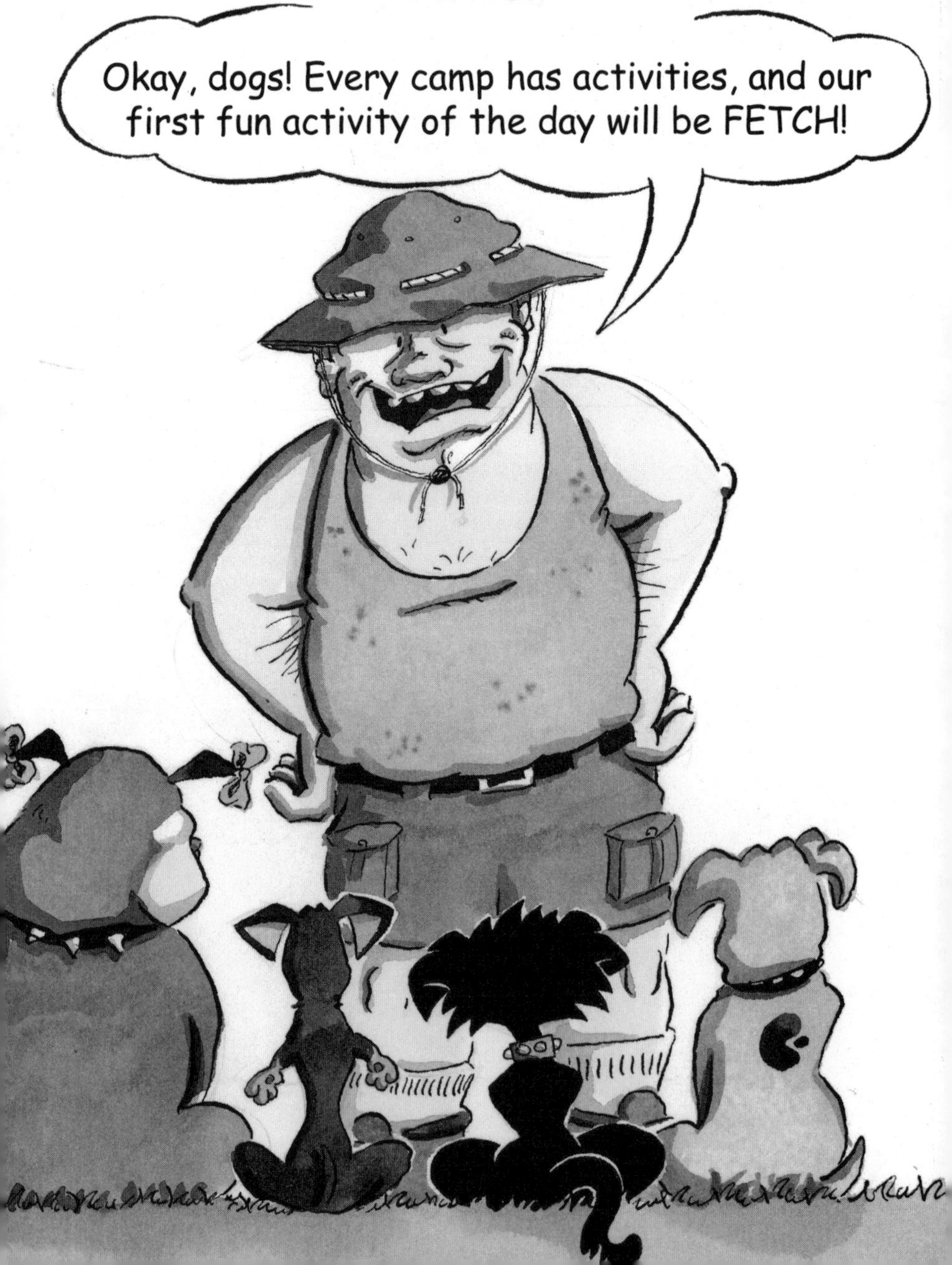
Okay, dogs! Every camp has activities, and our first fun activity of the day will be FETCH!

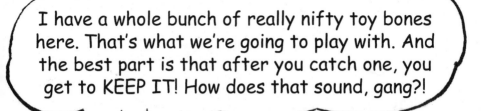

63

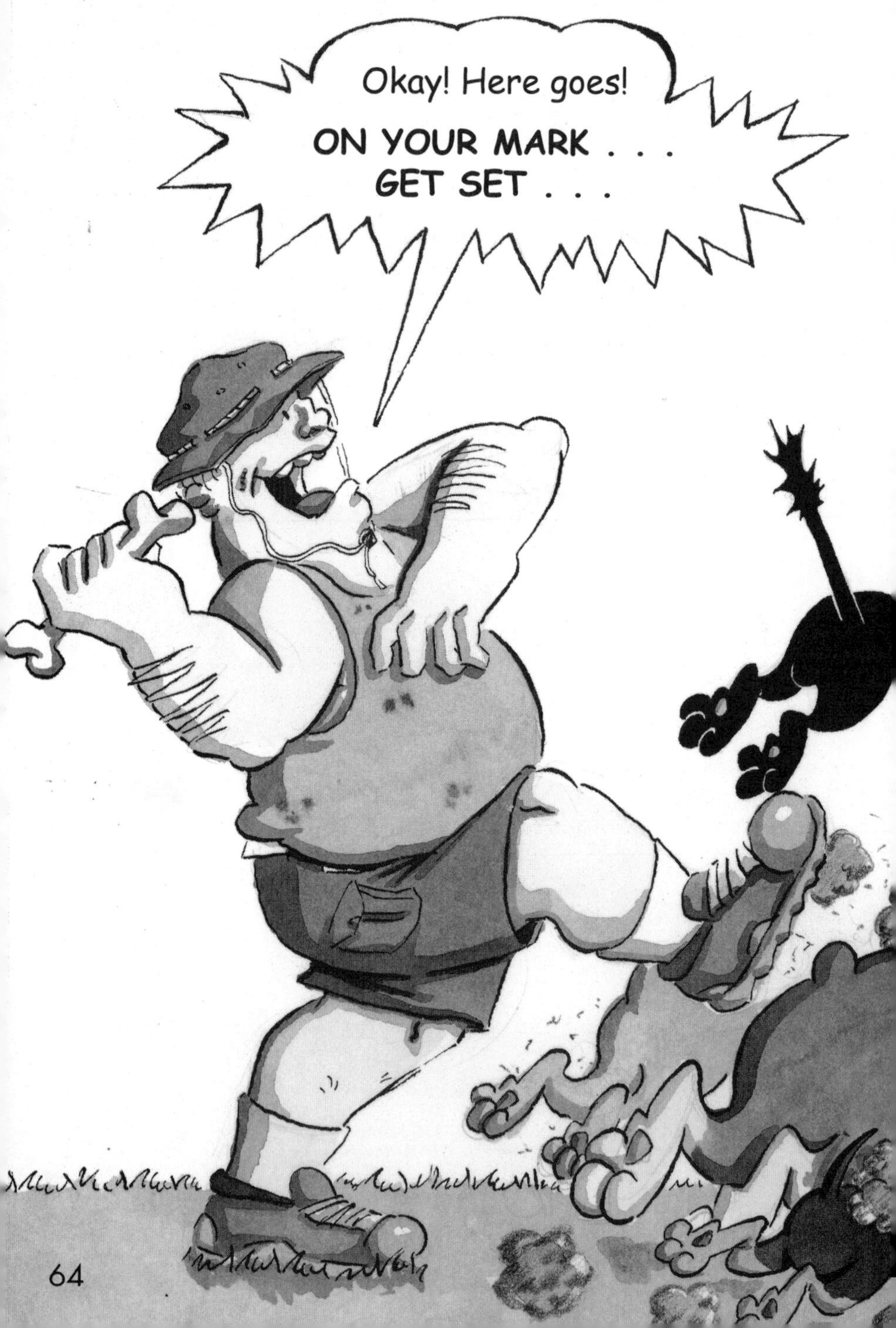
Okay! Here goes!
ON YOUR MARK . . .
GET SET . . .

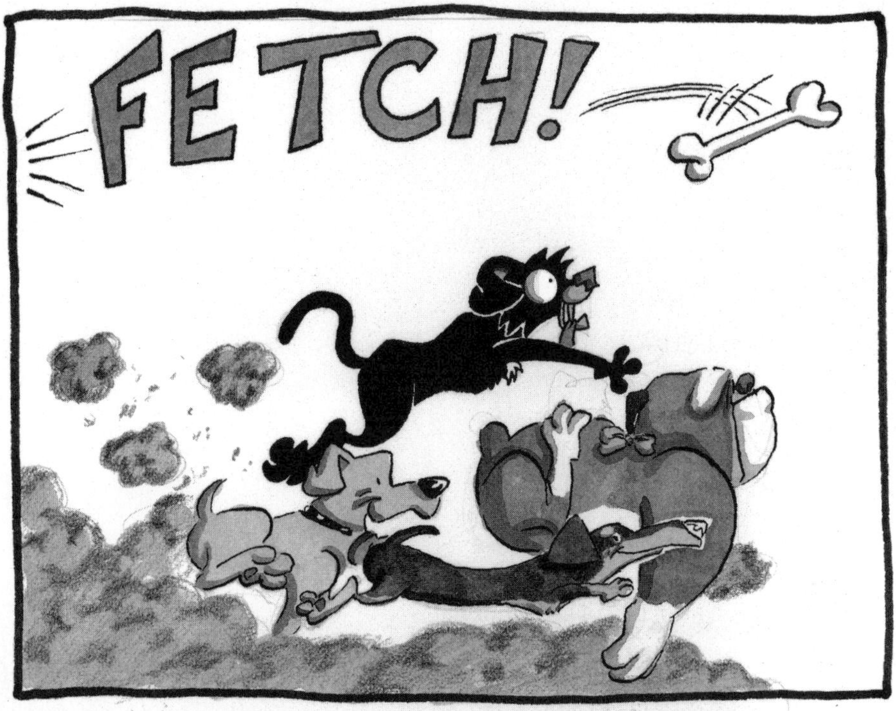
FETCH!

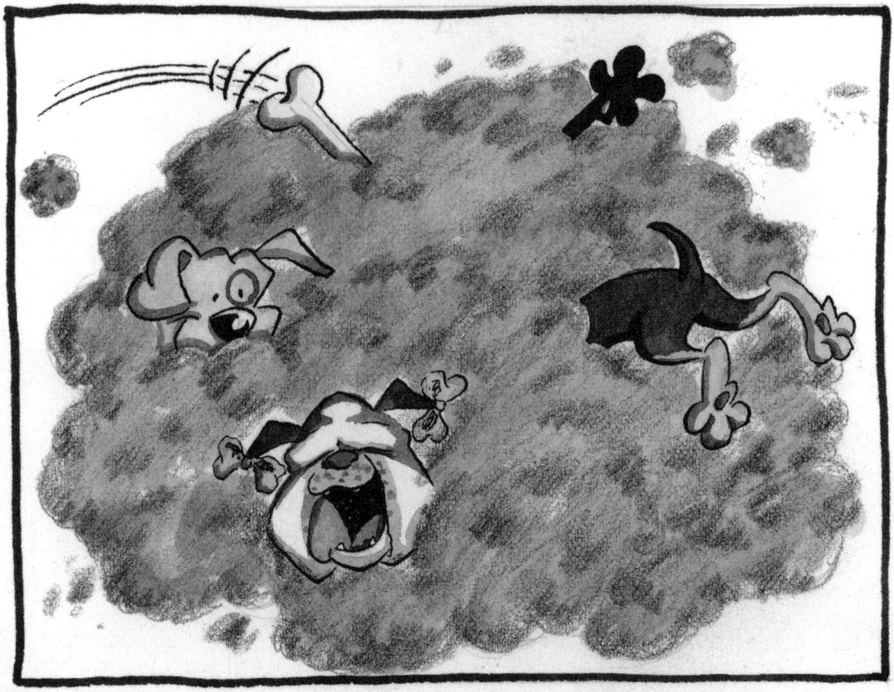

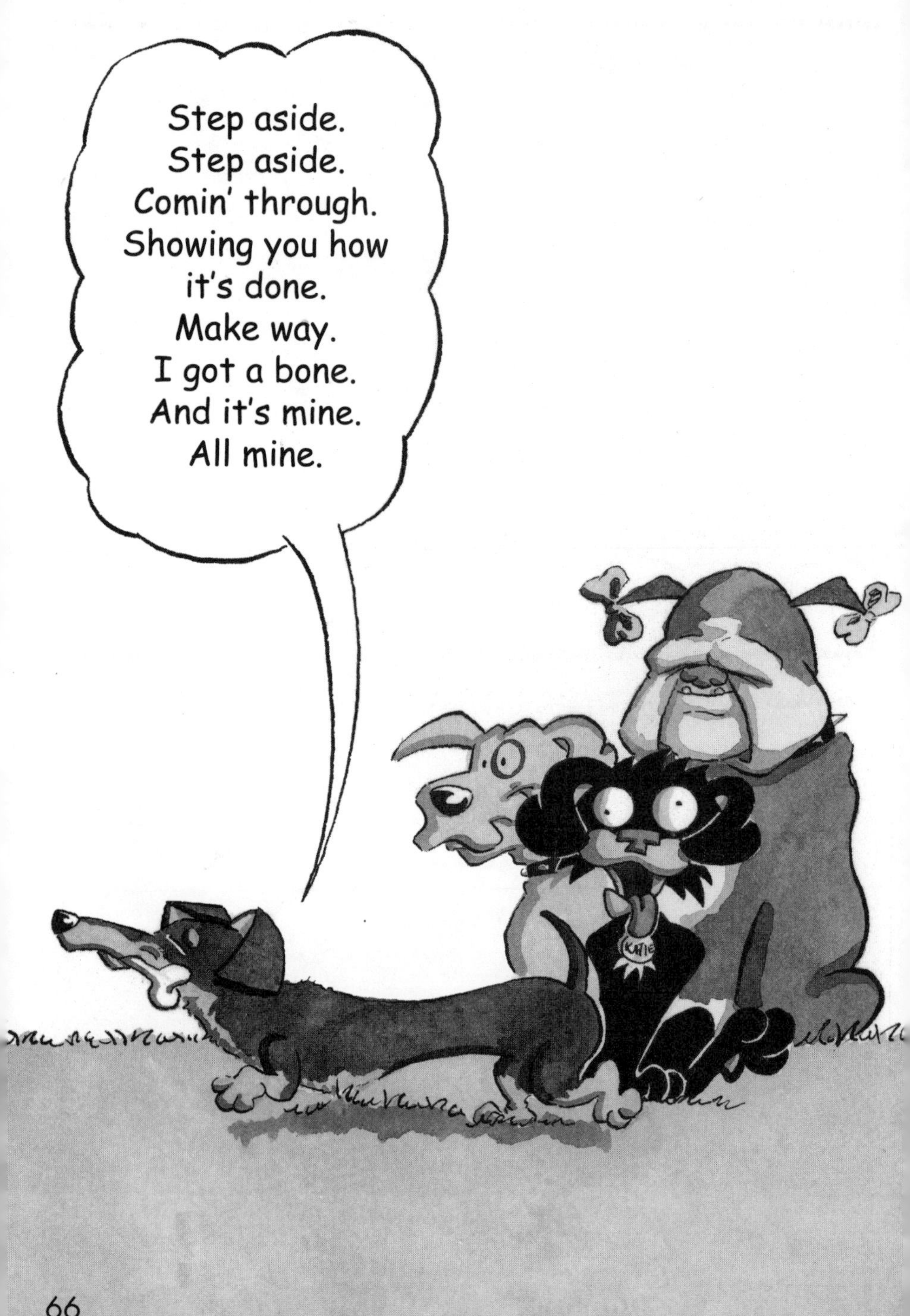
Step aside.
Step aside.
Comin' through.
Showing you how
it's done.
Make way.
I got a bone.
And it's mine.
All mine.
KATIE

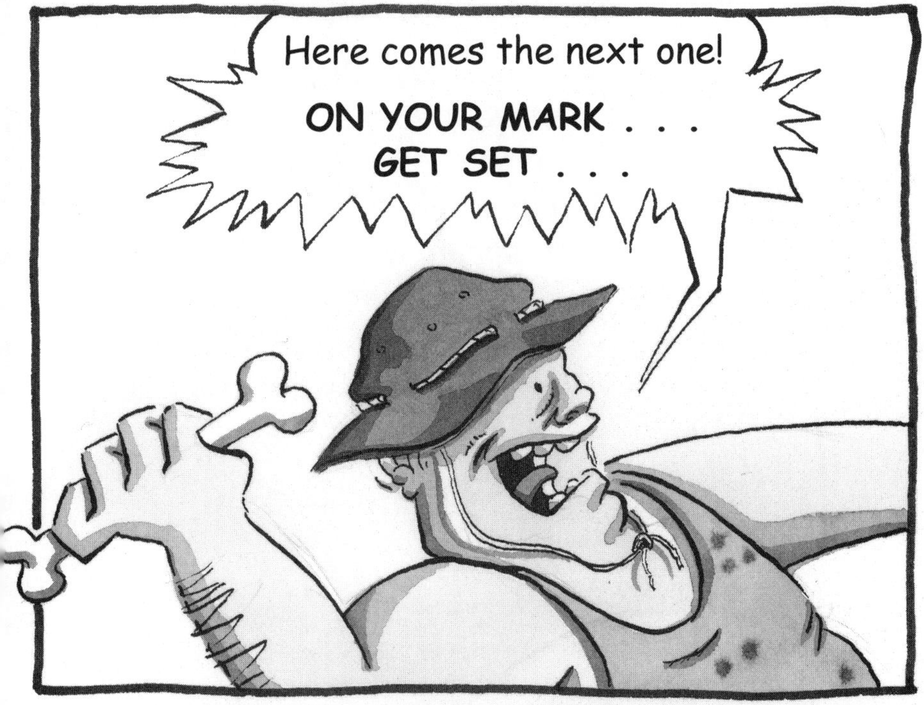
Here comes the next one!
ON YOUR MARK . . .
GET SET . . .

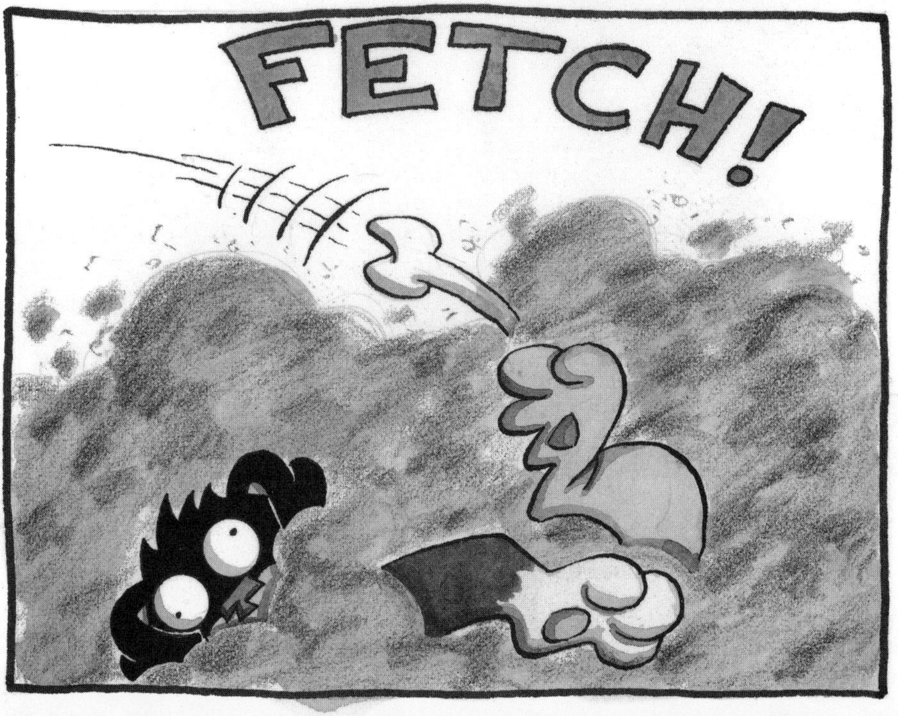
FETCH!

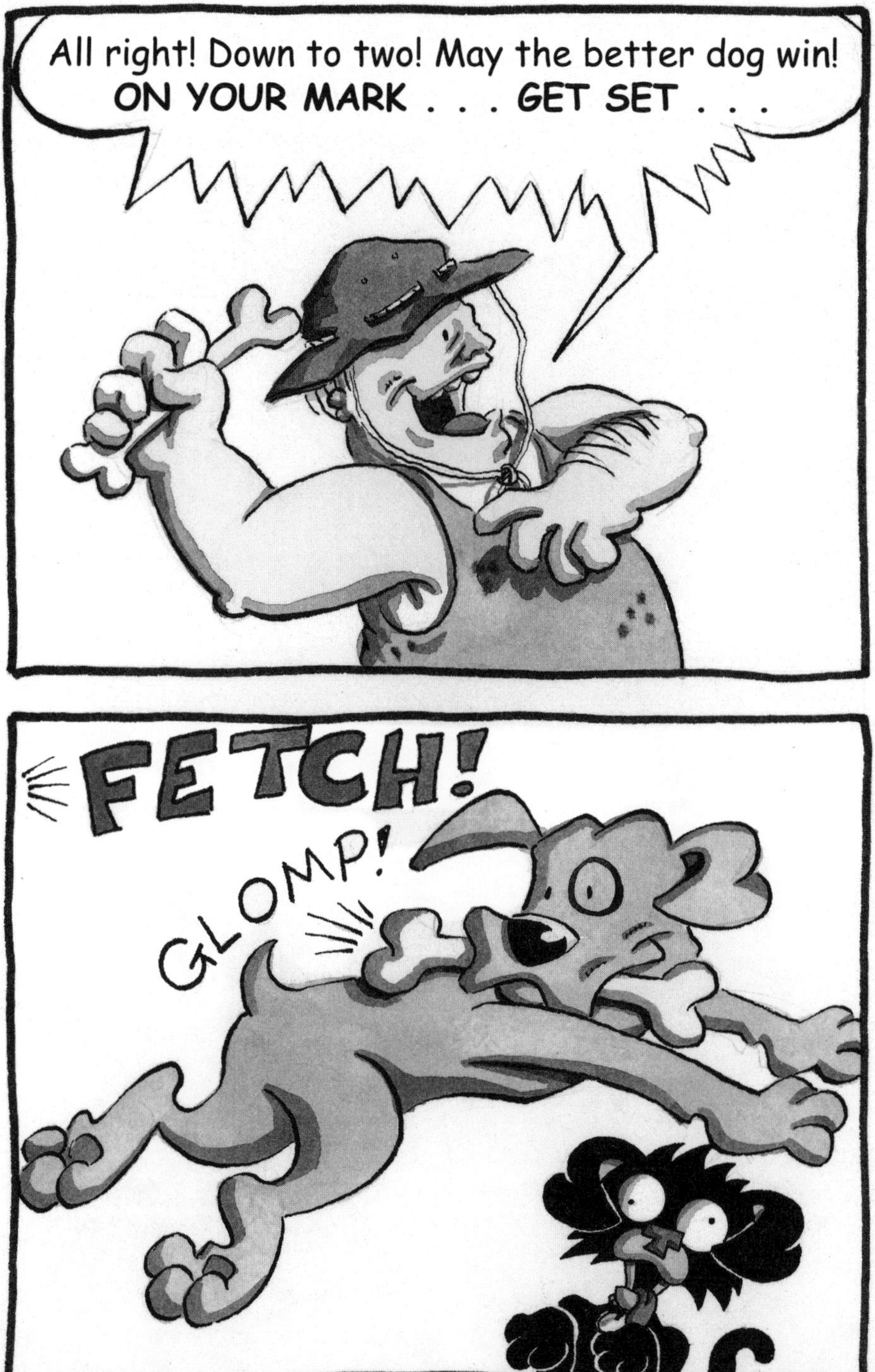
All right! Down to two! May the better dog win!
ON YOUR MARK . . . GET SET . . .
FETCH!
GLOMP!

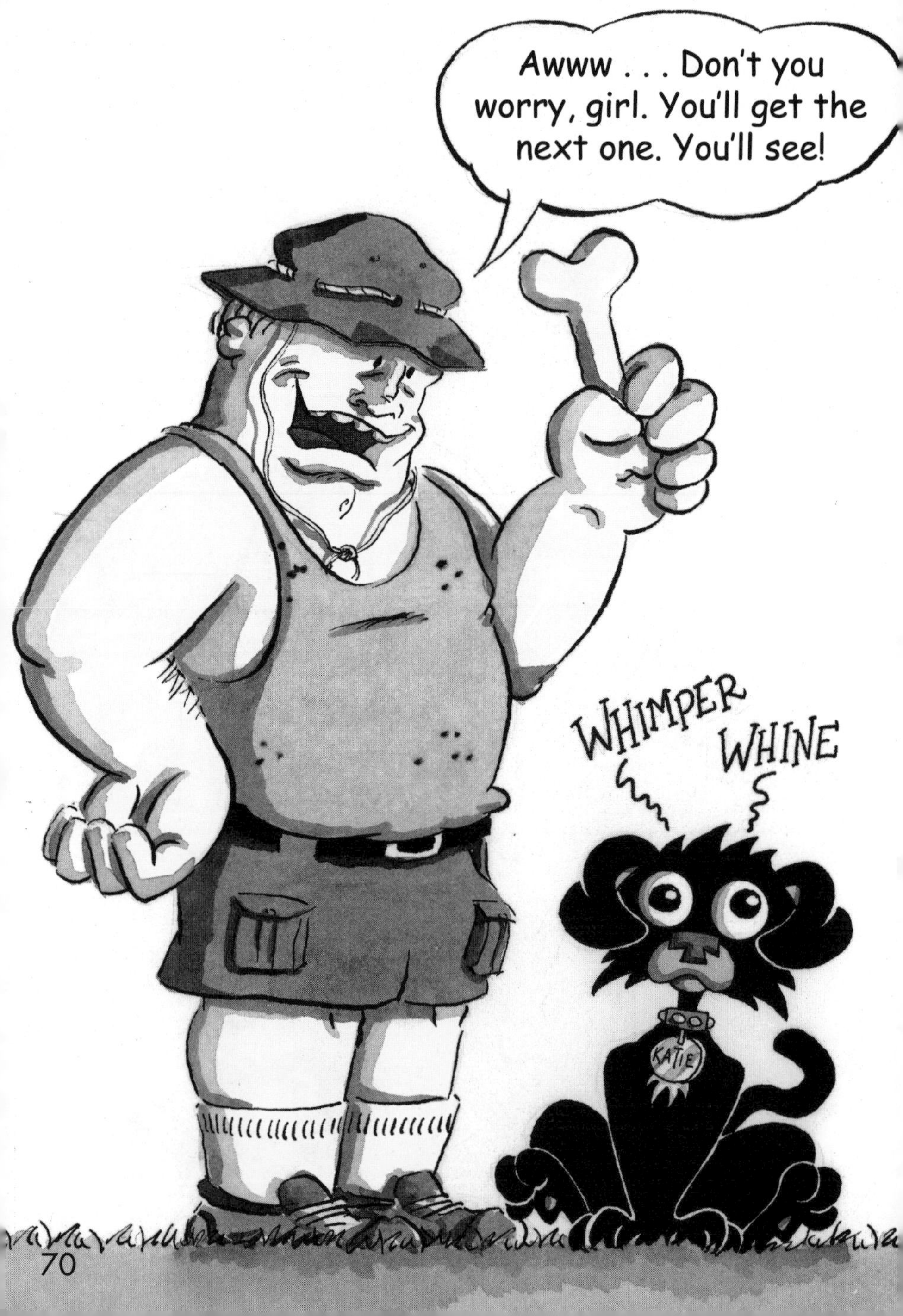
Awww . . . Don't you worry, girl. You'll get the next one. You'll see!
WHIMPER
WHINE
KATIE

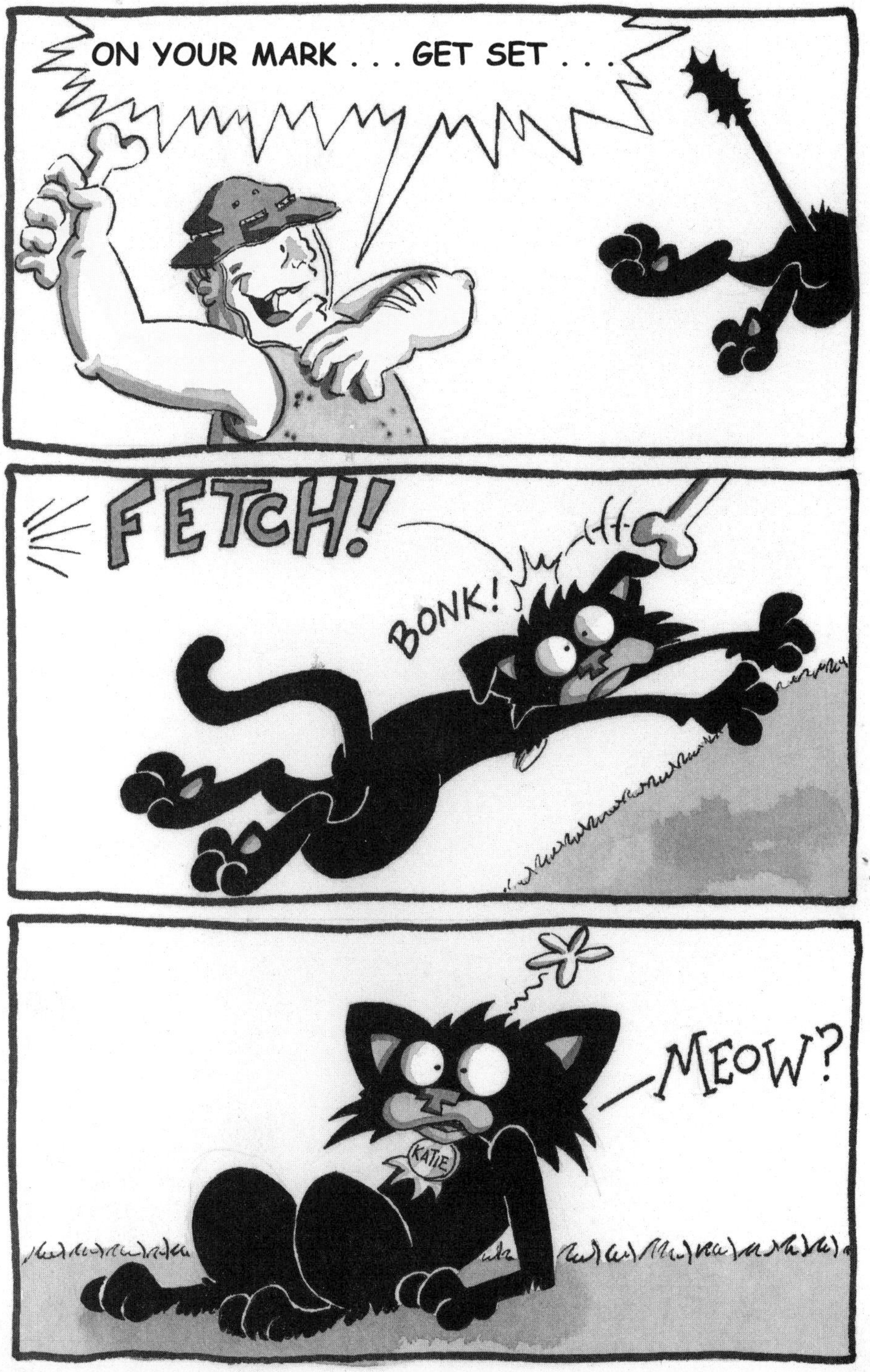
ON YOUR MARK . . . GET SET . . .
FETCH!
BONK!
KATIE
MEOW?

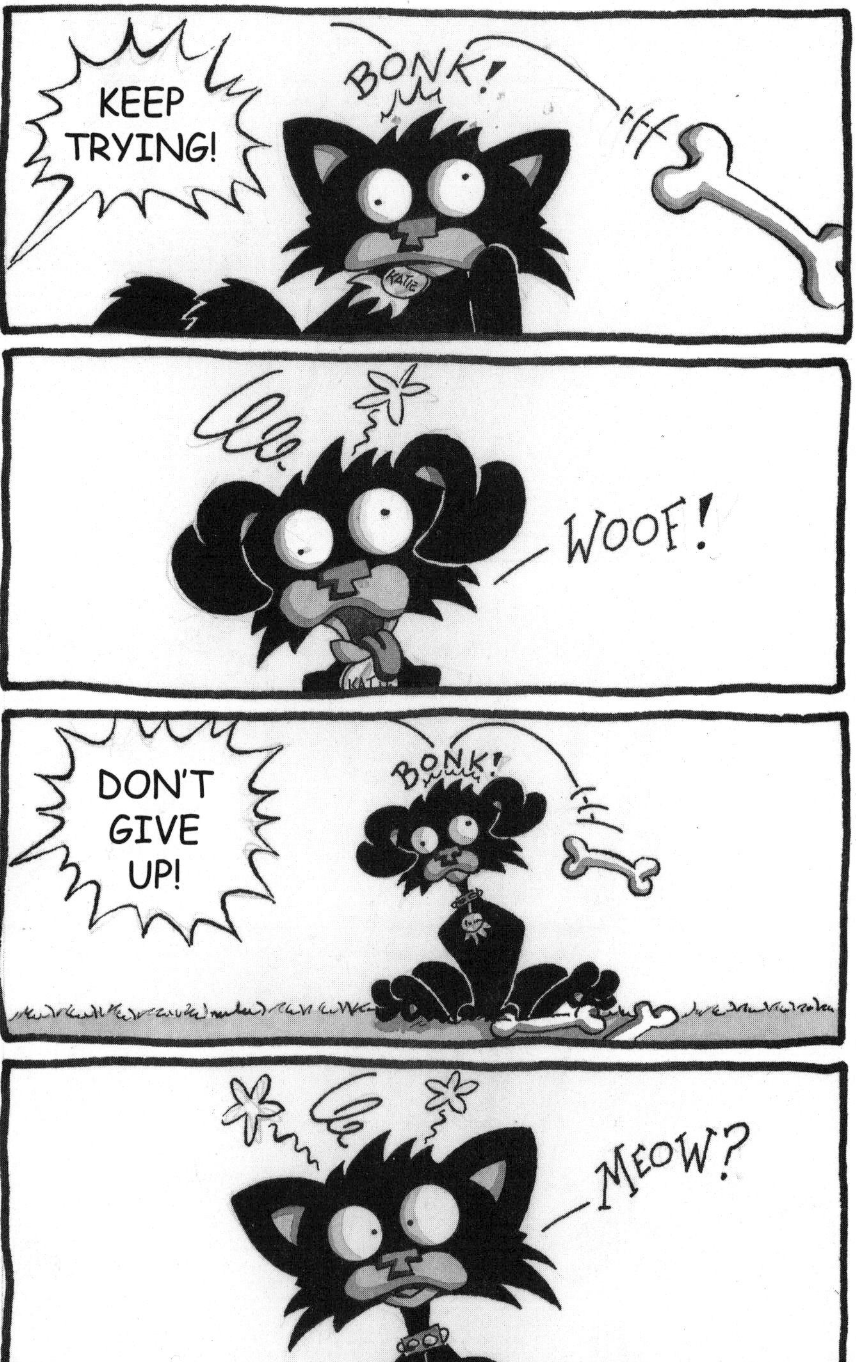
KEEP TRYING!
BONK!
WOOF!
DON'T GIVE UP!
BONK!
MEOW?

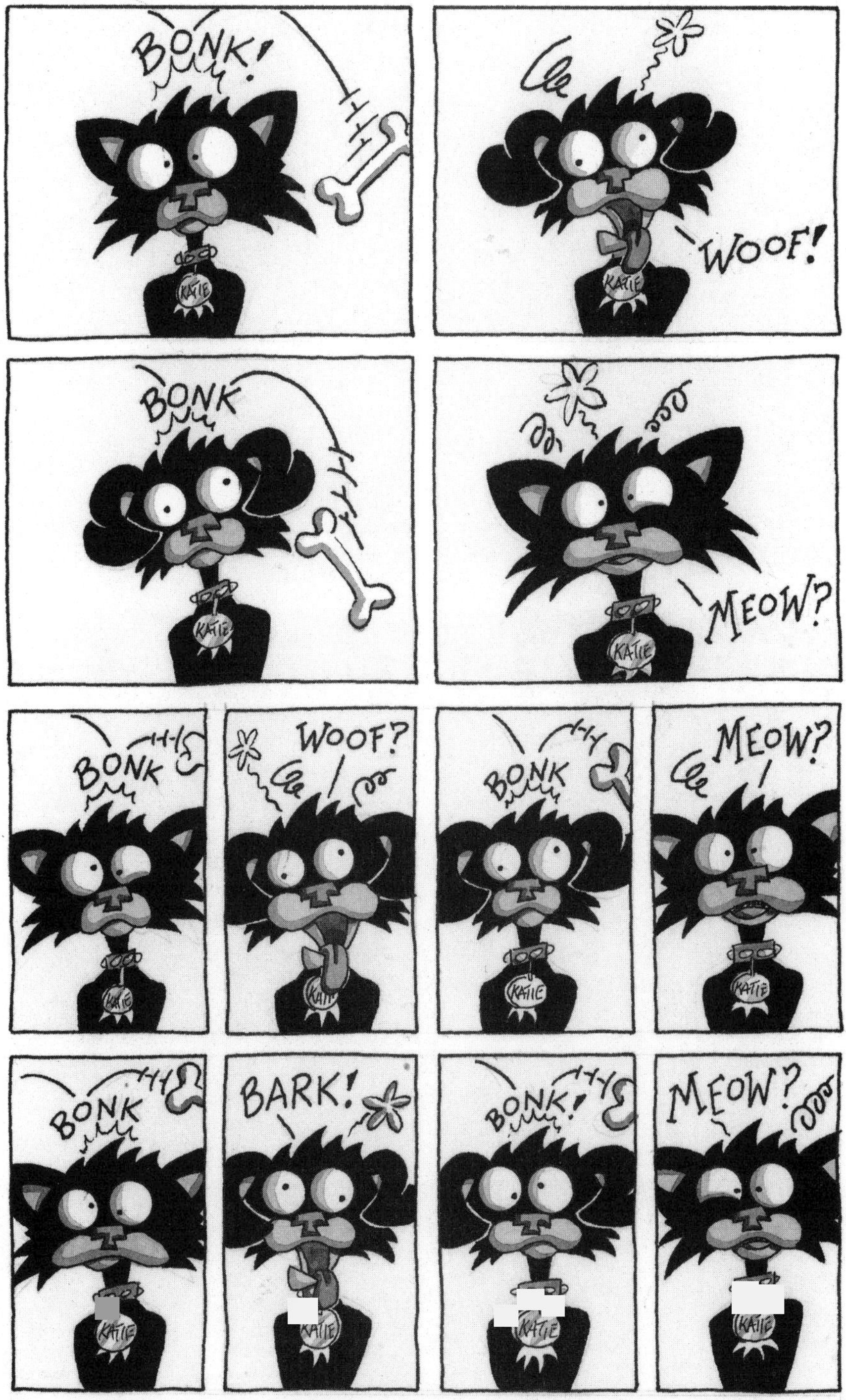
BONK!
KATIE
WOOF!
KATIE
BONK
KATIE
MEOW?
KATIE
BONK
KATIE
WOOF?
KATIE
BONK
KATIE
MEOW?
KATIE
BONK
KATIE
BARK!
KATIE
BONK!
KATIE
MEOW?
KATIE

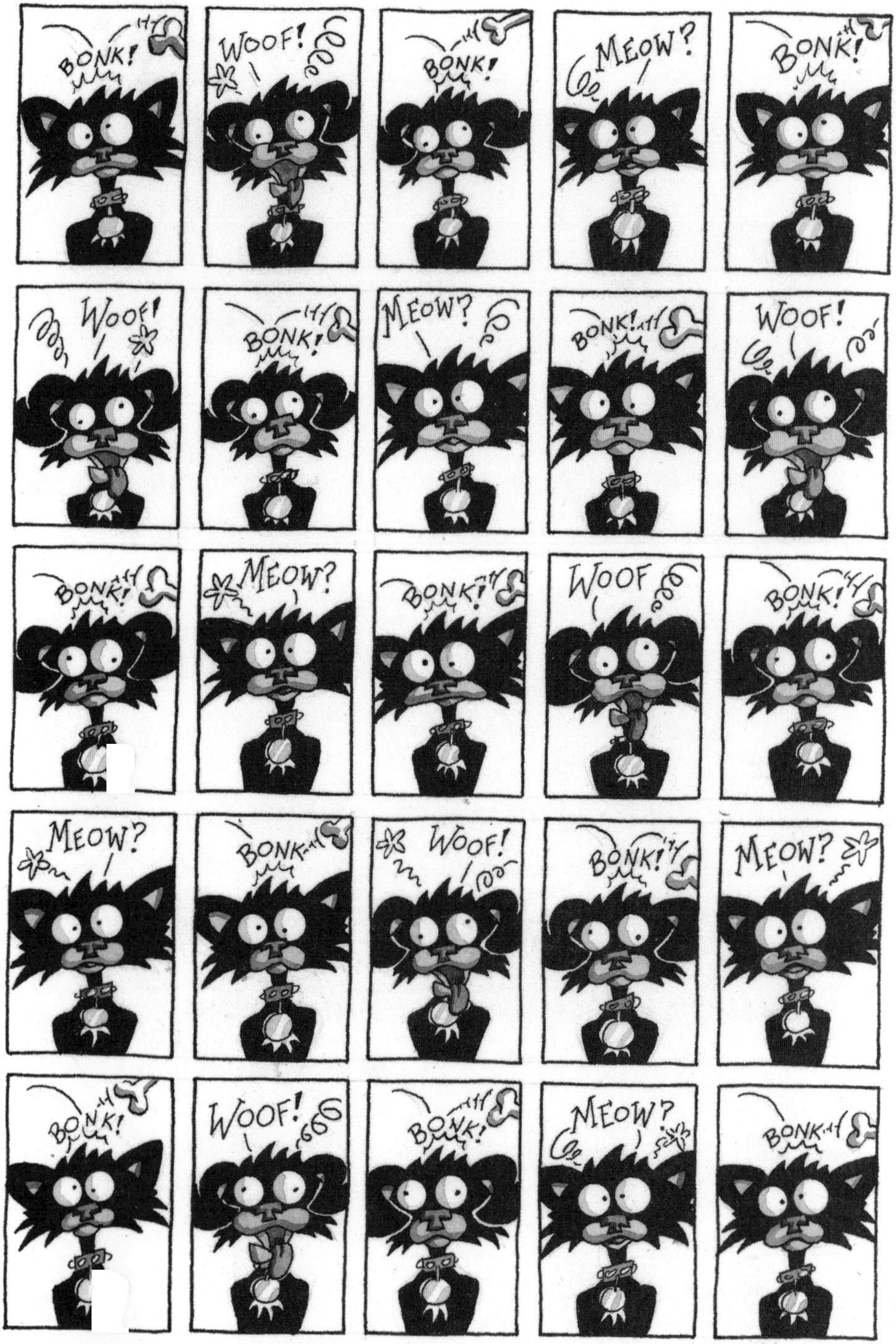
BONK!
WOOF!
BONK!
MEOW?
BONK!
WOOF!
BONK!
MEOW?
BONK!
WOOF!
BONK!
MEOW?
BONK!
WOOF
BONK!
MEOW?
BONK
WOOF!
BONK!
MEOW?
BONK!
WOOF!
BONK!
MEOW?
BONK

75

UNCLE MURRAY'S FUN FACTS

WHY ARE DOGS BETTER AT FETCHING THAN CATS?

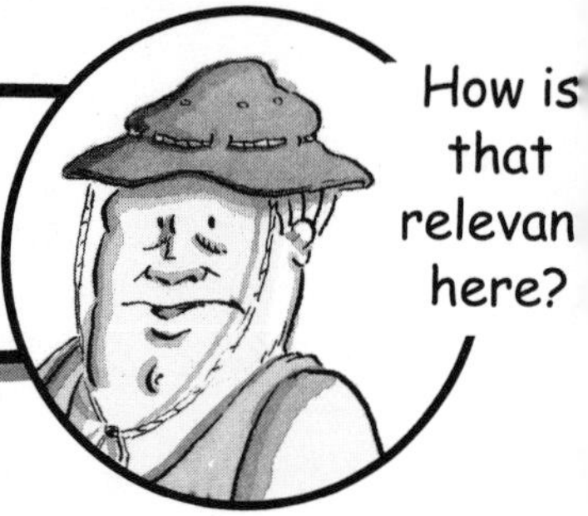
How is that relevan here?

Not all dogs like to play fetch. But those that do can become obsessed with the game.

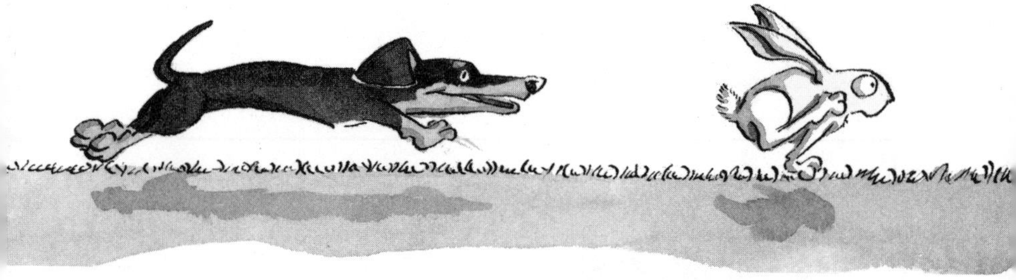

Why do dogs like to play fetch so much?
Built into a dog's brain is the instinct to fetch: to hunt and chase and capture smaller animals. Instinct is the knowledge an animal is born with that helps it to survive. No one teaches a bird how to fly. It just knows. No one teaches a dog how to fetch. It just knows. But without any smaller animals around, a stick or a tennis ball will do.

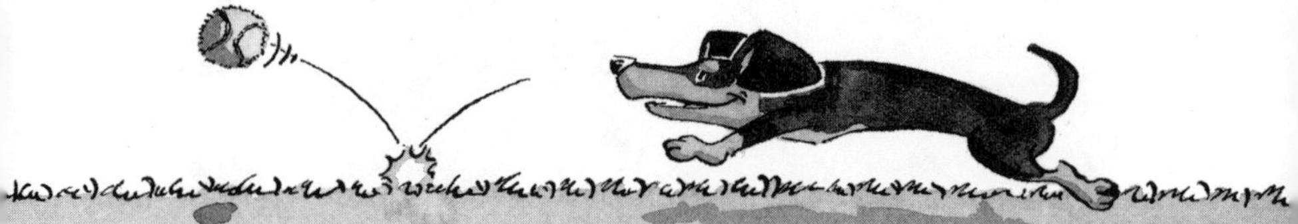

But cats are hunters, too. So why don't they play fetch?

A few of them do. Cats are natural born fetchers. Their mouths are perfectly designed to grab small items and animals and then carry them around. Think of a mother cat and how she will pick up and carry her kittens.

So why don't cats play fetch like dogs?

Cats just aren't generally as playful with people as dogs are. One reason is because cats like to conserve their energy. It's why they sleep so much. Their instinct tells them to rest as much as possible so they'll have the energy to hunt later.

Another reason is because they tend to be loners. Cats will be affectionate with their owners, but tend not to play with them the same way dogs do. This means that cats will often chase a toy you throw, but they'll rarely pick it up and bring it back.

More playful. More energetic. This all just goes to prove that dogs are better than cats. So, there.

•CHAPTER FIVE•

SWIMMING

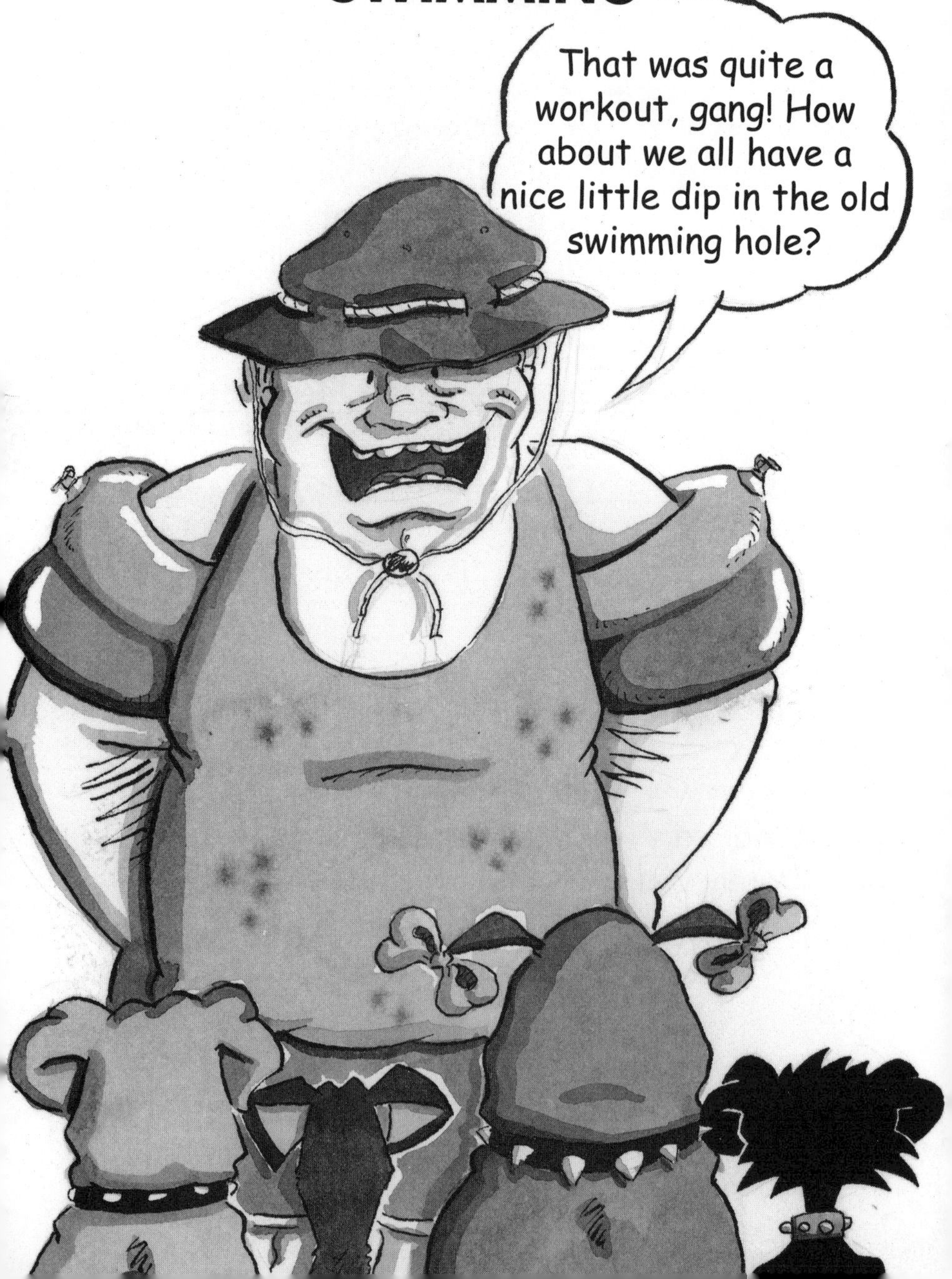

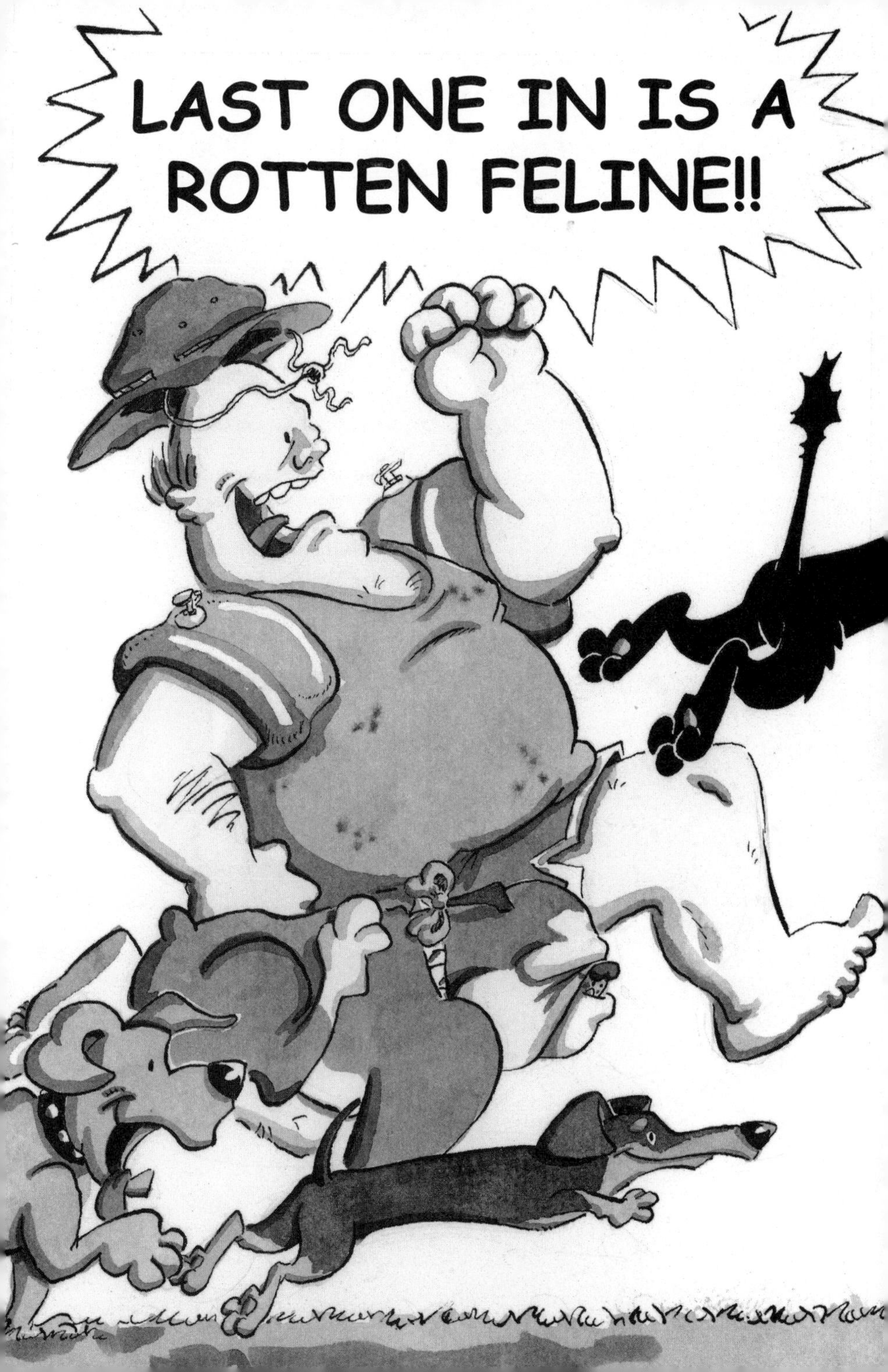
LAST ONE IN IS A ROTTEN FELINE!!

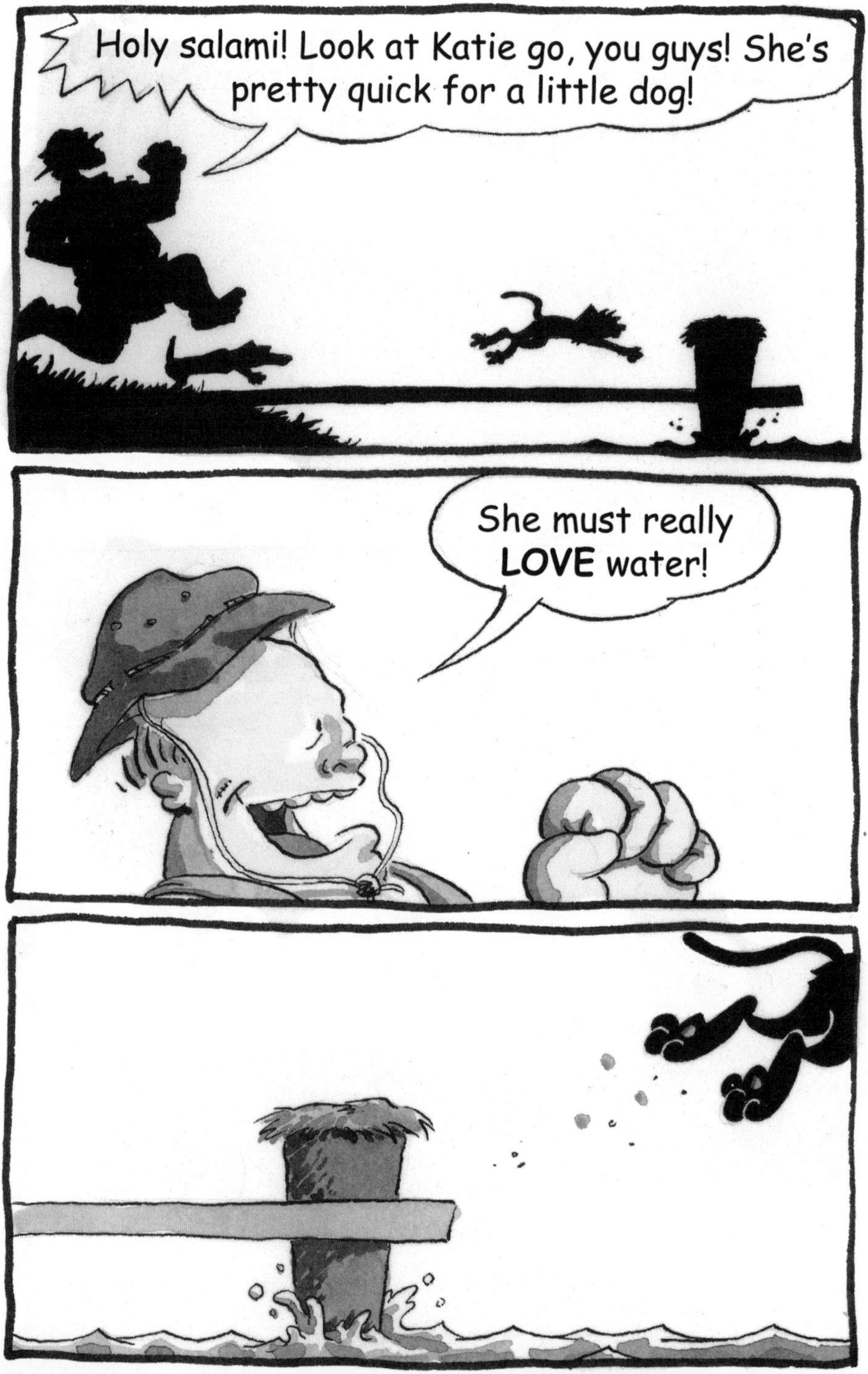
Holy salami! Look at Katie go, you guys! She's pretty quick for a little dog!
She must really **LOVE** water!

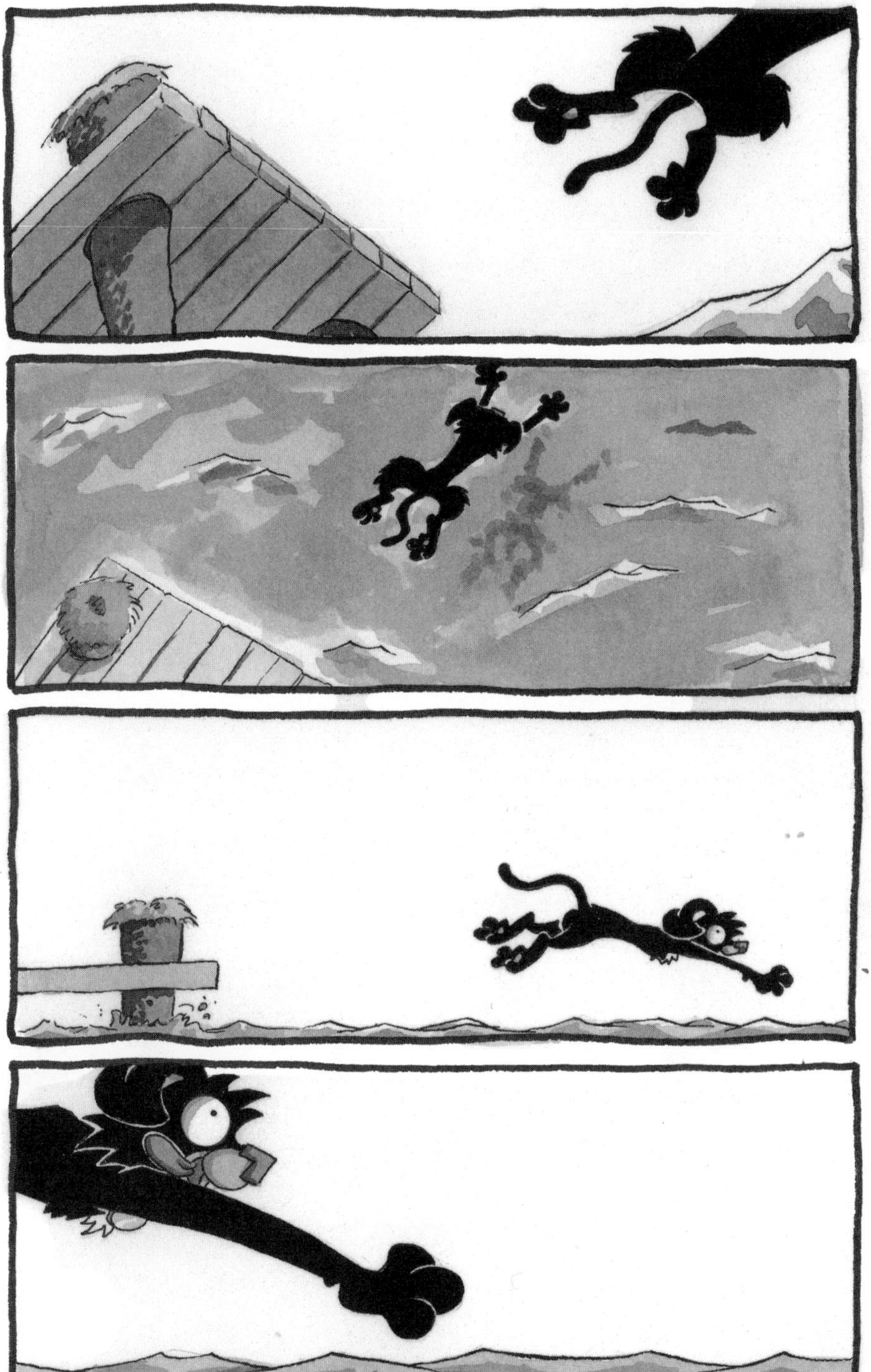

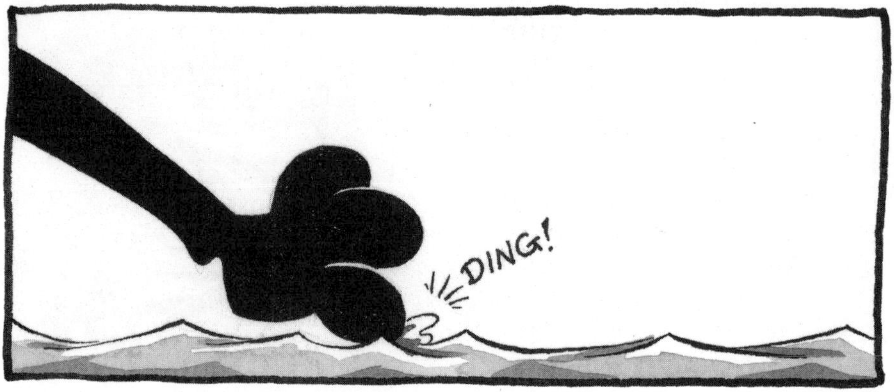
DING!

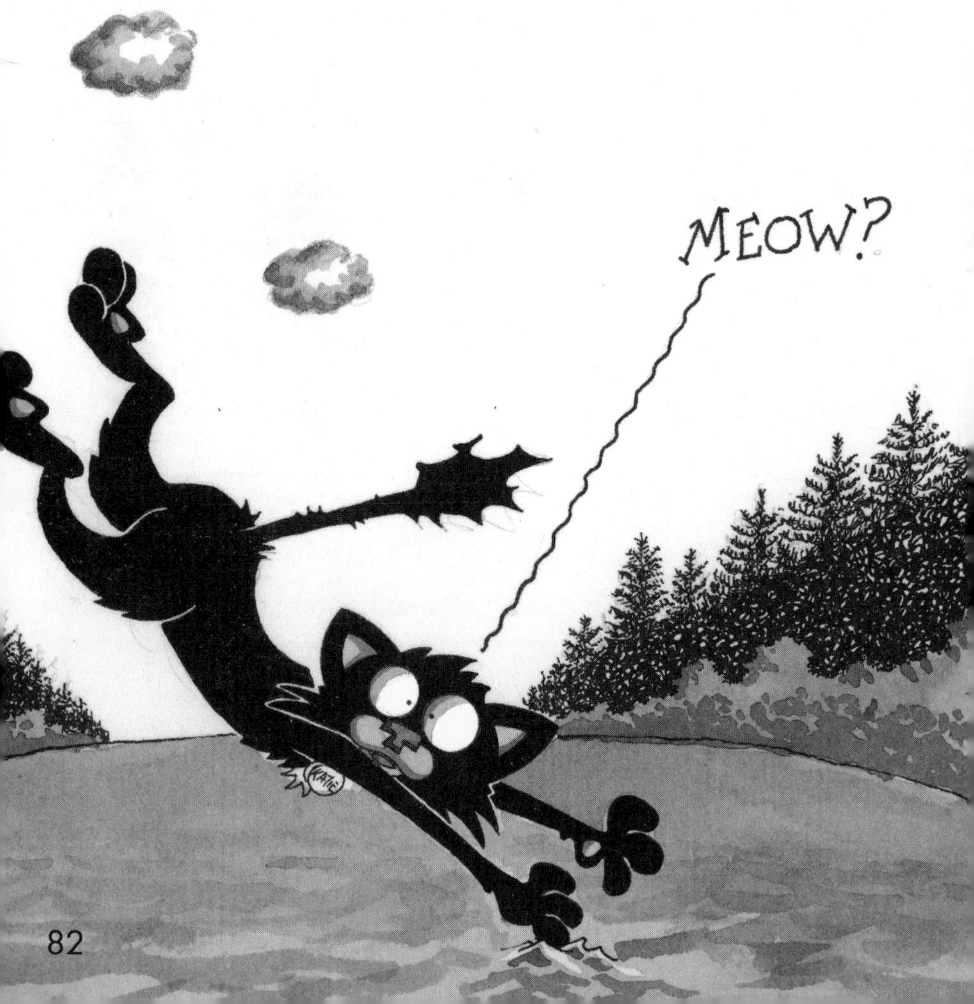
MEOW?

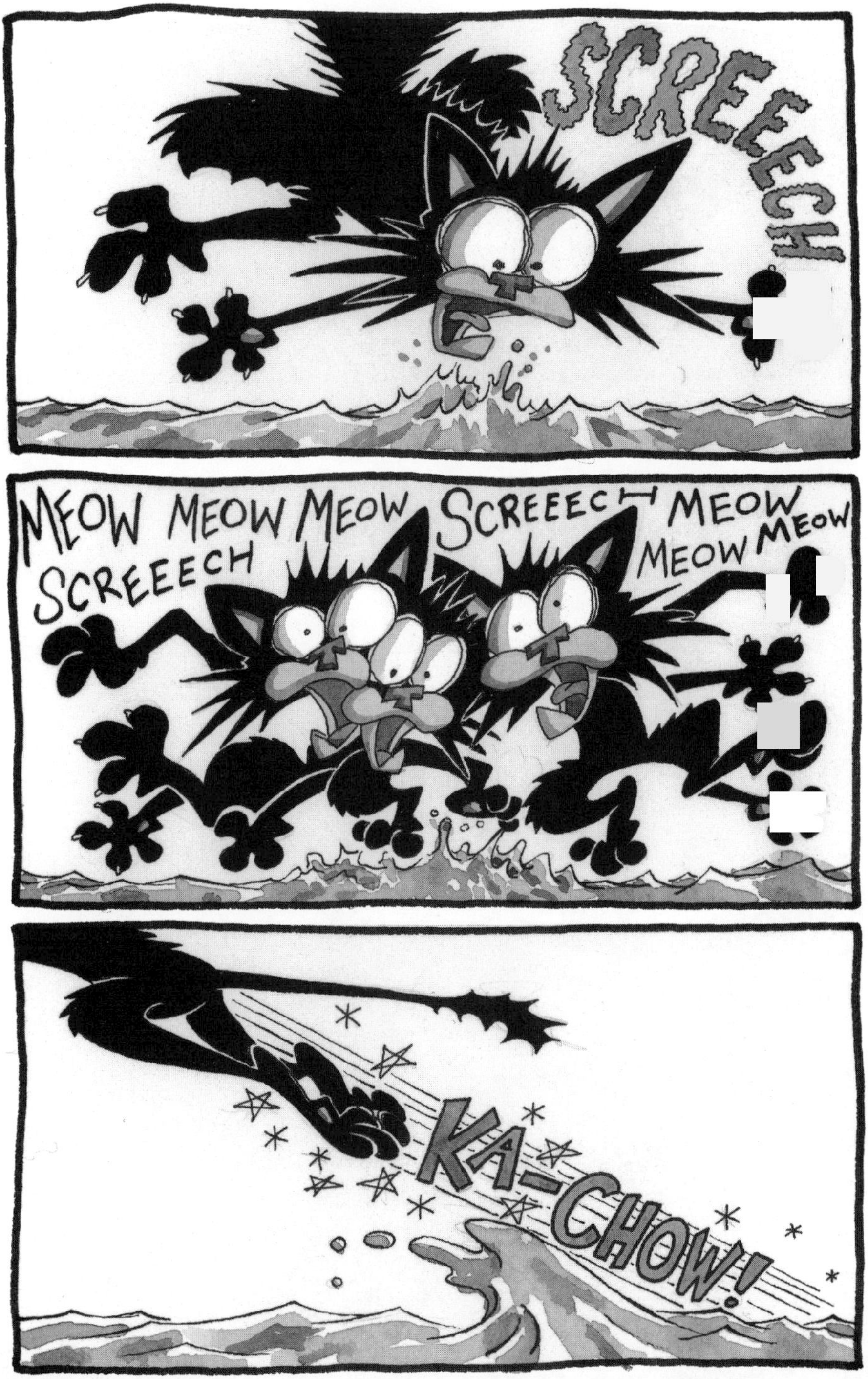
SCREEECH
MEOW MEOW MEOW
SCREEECH
SCREEECH
MEOW
MEOW MEOW
KA-CHOW!

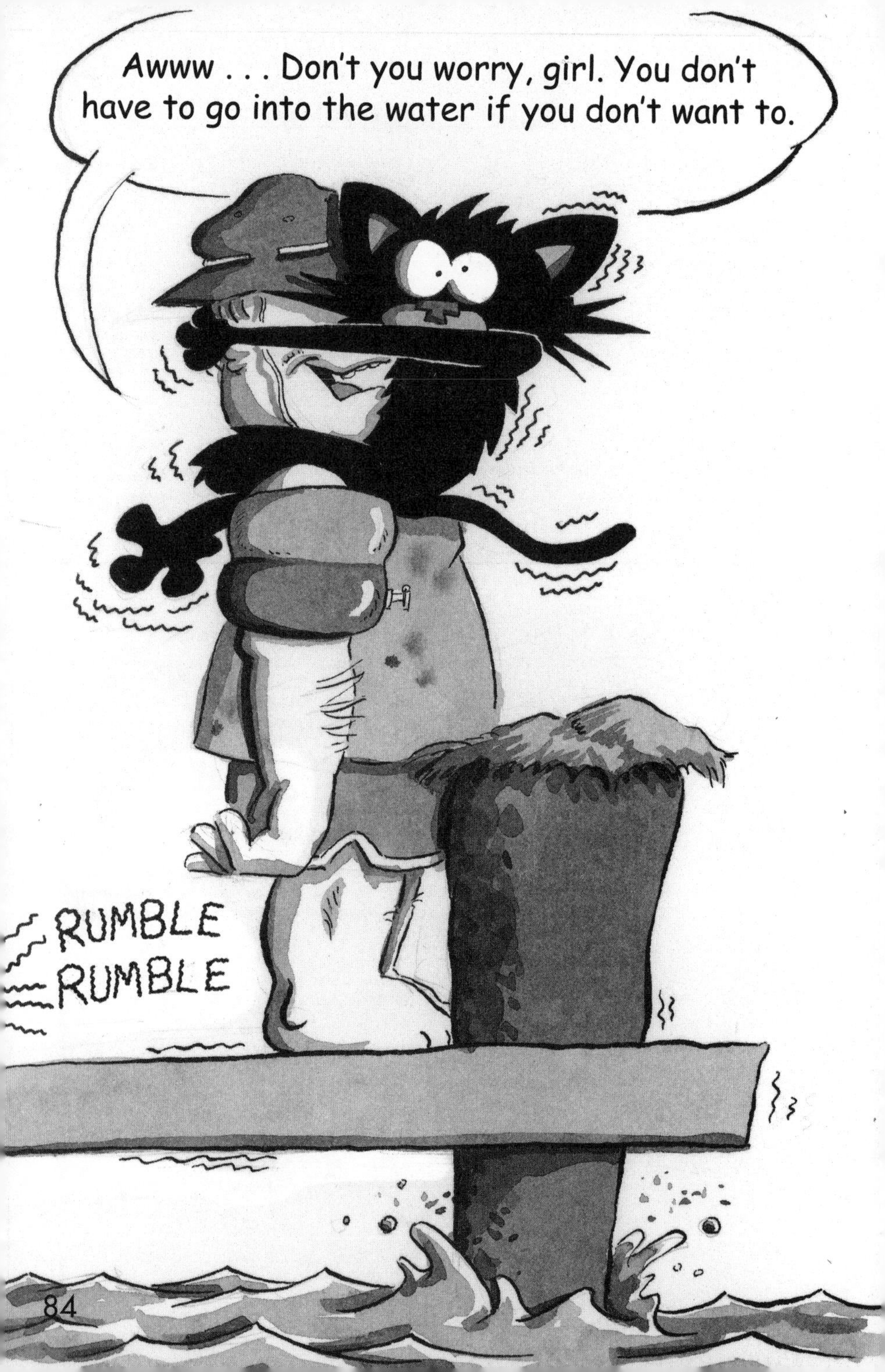
Awww . . . Don't you worry, girl. You don't have to go into the water if you don't want to.
RUMBLE
RUMBLE

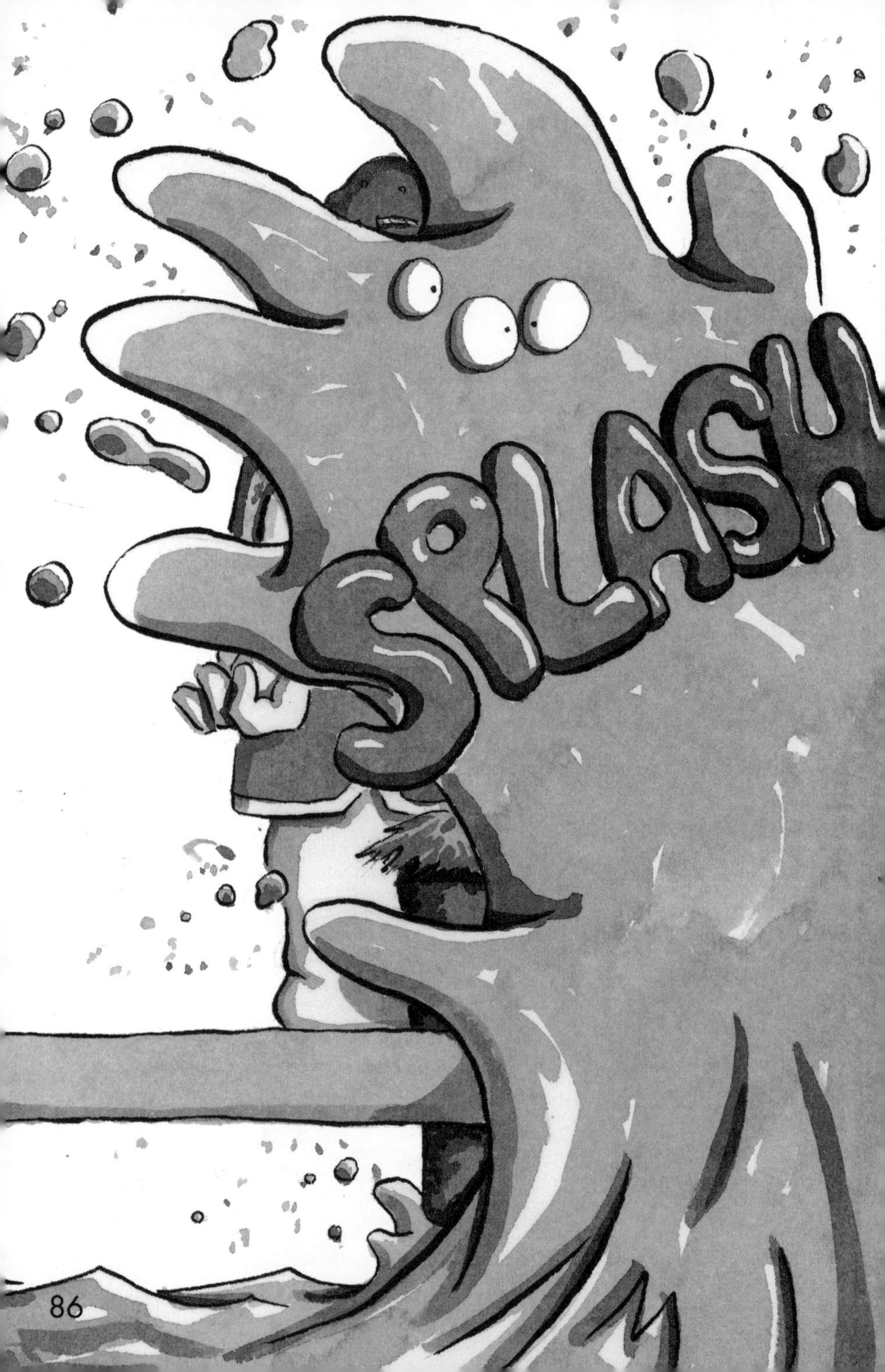
SPLASH

UNCLE MURRAY'S FUN FACTS

WHY DO DOGS LIKE TO SWIM MORE THAN CATS?

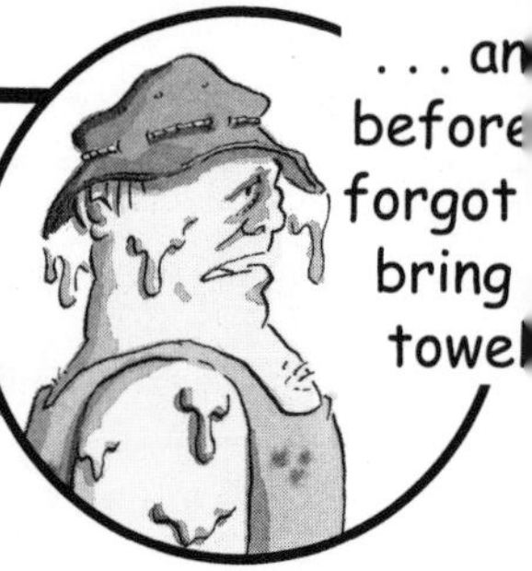
. . . an
befor
forgot
bring
towe

What's the first swim stroke kids learn? It's the dog paddle! Not the giraffe paddle or the rhinoceros paddle or the kitty paddle. The dog paddle.

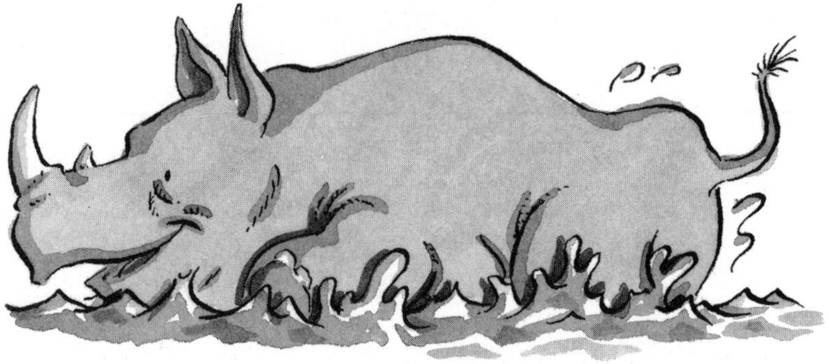

Do all dogs know how to swim?
Not all, but most dogs instinctively know how to swim. If a dog is put in deep water, its legs will begin trotting like a horse, moving in a motion like it's walking quickly. This will help the dog stay afloat. But you still have to be careful. Many dogs will try swimming, but just won't be able to float at all, so you have to be very careful before putting any dog in water that goes above its head.

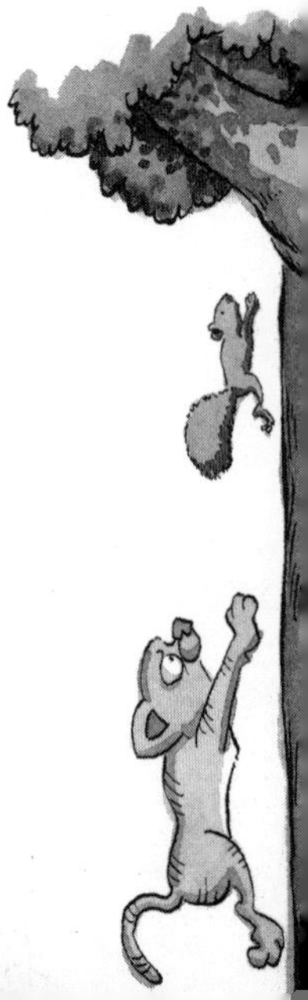

Do cats also know how to swim?
They do, but they don't like it. A cat's instinct tells it to hunt for food on the ground and in the woods and in the trees, which is why they're better at climbing than dogs.

But the really big reason dogs generally like to swim more than cats is because cats HATE TO GET WET.

A cat's fur is finer and softer than a dog's, so it doesn't dry as quickly. This means that if a cat gets soaking wet, it will stay wet for a long time and that can be very uncomfortable.

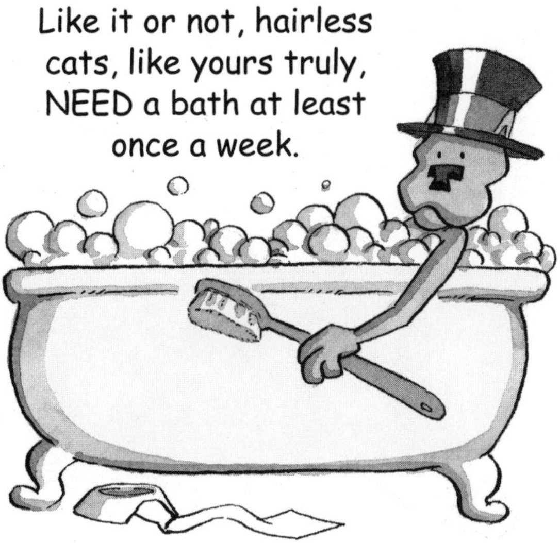
Like it or not, hairless cats, like yours truly, NEED a bath at least once a week.

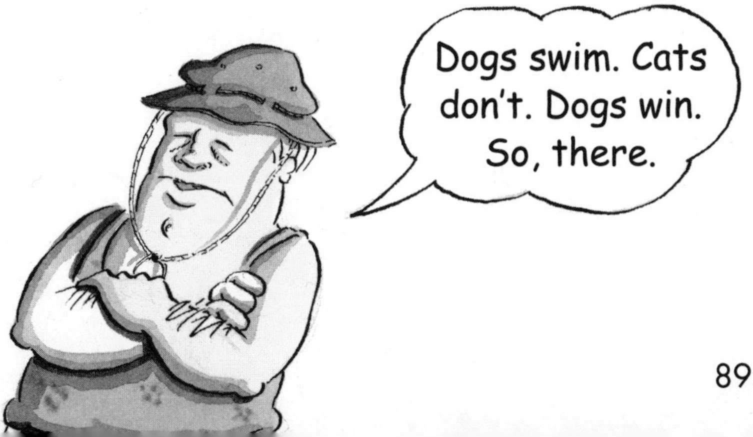
Dogs swim. Cats don't. Dogs win. So, there.

•CHAPTER SIX•
CAMPFIRE
Dogs, it's been a long day and we're going to have even more fun tomorrow. But I'm tired. I'm going to turn in. You guys can stay up for a while. Just don't forget to put out this fire before you go to sleep. And don't stay up too late telling ghost stories. Heh-heh. Good night!

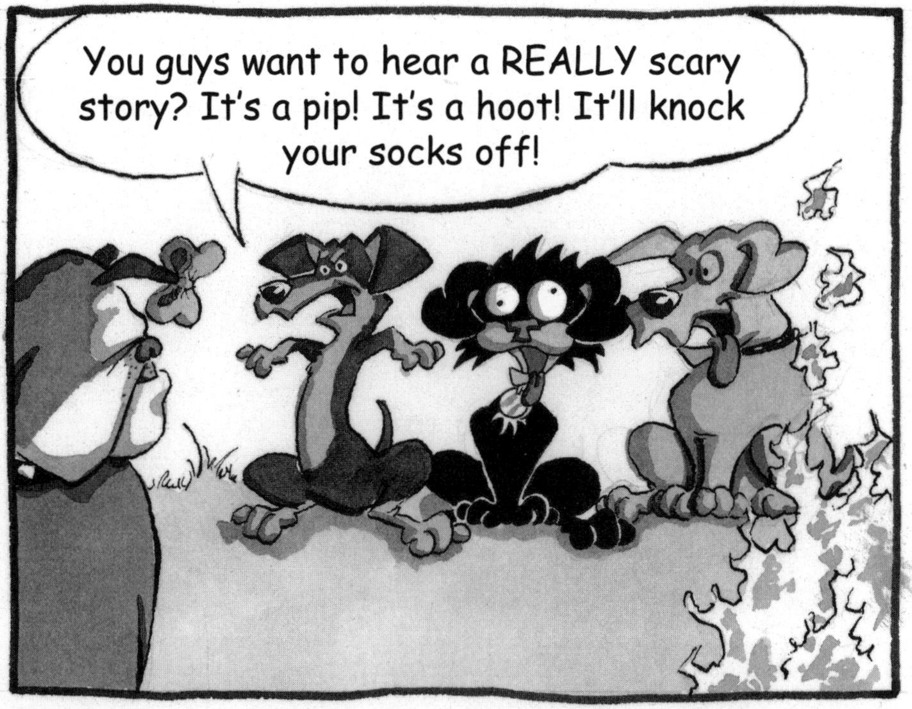
You guys want to hear a REALLY scary story? It's a pip! It's a hoot! It'll knock your socks off!

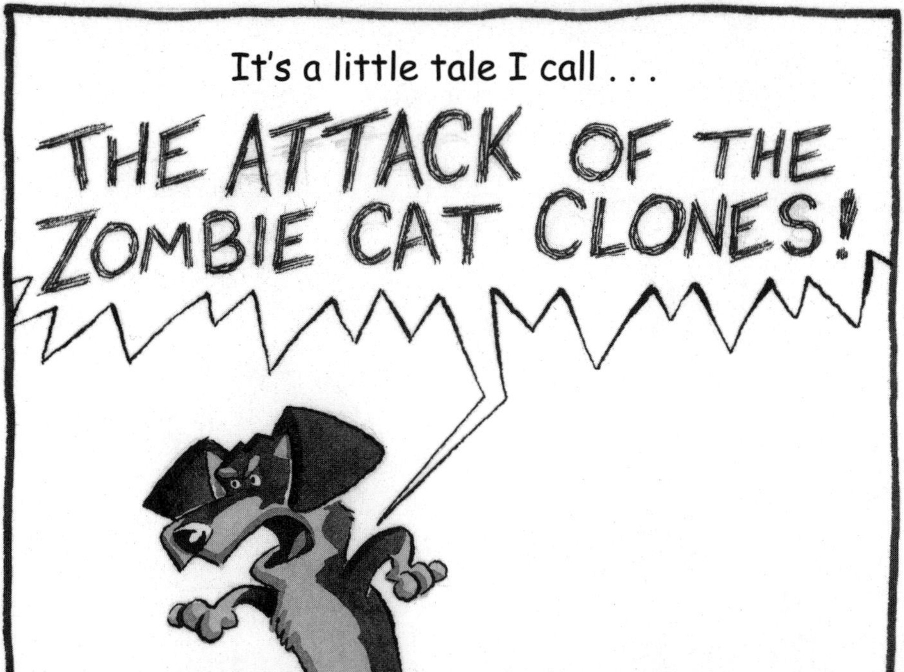
It's a little tale I call . . .
THE ATTACK OF THE ZOMBIE CAT CLONES!

Once there was a brave dog. Swell guy. Smart. Handsome, too. No trouble with the ladies. Smelled nice.

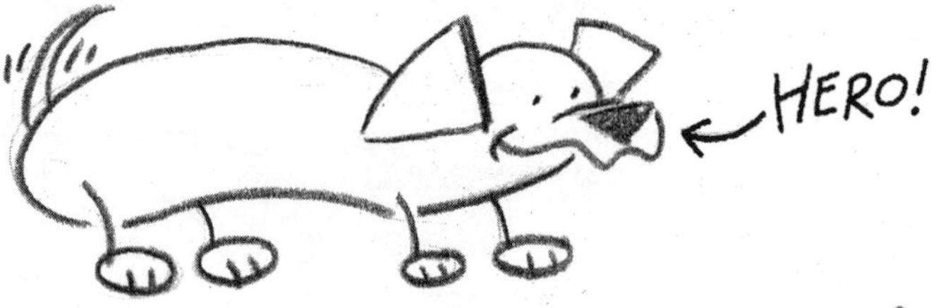
HERO!

But the poor guy, he had to live with this cat. Bad news, right? It was a cat. Looked weird. Smelled weirder. Litter box. Hair balls. The whole ugly business.

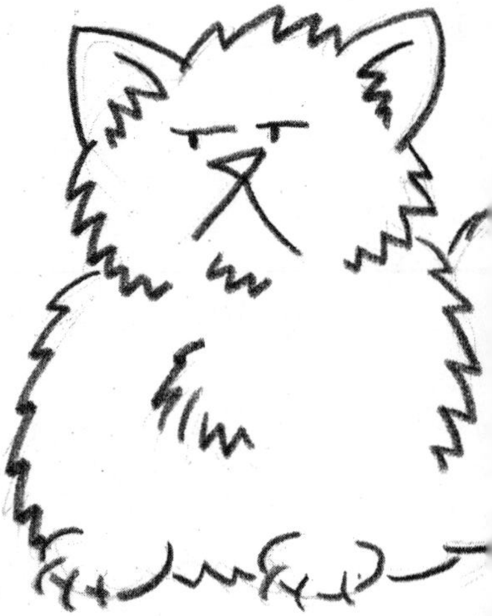

What could the dog do?
Nothing! That's what.
He just had to live with it.

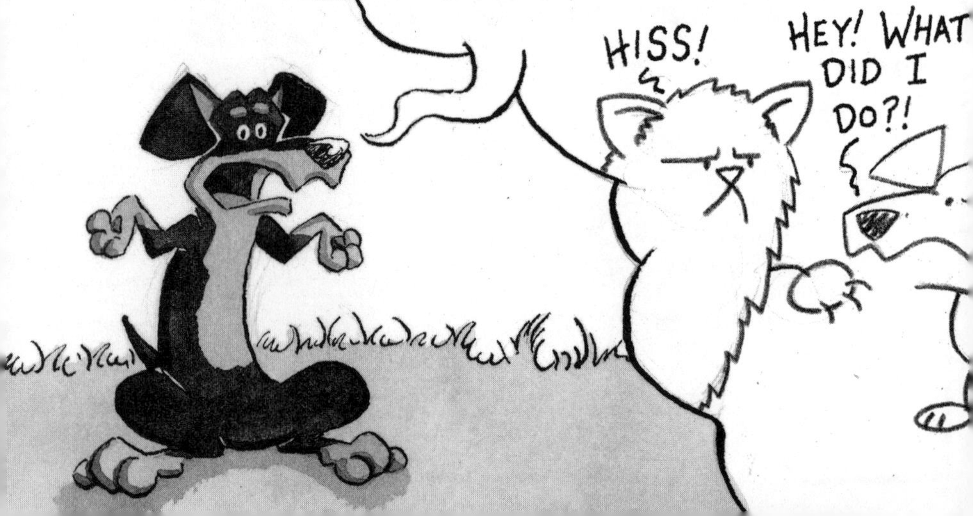
HISS!
HEY! WHAT DID I DO?!

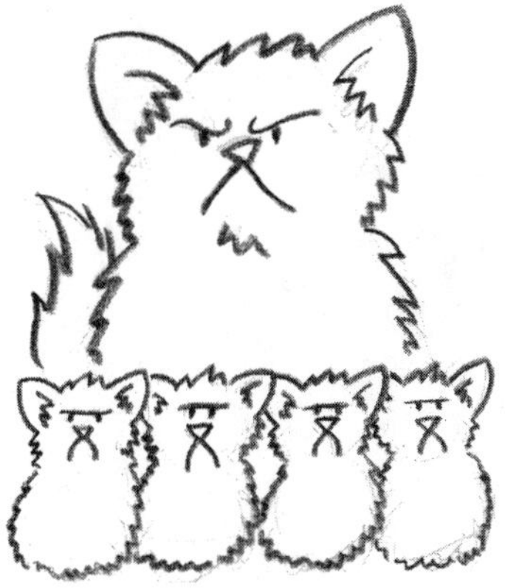

But then, one day—just when the dog thought things couldn't get worse, they got worse. WAY WORSE. One day, it was as if the cat EXPLODED! All of a sudden, there were these teeny, little cats all over the place. Plus, the original.

They were in the food. They were in the water.

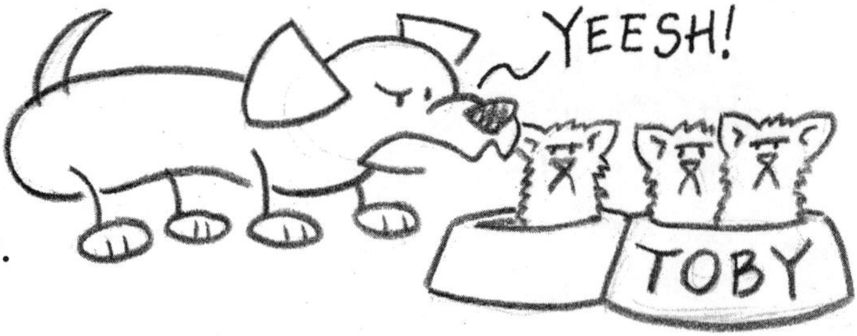
YEESH!
TOBY

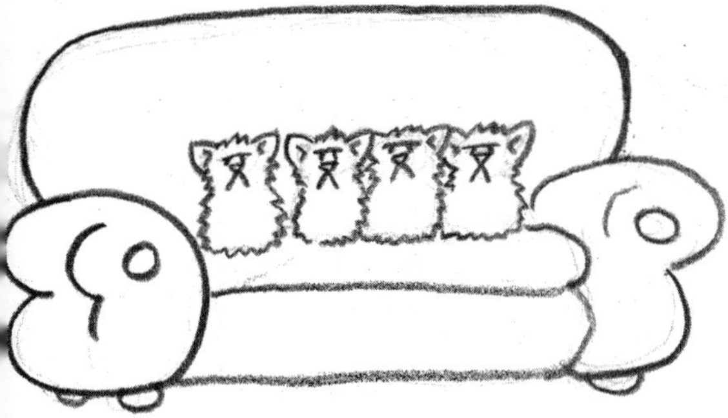

They were on the bed. They were on the couch.

Did I mention the food? They were in the FOOD, for crying out loud!

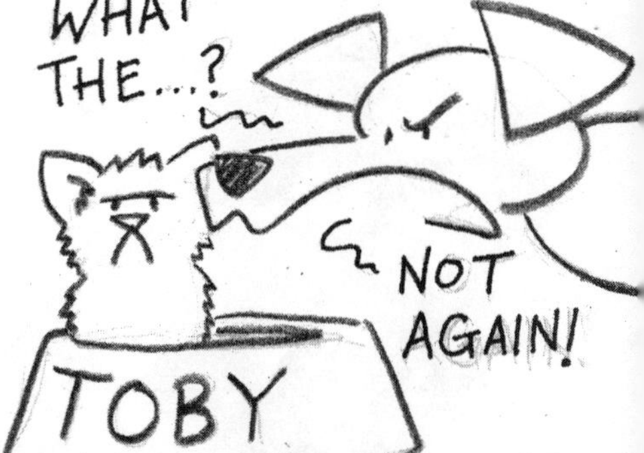
WHAT THE...?
NOT AGAIN!
TOBY

The dog did his absolute best to endure this whole gruesome situation. But these things, they had no sense of boundaries!

They played with his ears!

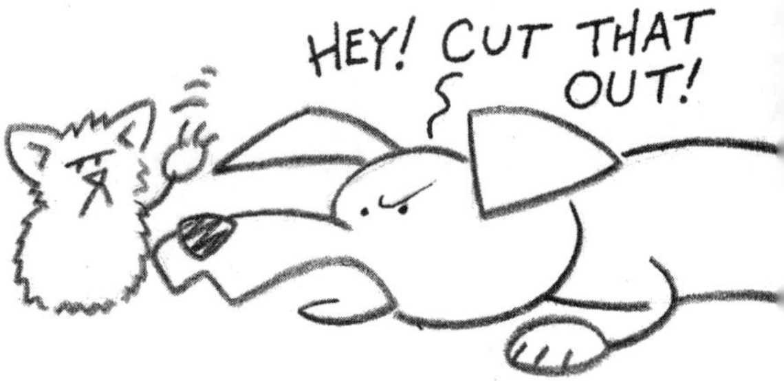
HEY! CUT THAT OUT!

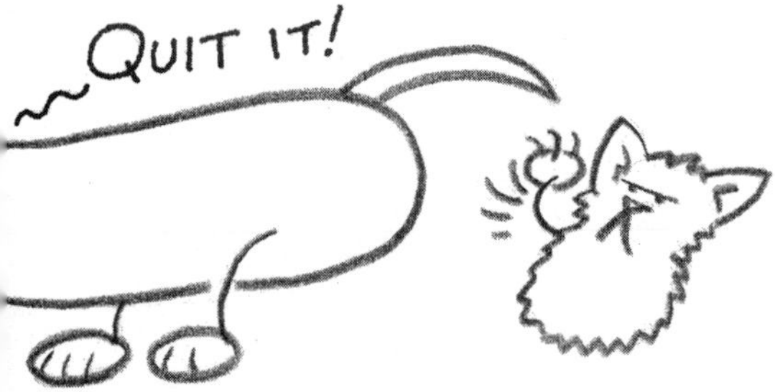
QUIT IT!

They played with his tail!

They tormented him day and night!

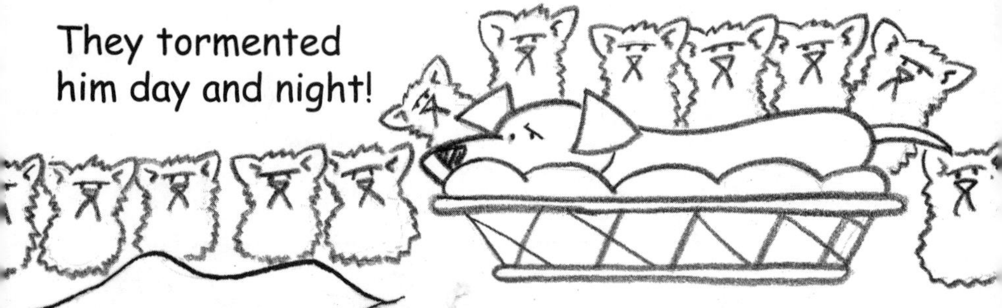

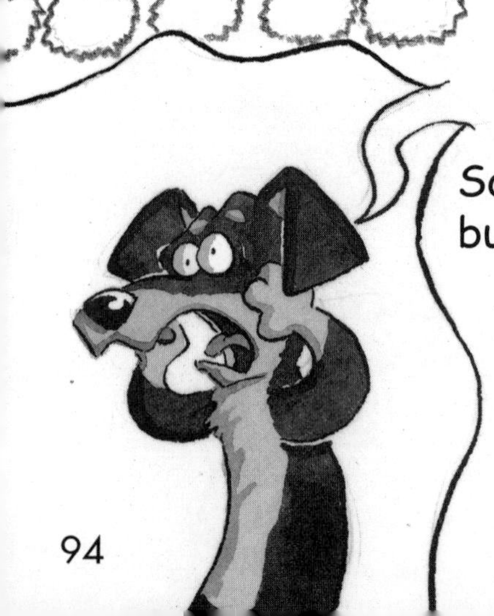

Soon the poor dog had no choice but to go completely . . .

INSANE!

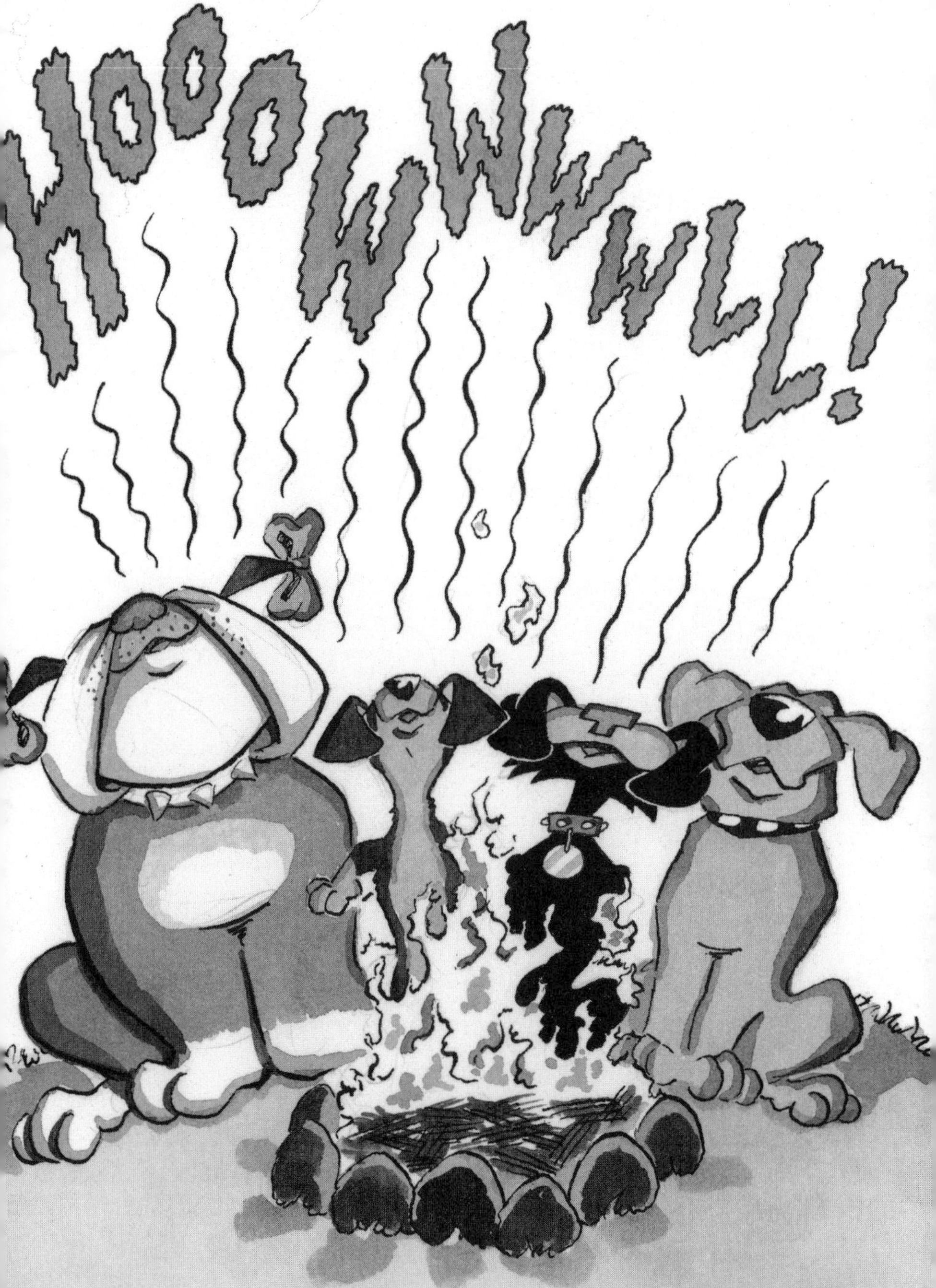
HOOOWWWWLL!

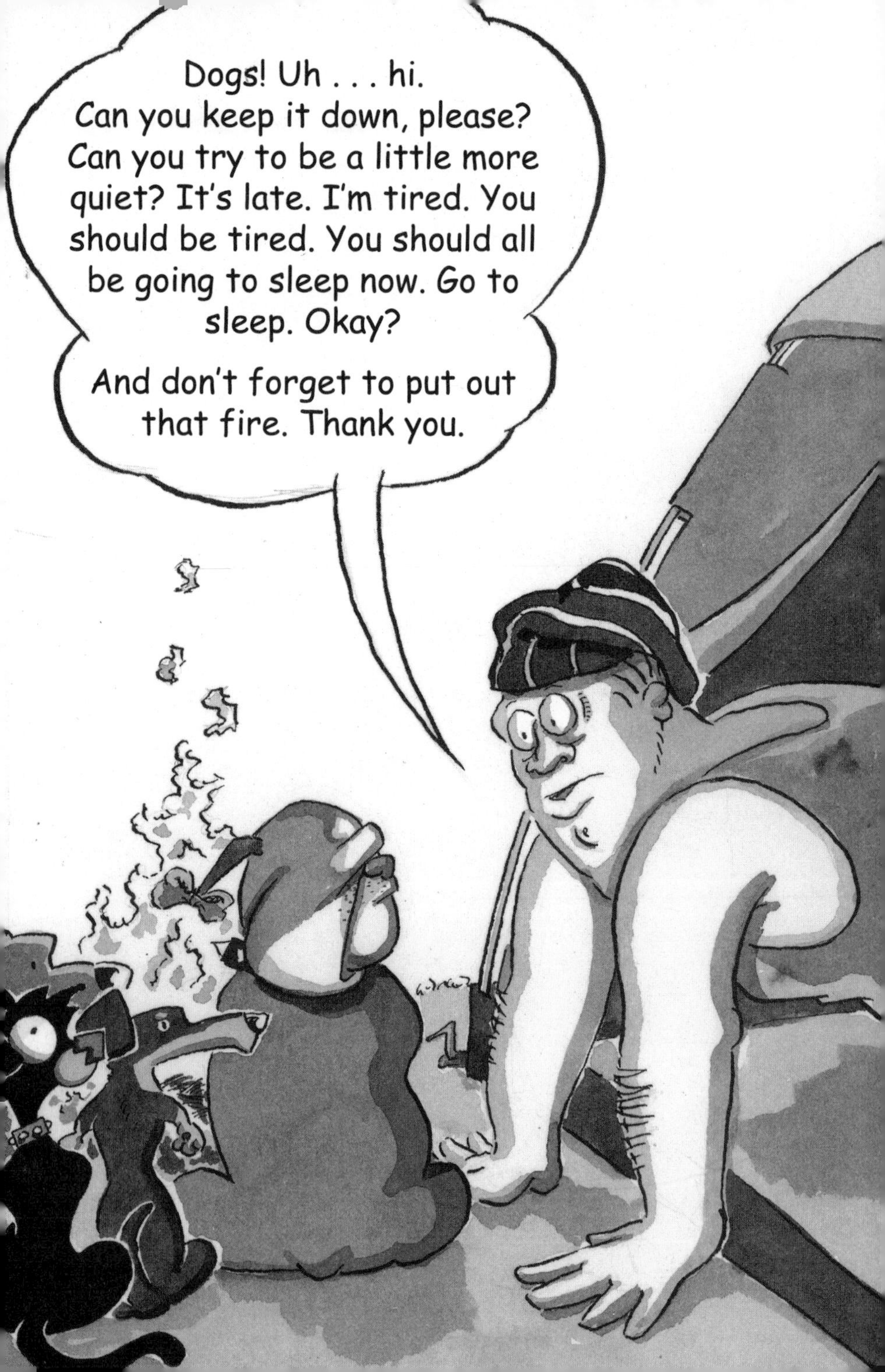
Dogs! Uh . . . hi.
Can you keep it down, please? Can you try to be a little more quiet? It's late. I'm tired. You should be tired. You should all be going to sleep now. Go to sleep. Okay?
And don't forget to put out that fire. Thank you.

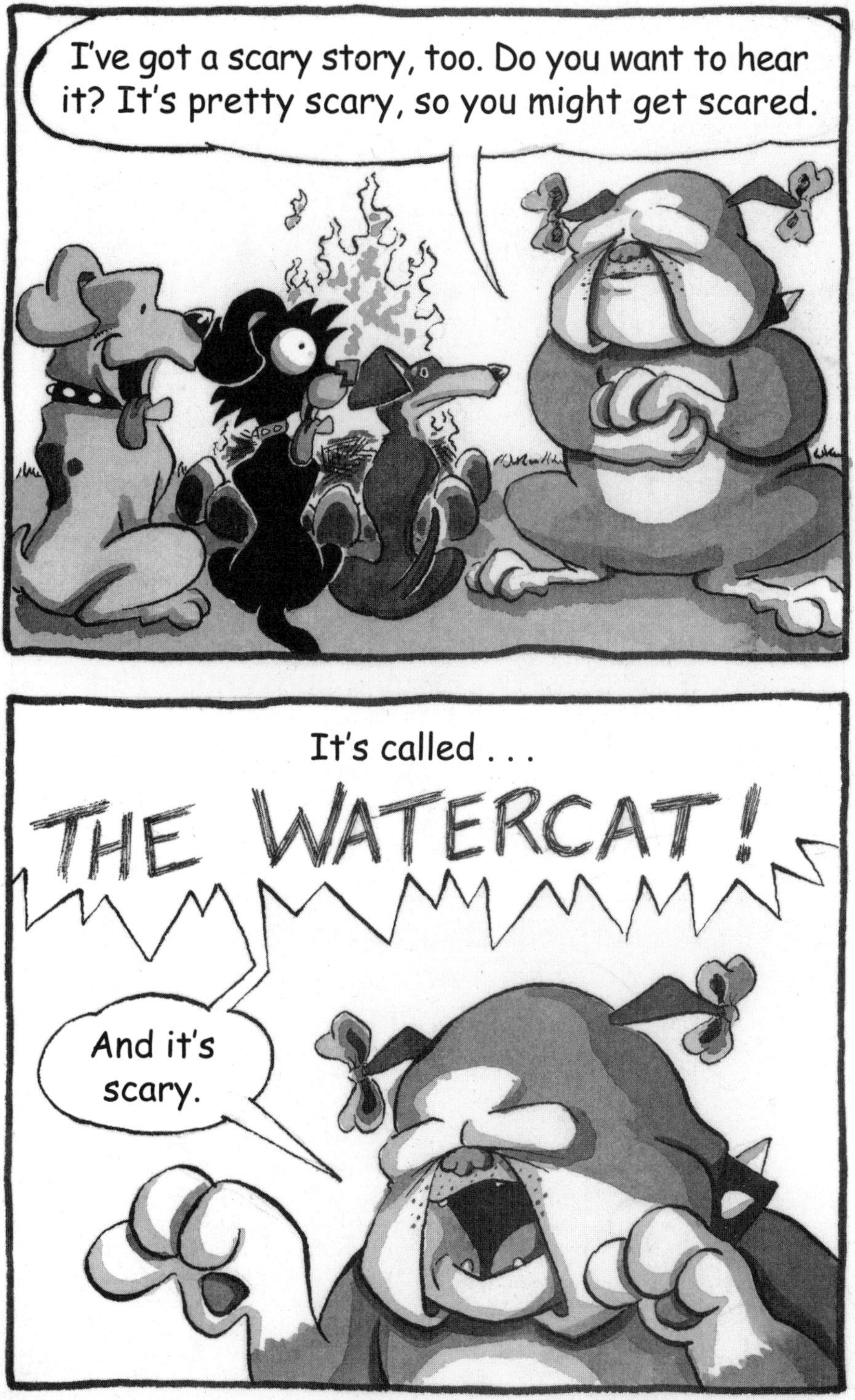
I've got a scary story, too. Do you want to hear it? It's pretty scary, so you might get scared.
It's called . . .
THE WATERCAT!
And it's scary.

Once there was a dog. She was
a very good dog. She chewed
up a shoe a couple of times,
but only because the shoe
was asking for it. She
rarely had an
accident in the
house. She was
a good dog.

GOOD DOG

BAD SHOE

Then, one day, the dog's
owner brought a horrible
creature into the house.
It was orange and scaly
and had a huge flat tail.
The poor dog knew im-
mediately it could only be
a WATERCAT!

The worst feature of the watercat was its
eyes—its huge, cold empty eyes that stared deep
into the dog's soul! All day, every day, the
watercat would float about in its
home staring, STARING at the dog.

It stared at the dog when she was drinking out of the toilet, (which the dog knew she wasn't supposed to do). It stared at the dog when she sat on the sofa (which the dog knew she wasn't supposed to be on).

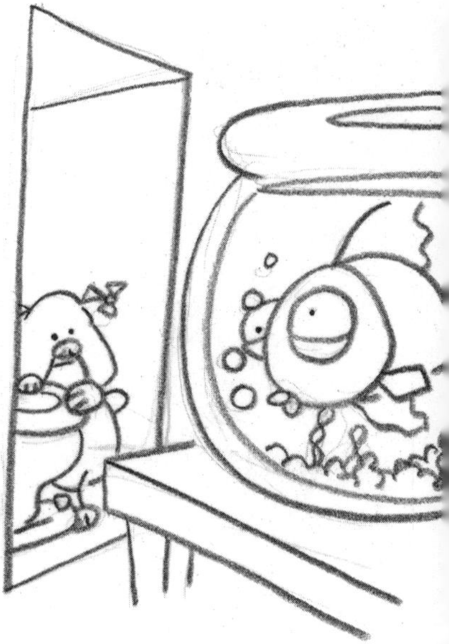

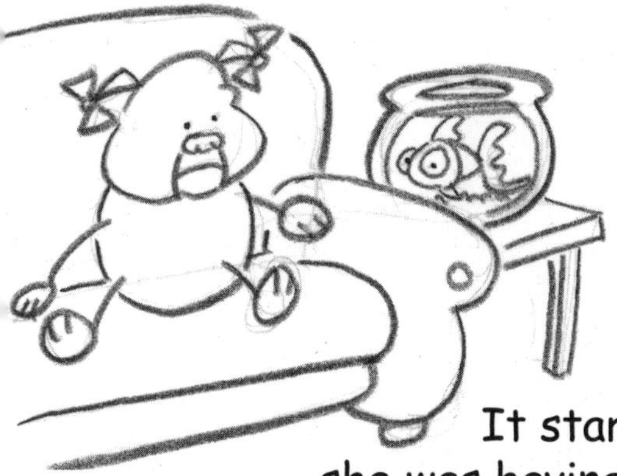

It stared at the dog when she was having an argument with the shoe (which the dog knew she wasn't supposed to do).

That's when the dog realized that the watercat was placed there by her owners to watch her every move and report her every crime! It was enough to make the poor dog go completely

INSANE!

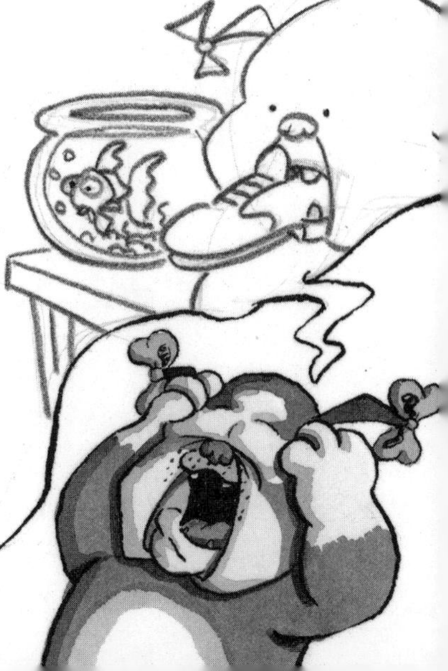

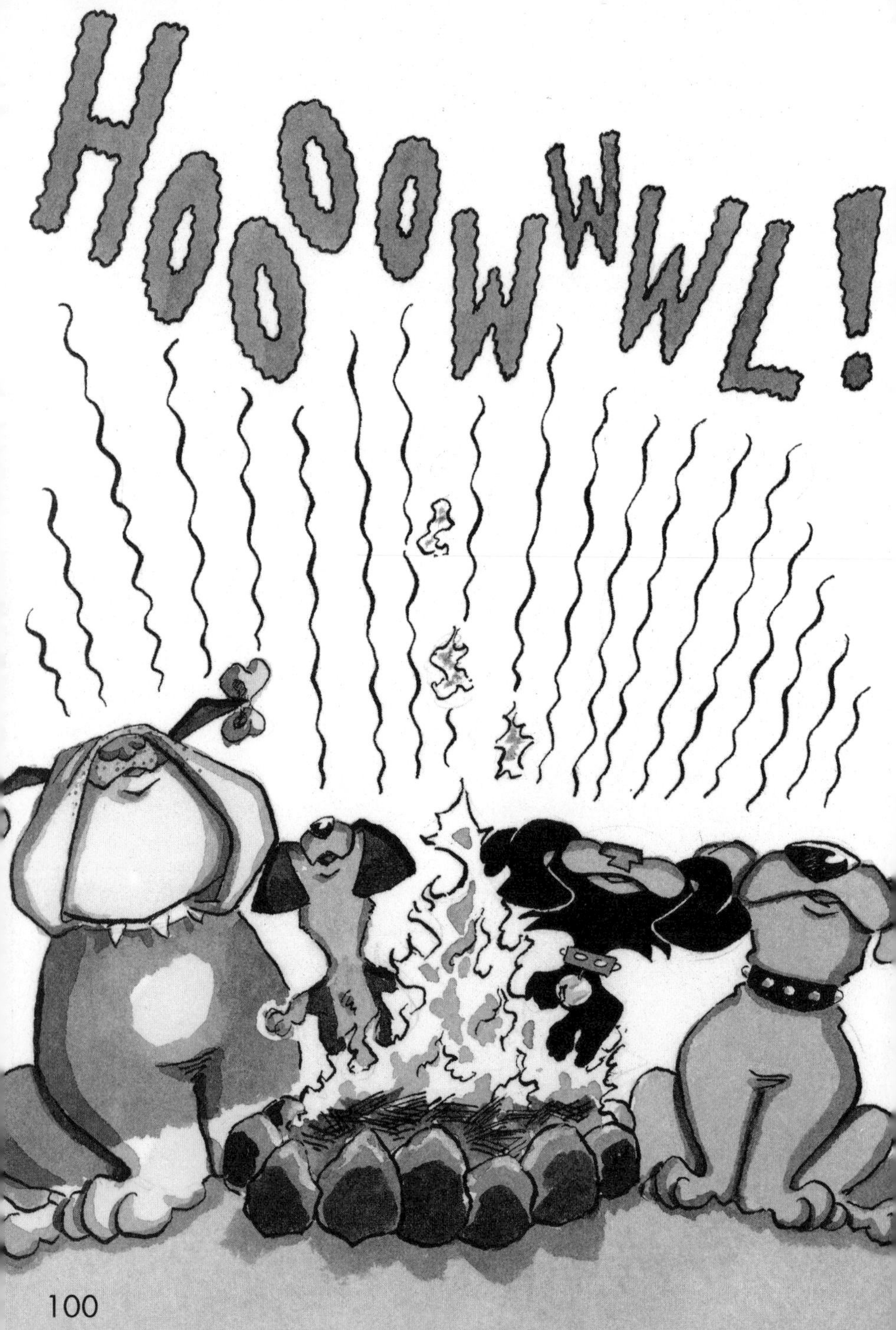
HOOOOWWWL!

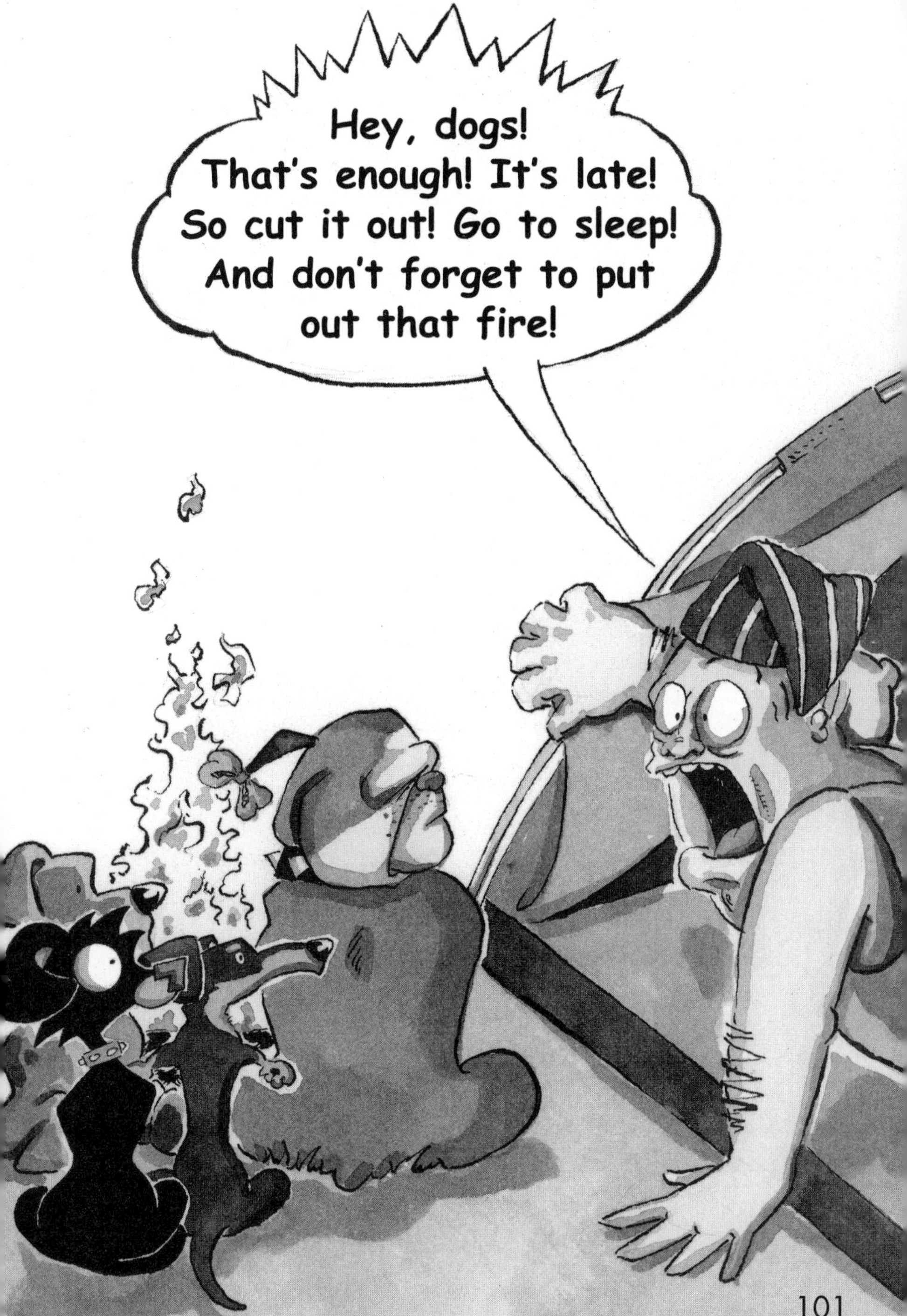
Hey, dogs!
That's enough! It's late!
So cut it out! Go to sleep!
And don't forget to put
out that fire!

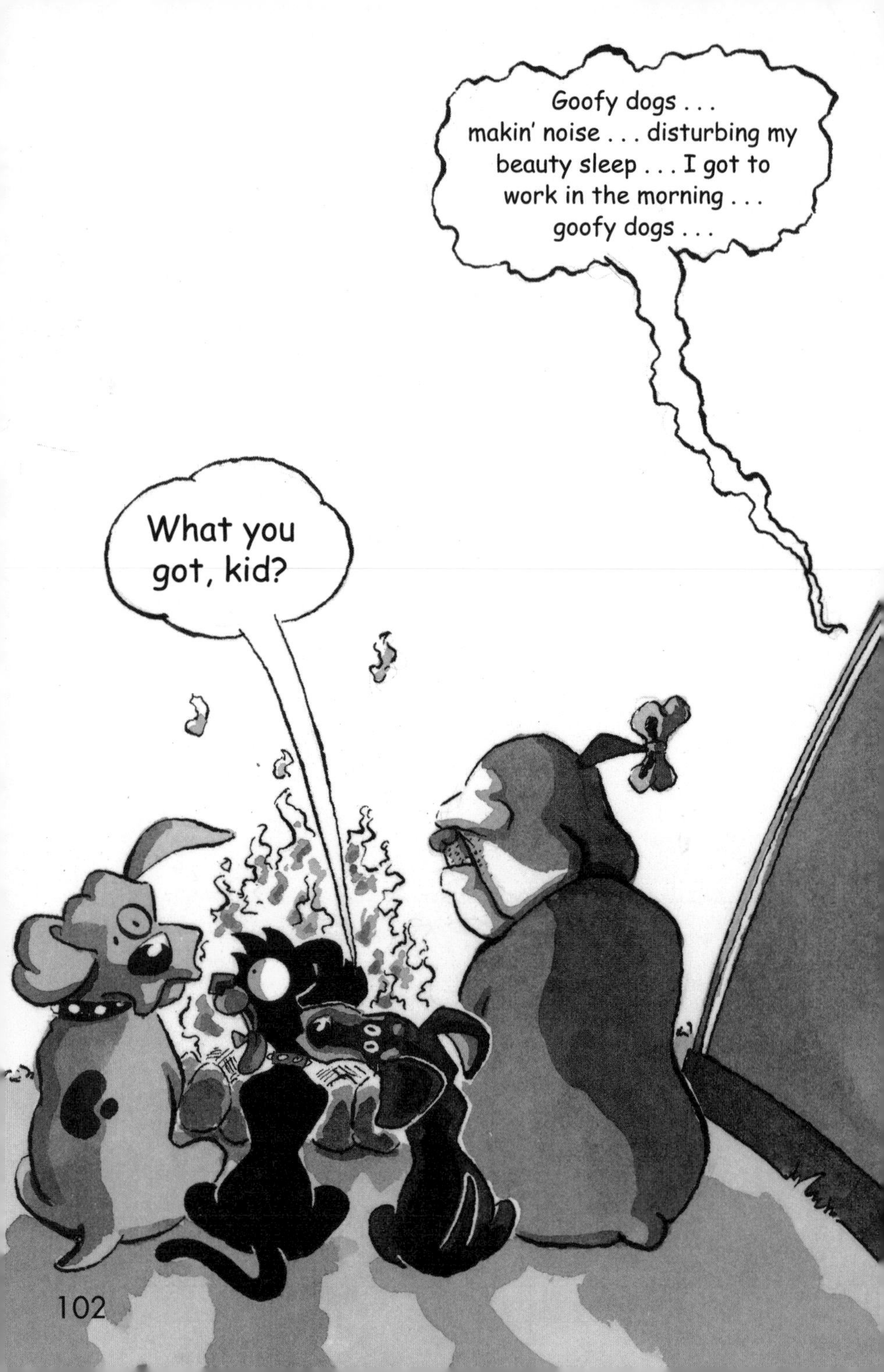
Goofy dogs . . . makin' noise . . . disturbing my beauty sleep . . . I got to work in the morning . . . goofy dogs . . .
What you got, kid?

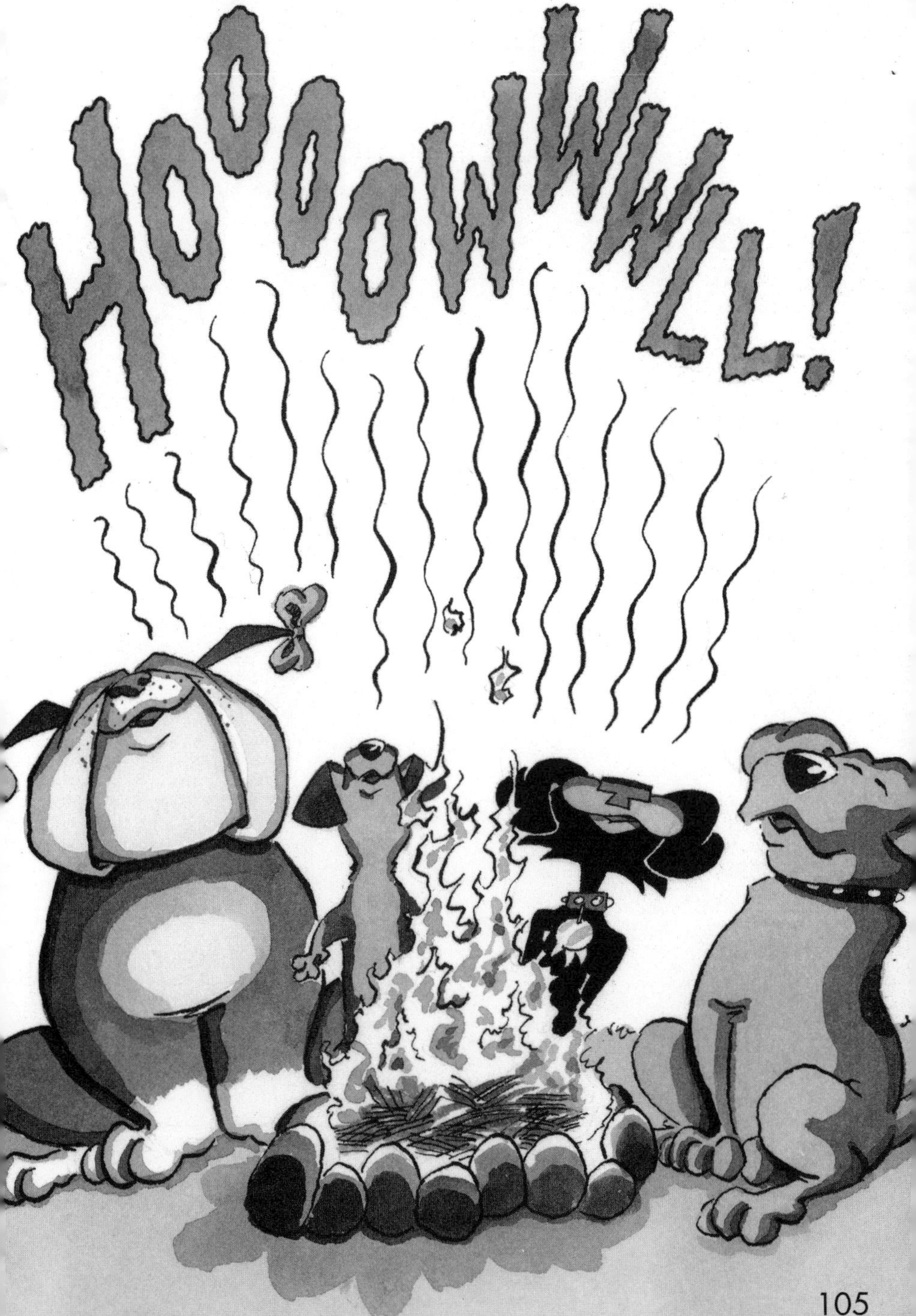
HOOOOWWWLL!

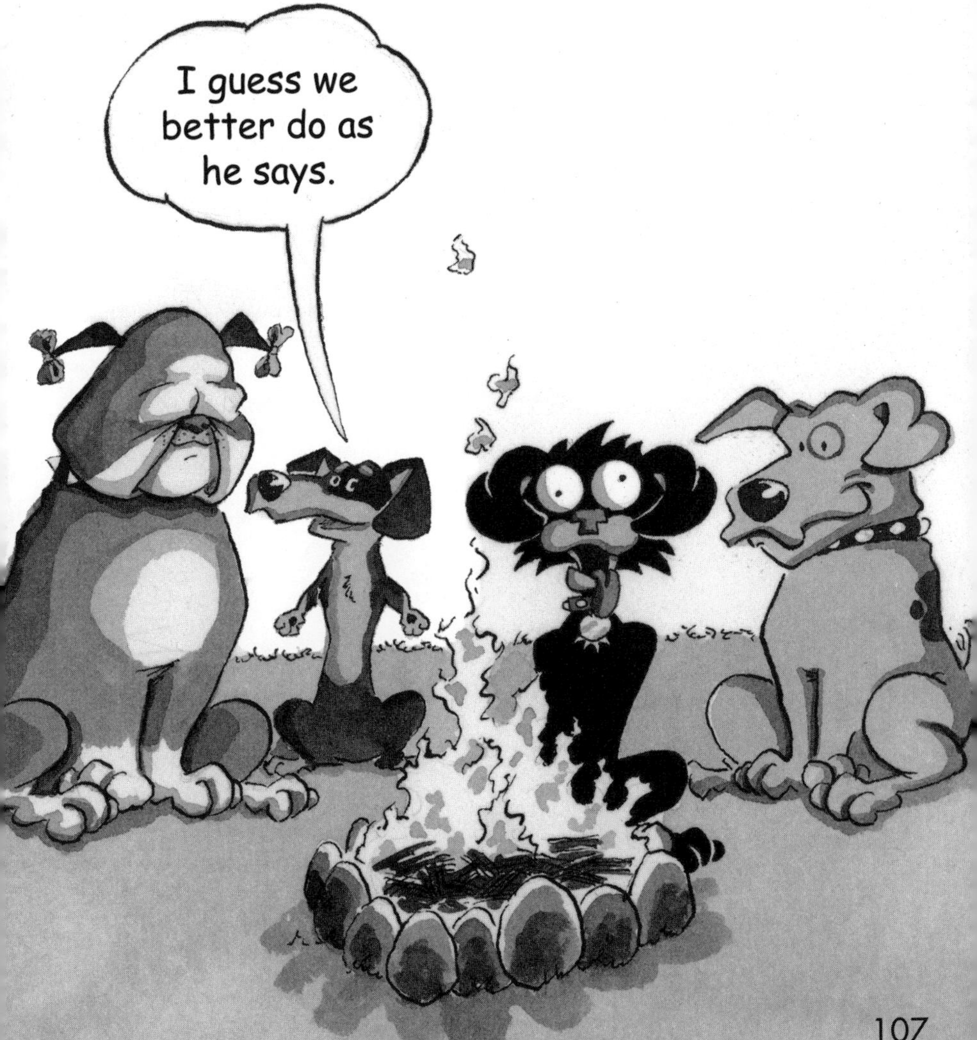
I guess we better do as he says.

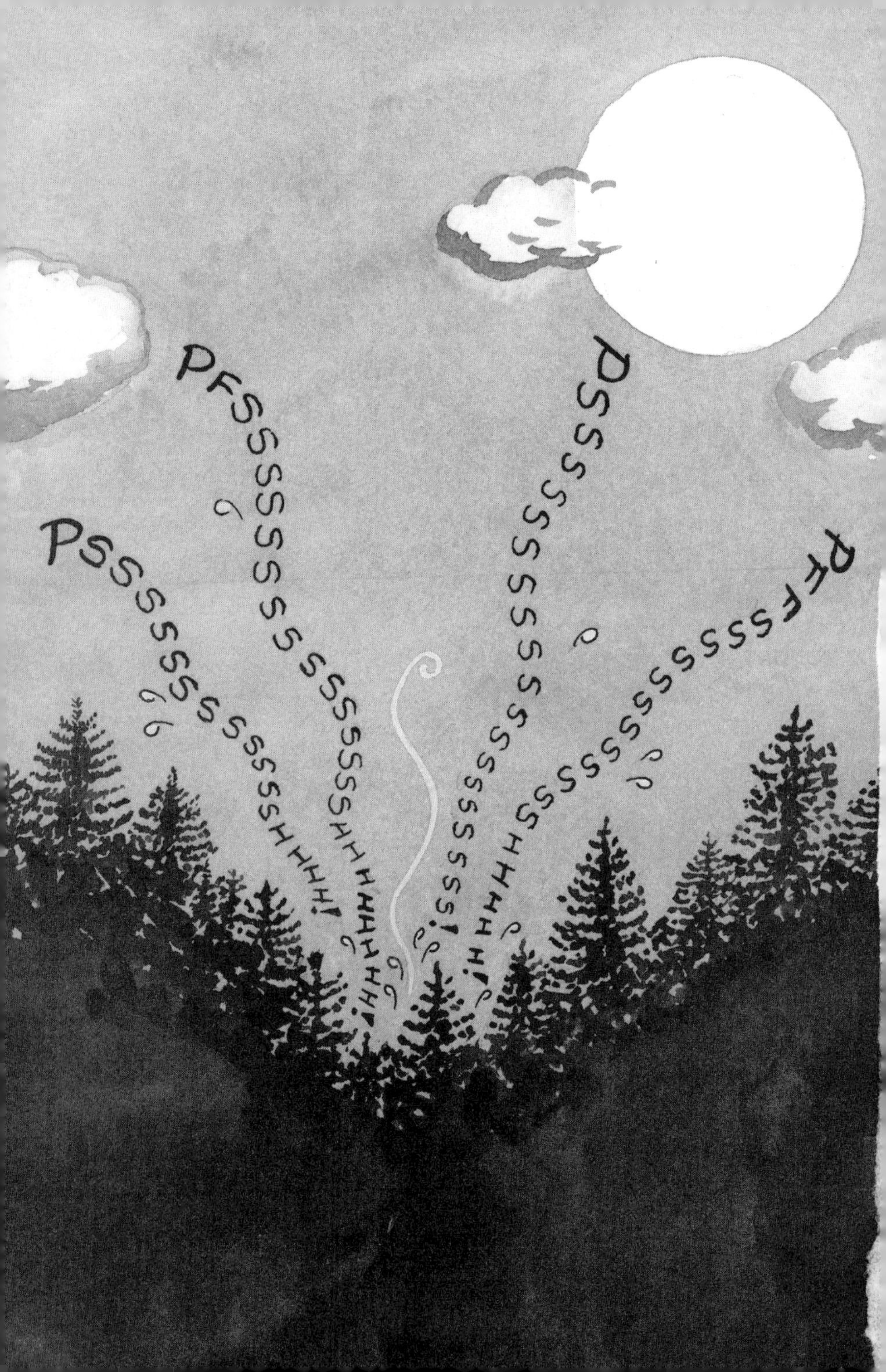
PSSSSSSSSSSSSSHHHH!
PFSSSSSSSSSSSSSSSSHHHHHHH!
PSSSSSSSSSSSSSSSSSSS!
PFSSSSSSSSSSSSSSHHHHH!

•CHAPTER SEVEN•

NATURE HIKE

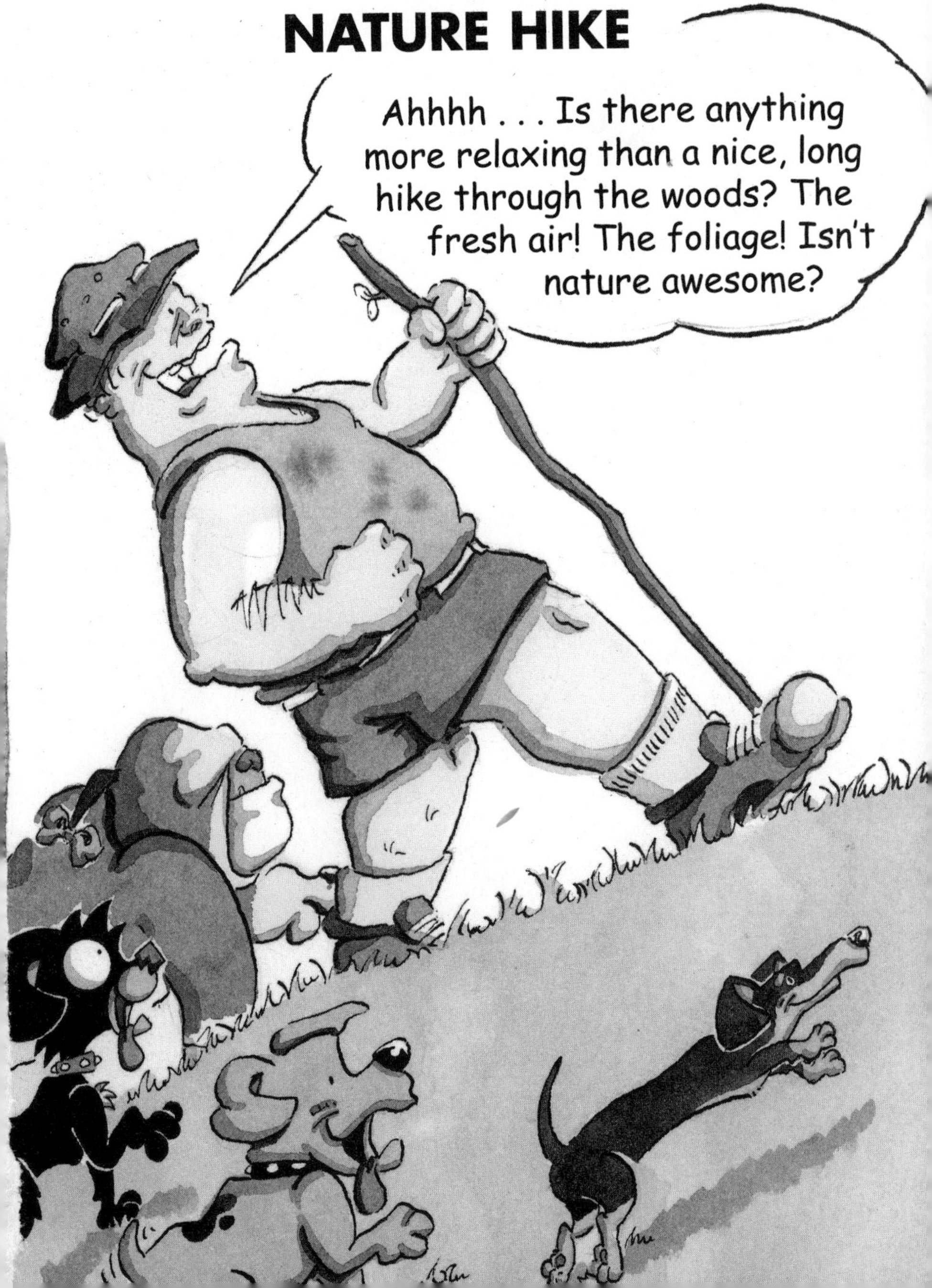

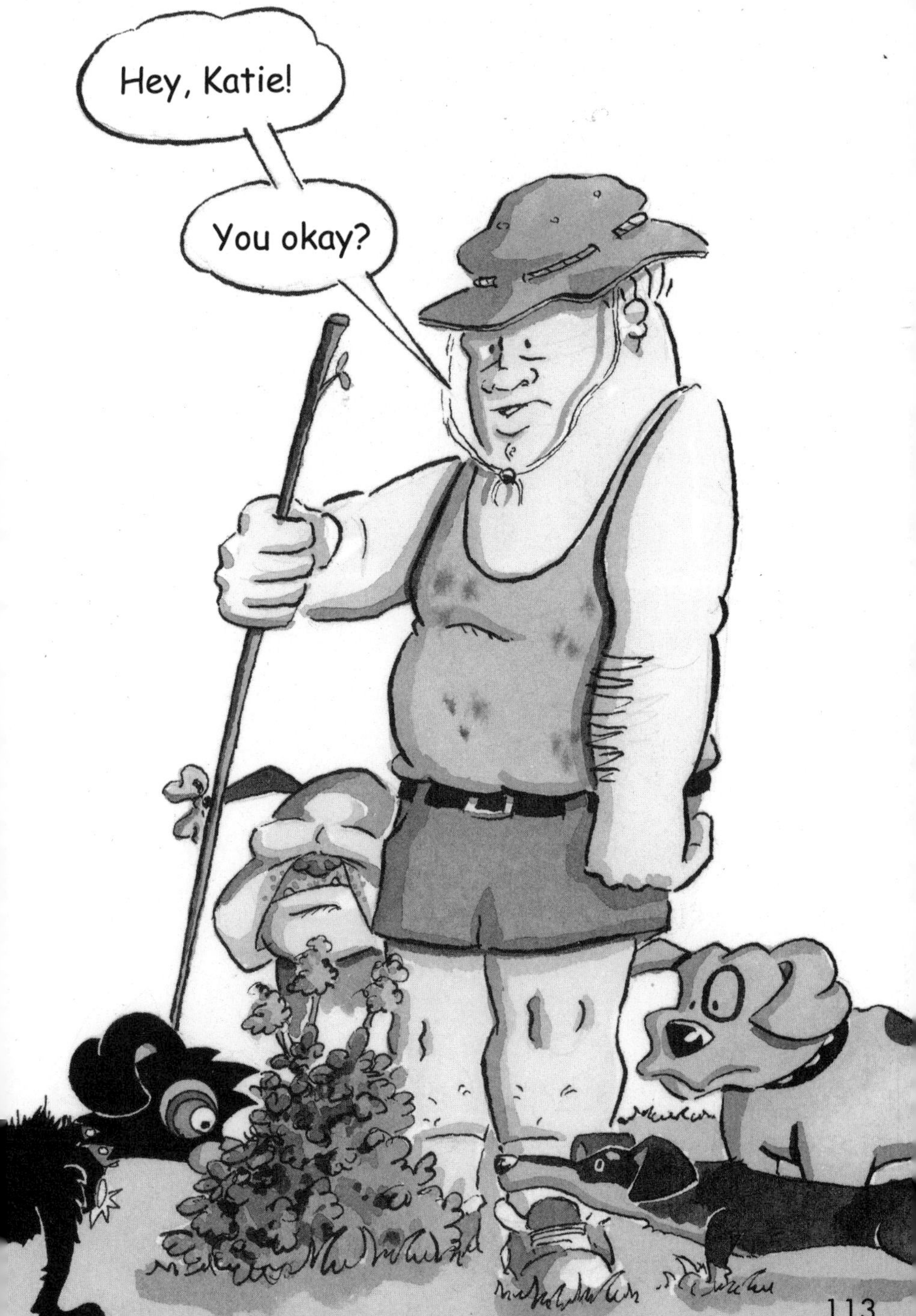
Hey, Katie!
You okay?

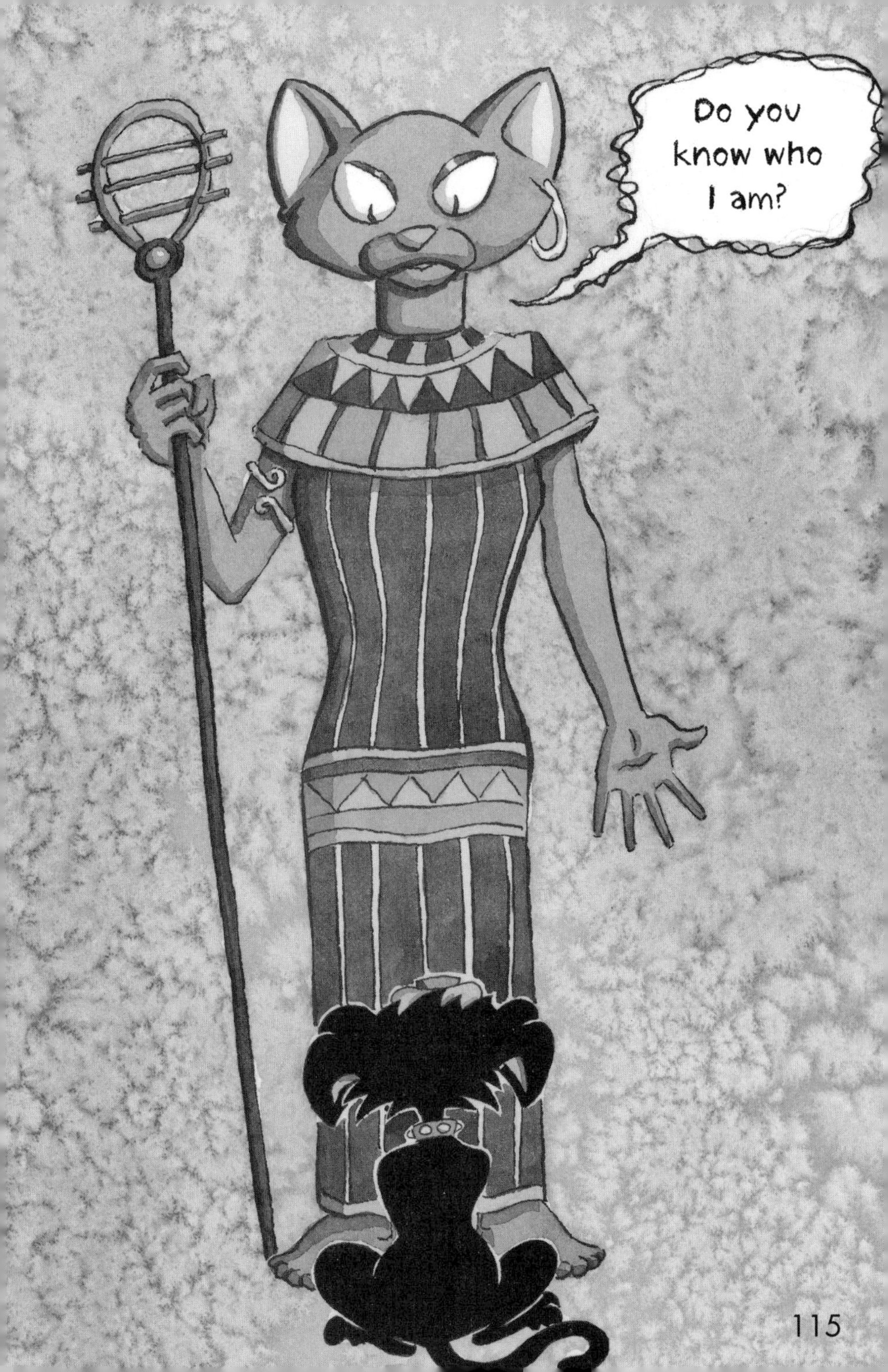
Do you know who I am?

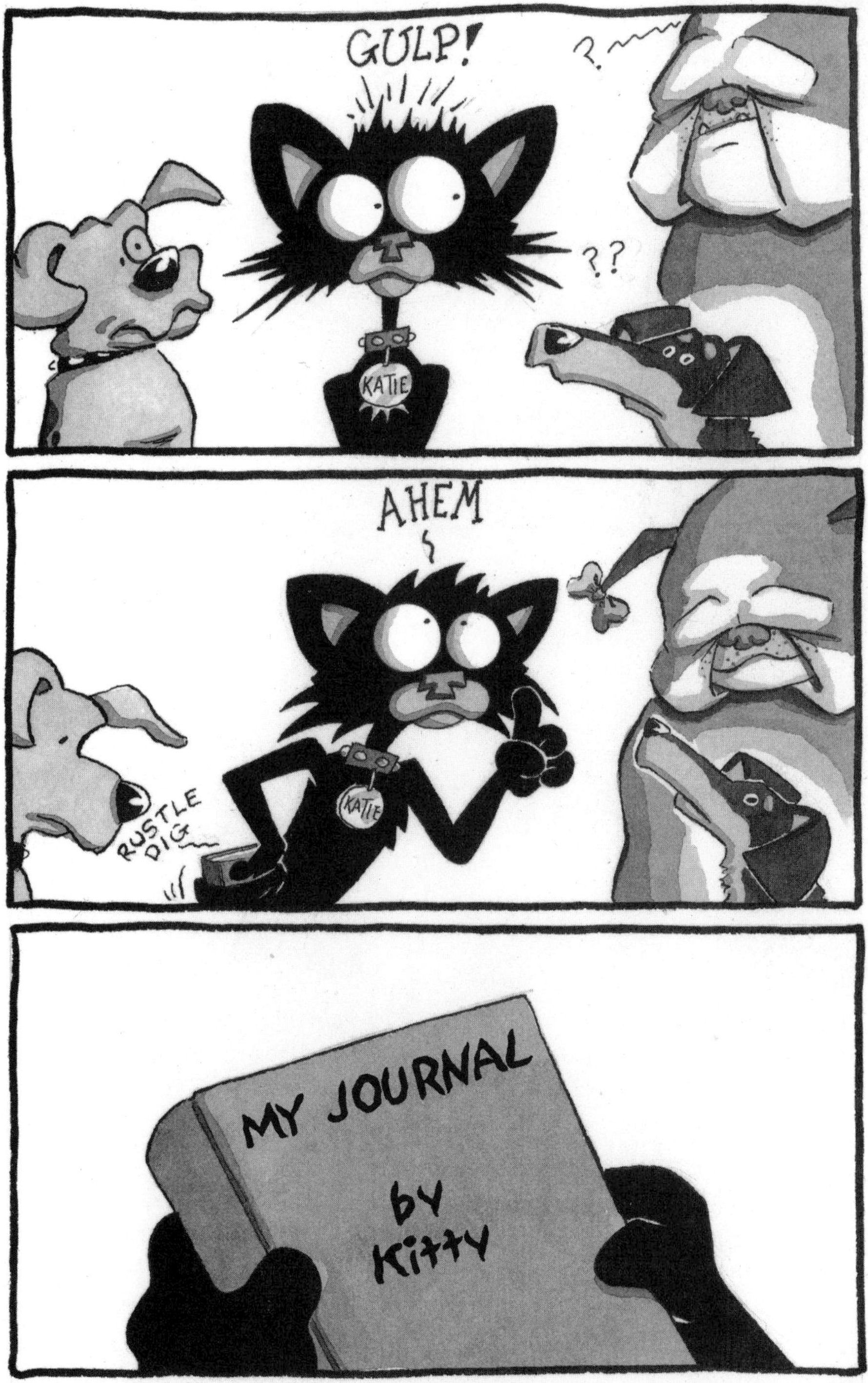
GULP!
?
??
KATIE
AHEM
KATIE
RUSTLE
DIG
MY JOURNAL
by
Kitty

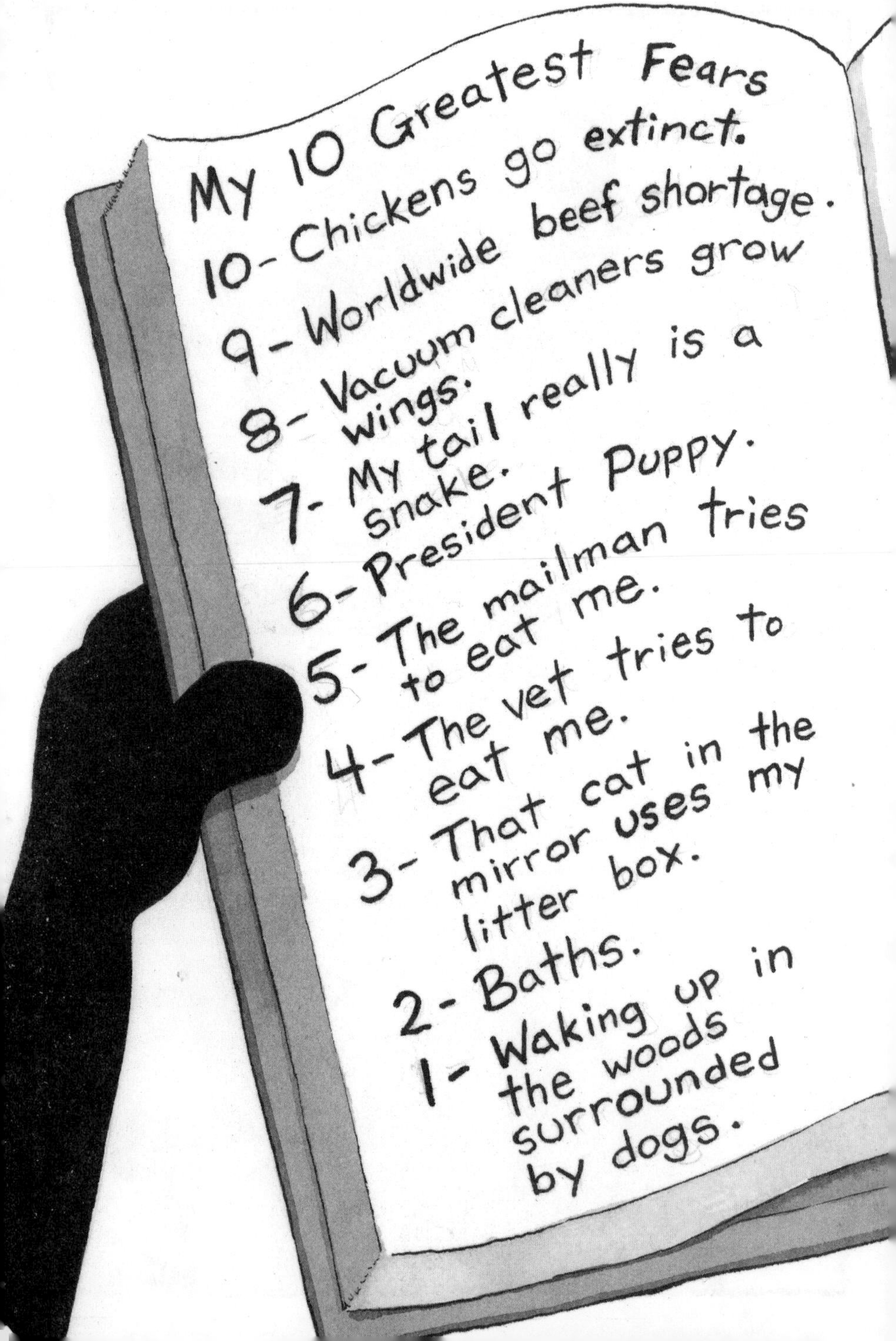
My 10 Greatest Fears
10- Chickens go extinct.
9- Worldwide beef shortage.
8- Vacuum cleaners grow wings.
7- My tail really is a snake.
6- President Puppy.
5- The mailman tries to eat me.
4- The vet tries to eat me.
3- That cat in the mirror uses my litter box.
2- Baths.
1- Waking up in the woods surrounded by dogs.

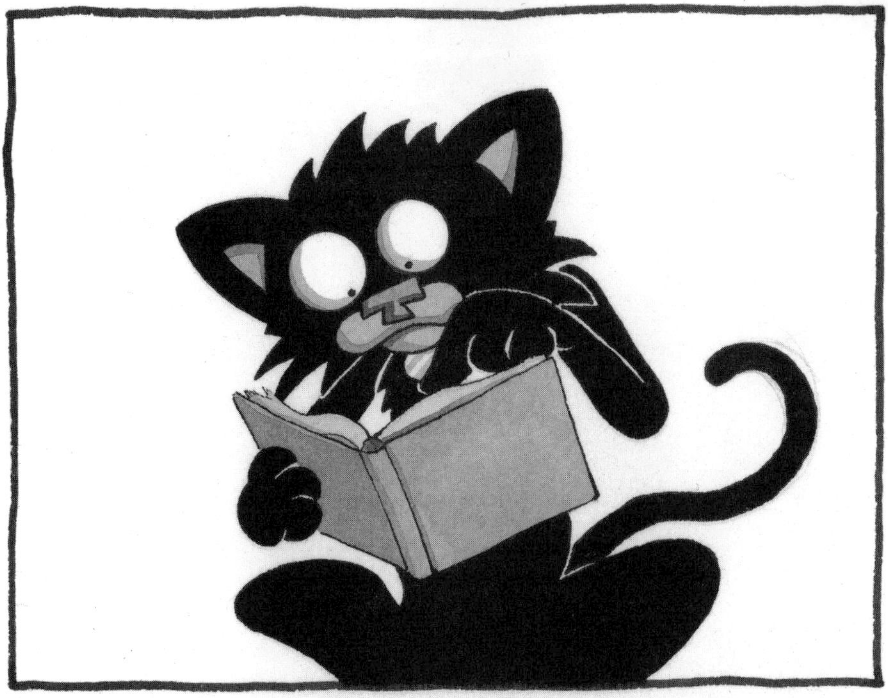

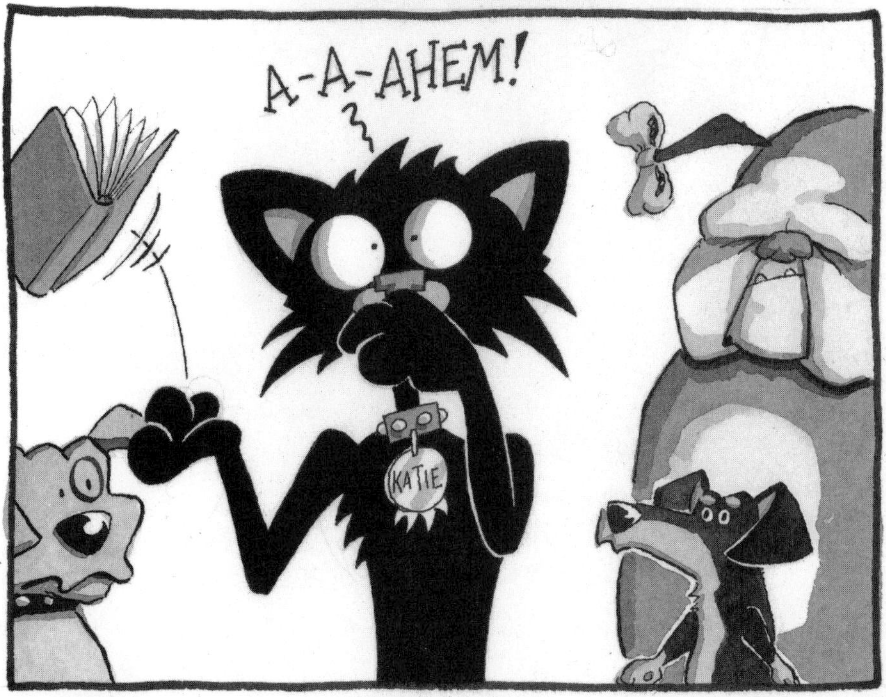
A-A-AHEM!
KATIE

UNCLE MURRAY'S FUN FACTS

This is really not a good time!

WHY DO CATS LIKE CATNIP?

Only about 50 percent of cats actually respond to catnip, but for those that do—watch out!

What is catnip?

Catnip is a type of mint that contains nepetalactone, a chemical which can have a powerful effect on cats.

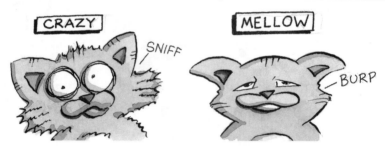

CRAZY
SNIFF
MELLOW
BURP

How do cats respond to it?

Cats can either sniff catnip or eat it. Cats who smell catnip have been known to roll in it, rub their faces in it, and can sometimes become very hyper and energetic. Interestingly, when a cat eats catnip, the opposite can happen: The cat can become very mellow and sleepy.

Why does this happen?

To be honest, even scientists don't know exactly why nepetalactone can have such a dramatic effect on a

cat's behavior. All they know is that this chemical can make a cat go bonkers for as little as ten minutes to as much as two hours. This chemical has even been known to affect big cats like leopards and tigers.

Does catnip affect dogs?
Dogs don't go crazy over the scent of catnip like cats do, but they will get sleepy if they eat it. Some people will put a few catnip leaves in a dog's water bowl to help it calm down.

Is there such a thing as "dognip"?
The smell of anise seed, the same herb that flavors licorice, can make some dogs go completely nuts in the same way catnip can affect cats. But you have to be careful. The ASPCA warns that too much anise can really bother a dog's stomach.

•CHAPTER EIGHT•

LOST

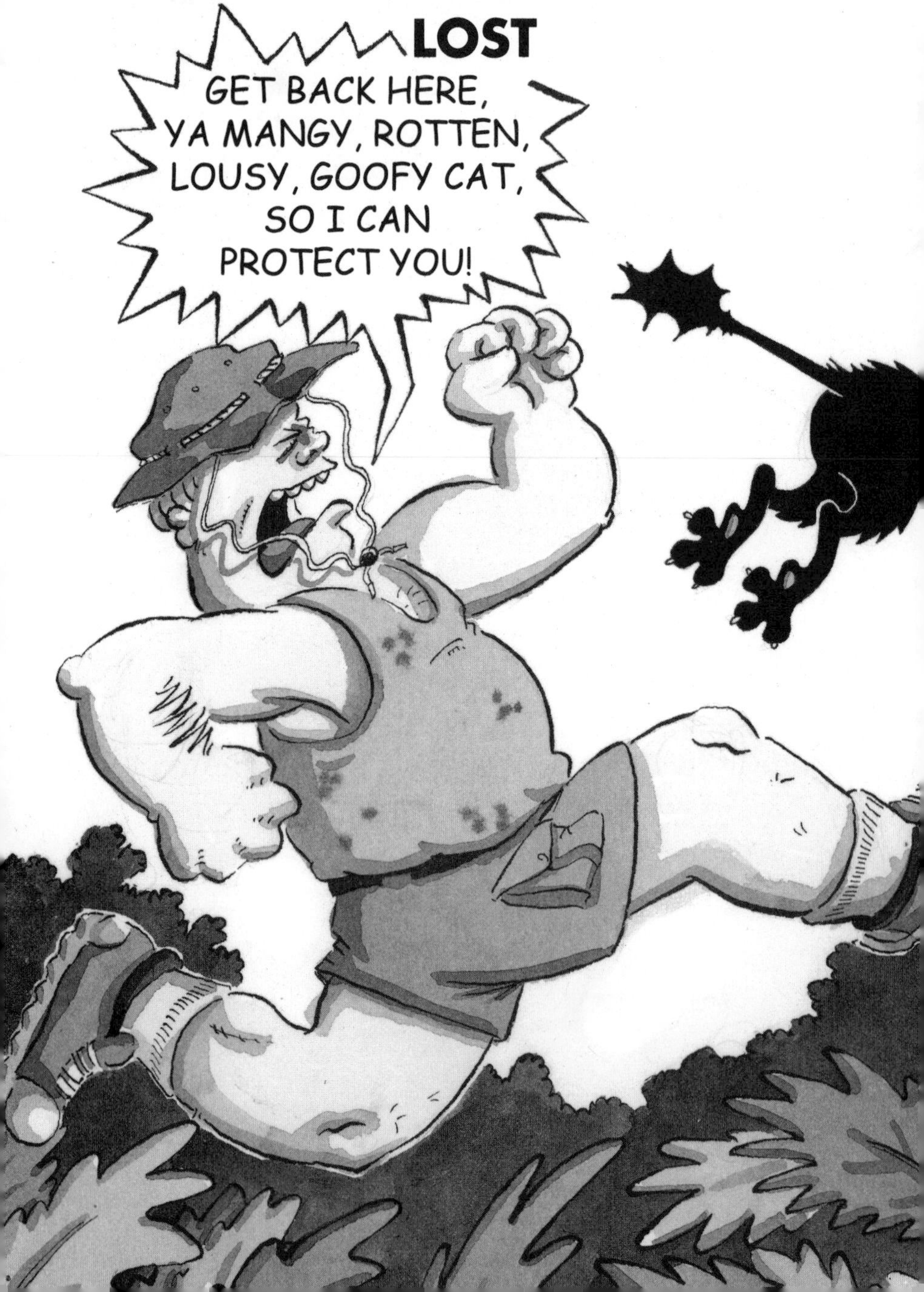
GET BACK HERE, YA MANGY, ROTTEN, LOUSY, GOOFY CAT, SO I CAN PROTECT YOU!

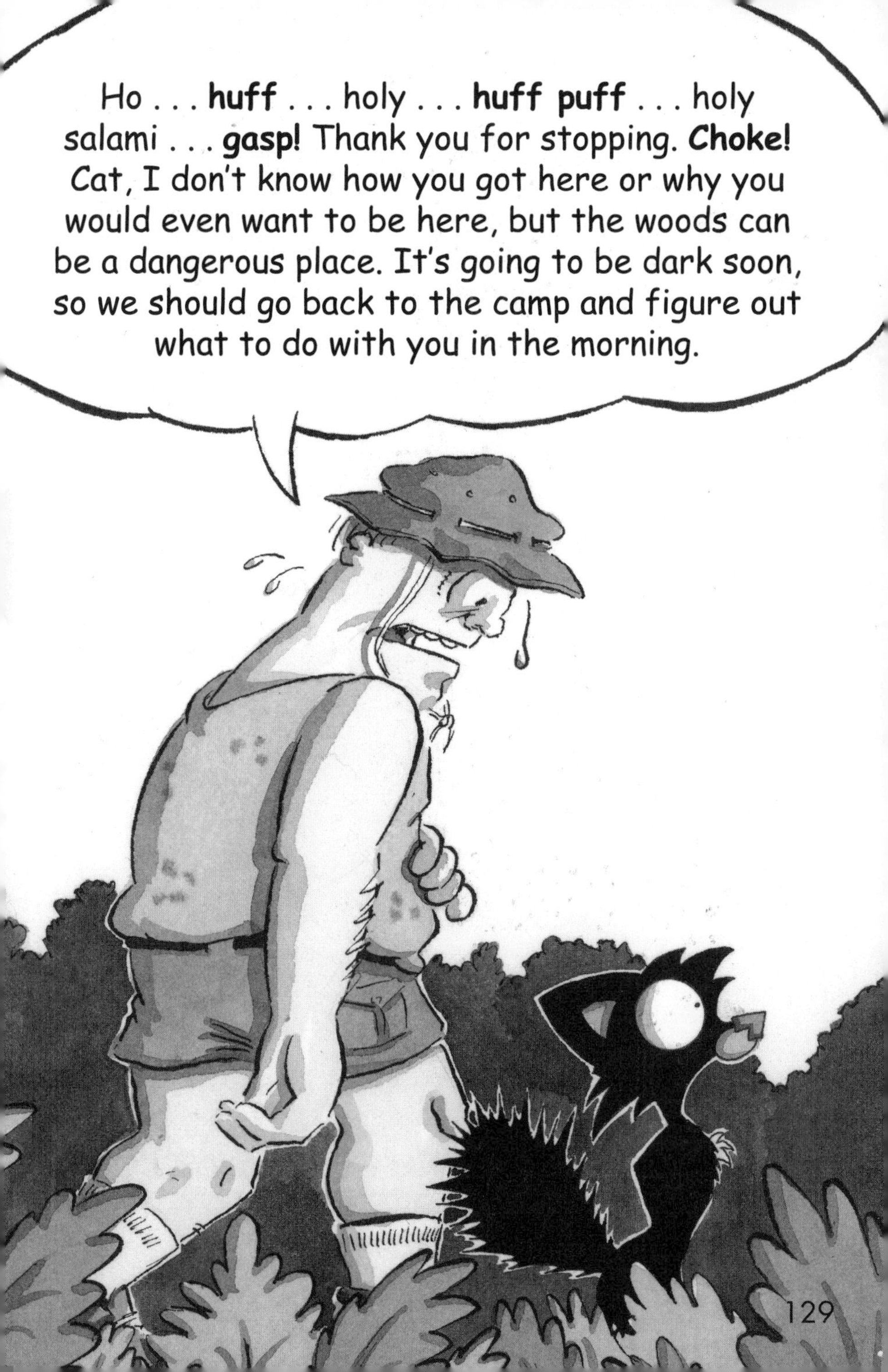
Ho . . . **huff** . . . holy . . . **huff puff** . . . holy salami . . . **gasp!** Thank you for stopping. **Choke!** Cat, I don't know how you got here or why you would even want to be here, but the woods can be a dangerous place. It's going to be dark soon, so we should go back to the camp and figure out what to do with you in the morning.

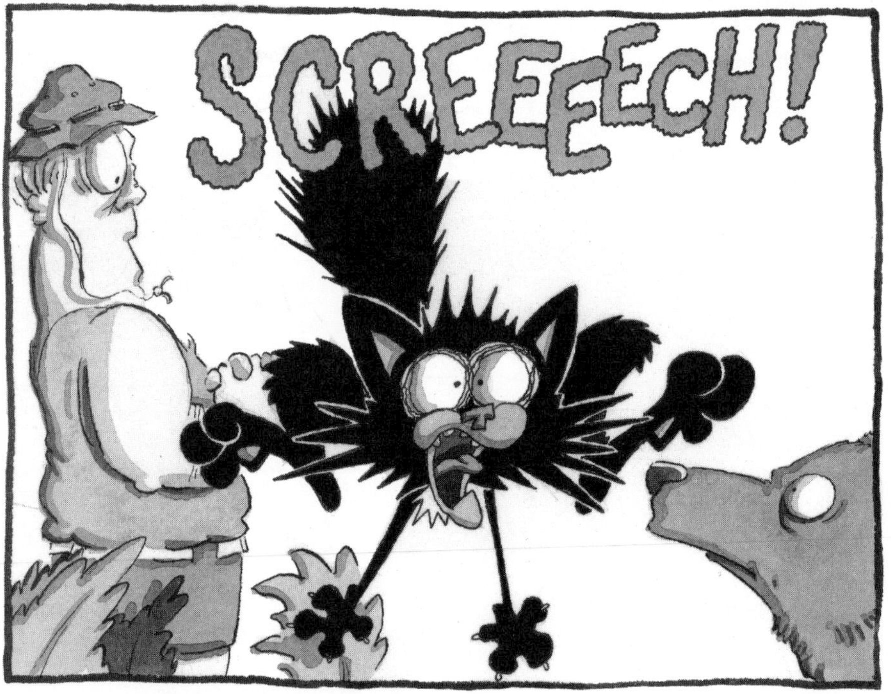
SCREEEECH!

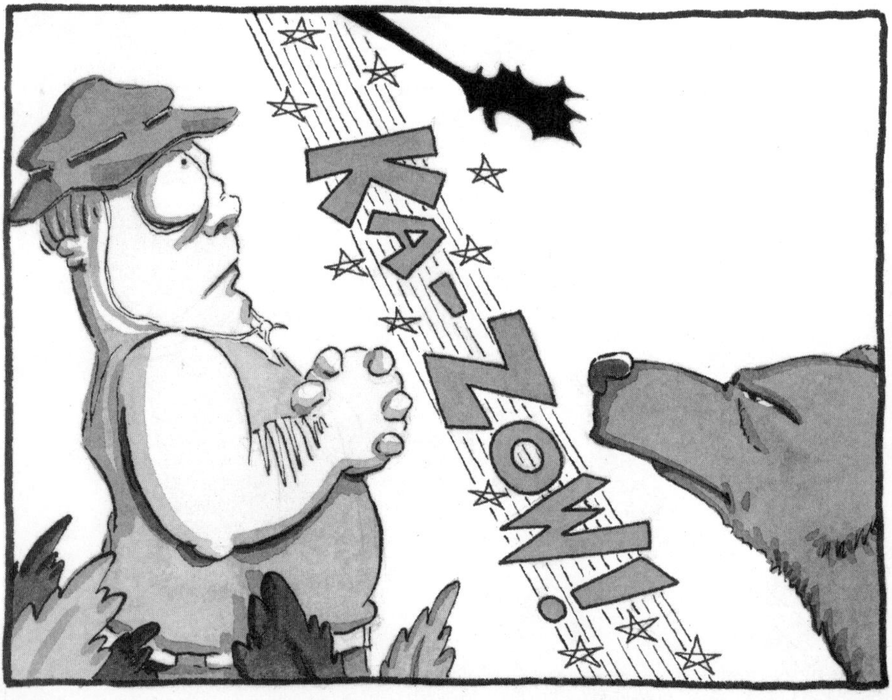
KA-ZOW!

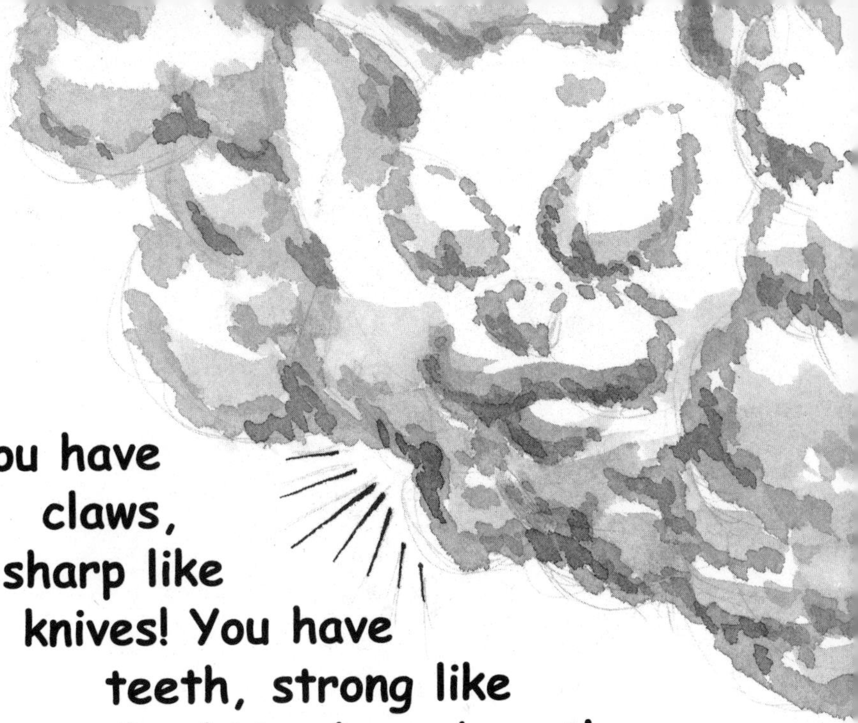

You have
claws,
sharp like
knives! You have
teeth, strong like
spikes! You have breath,
powerful like garlic left outside
on a hot day! No mere man can
frighten you! No mere
beast can defeat you!

Tell me who you are!

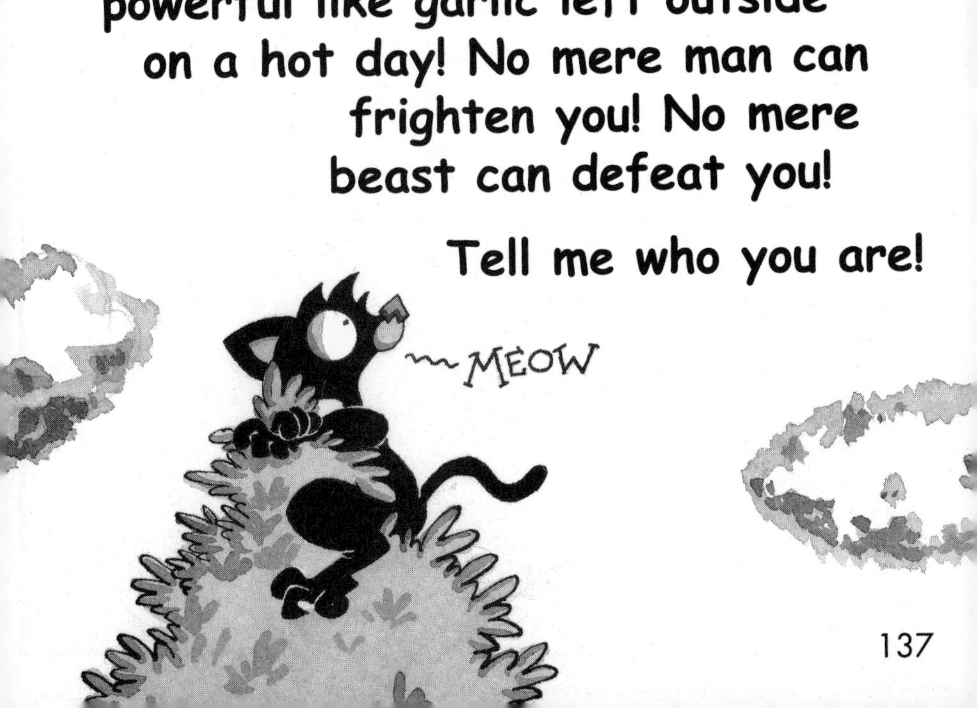
MEOW

MEANWHILE . . .

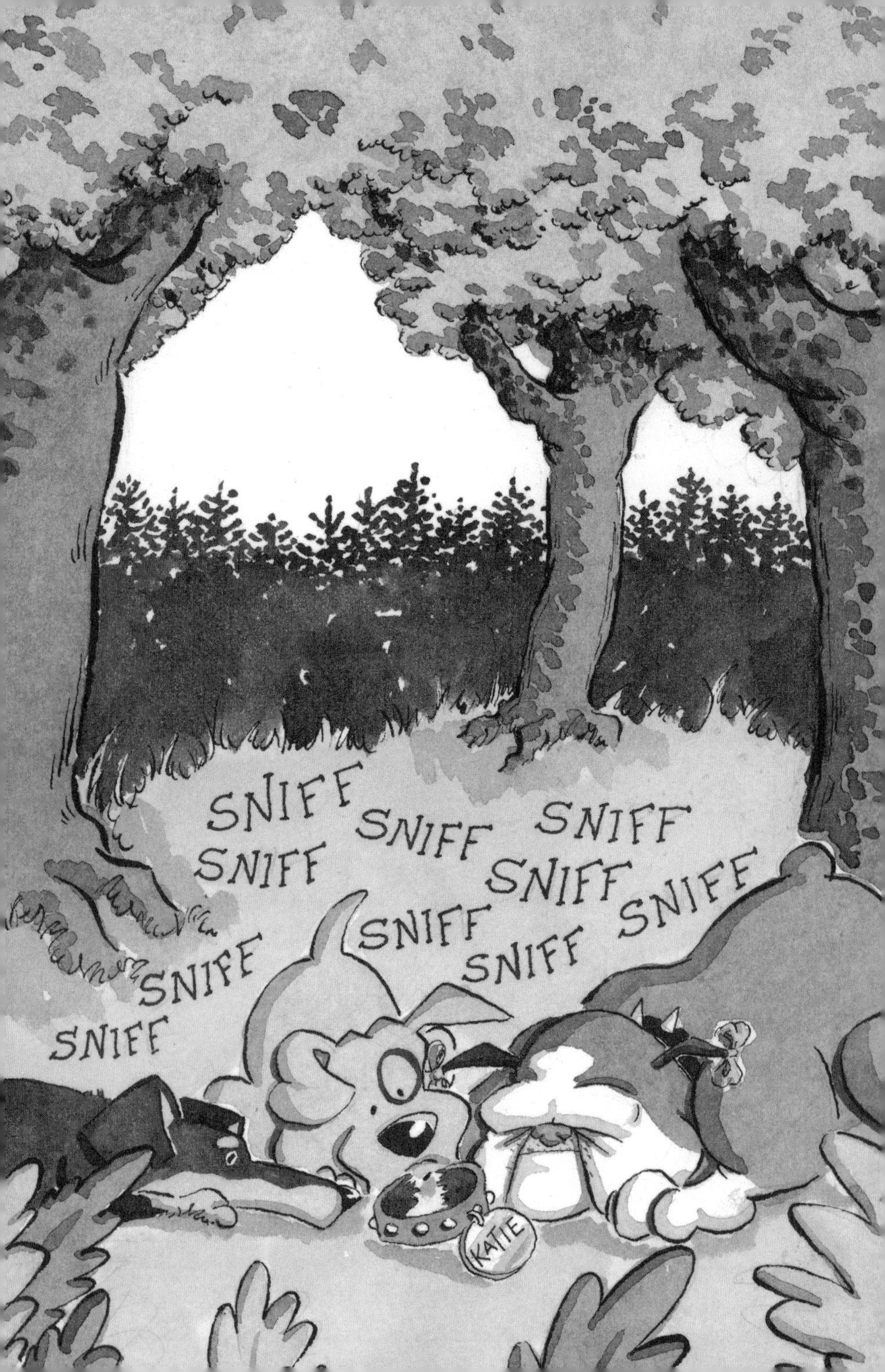
SNIFF
SNIFF
SNIFF
SNIFF
SNIFF
SNIFF
SNIFF
SNIFF
SNIFF
SNIFF
KATIE

•CHAPTER TEN•

REUNITED

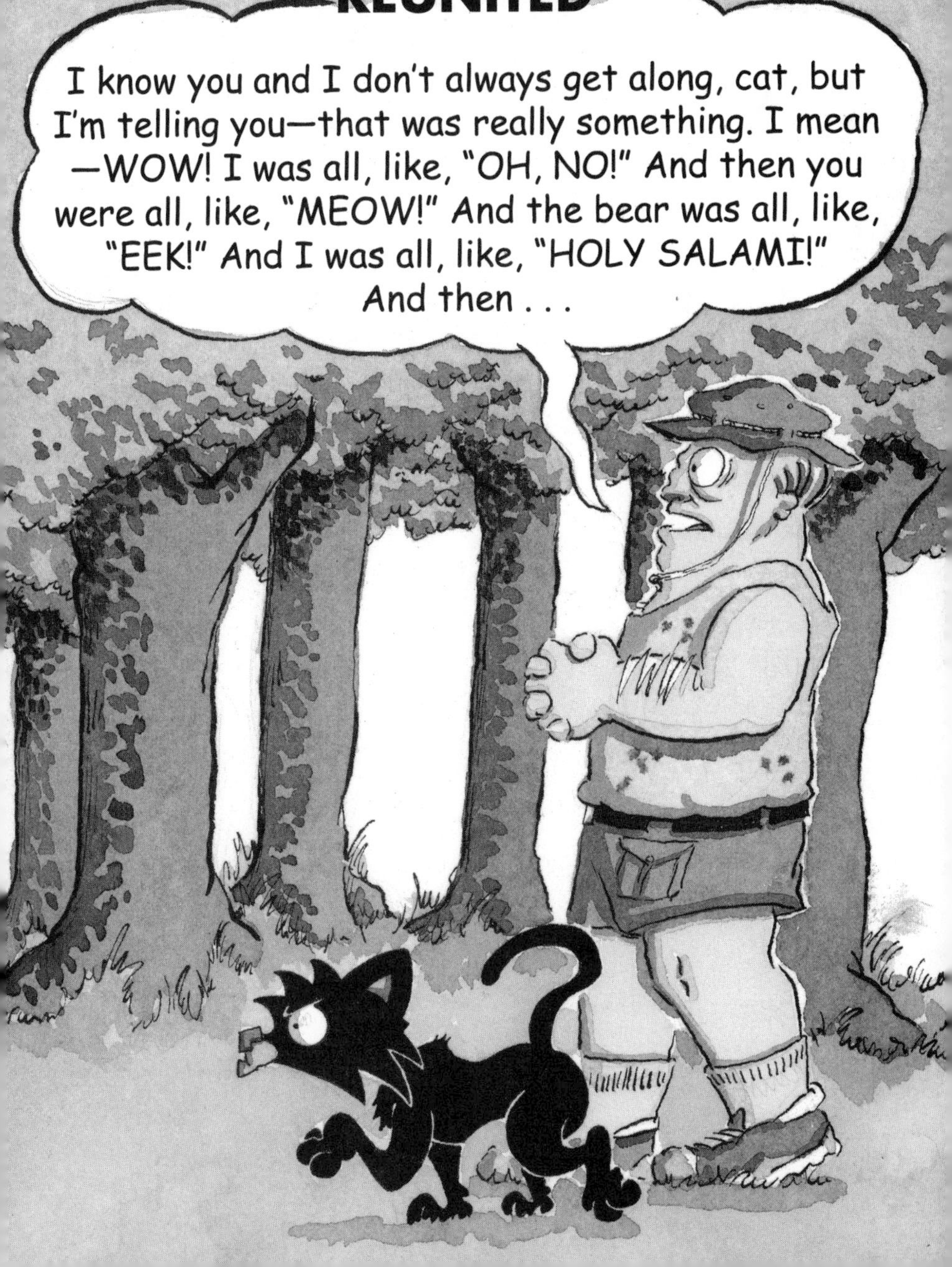

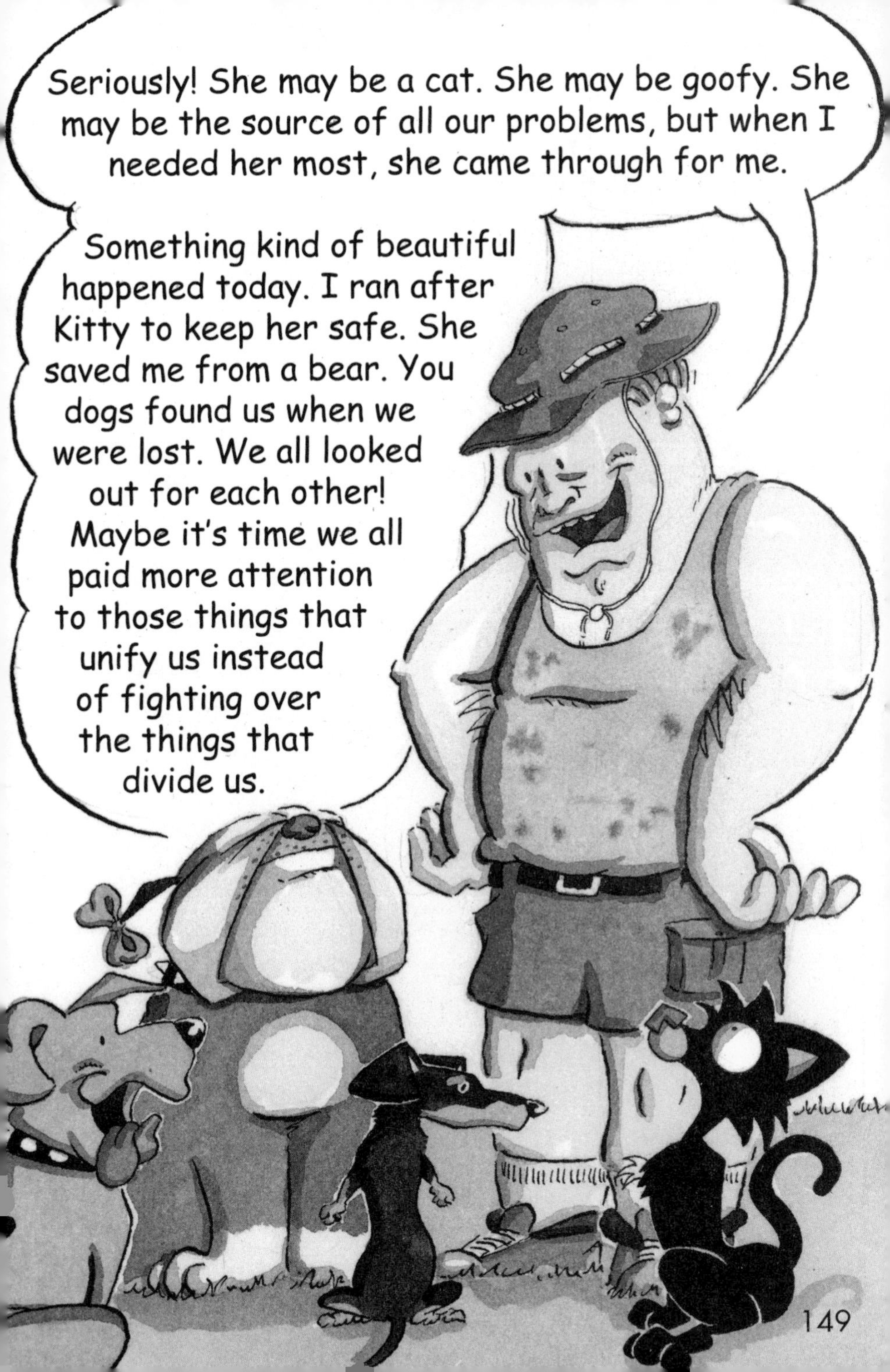
Seriously! She may be a cat. She may be goofy. She may be the source of all our problems, but when I needed her most, she came through for me.
Something kind of beautiful happened today. I ran after Kitty to keep her safe. She saved me from a bear. You dogs found us when we were lost. We all looked out for each other! Maybe it's time we all paid more attention to those things that unify us instead of fighting over the things that divide us.

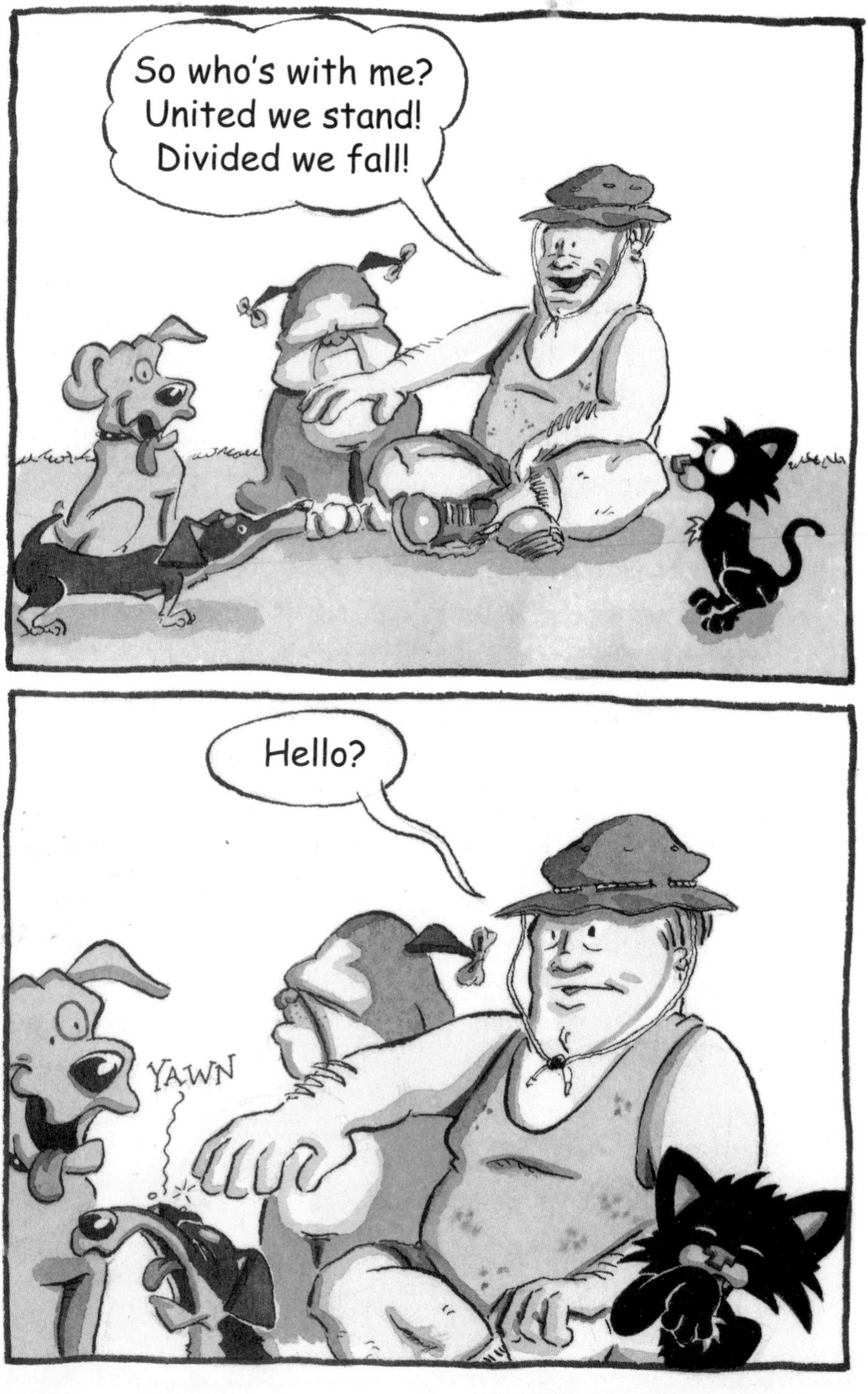
So who's with me? United we stand! Divided we fall!
Hello?
YAWN

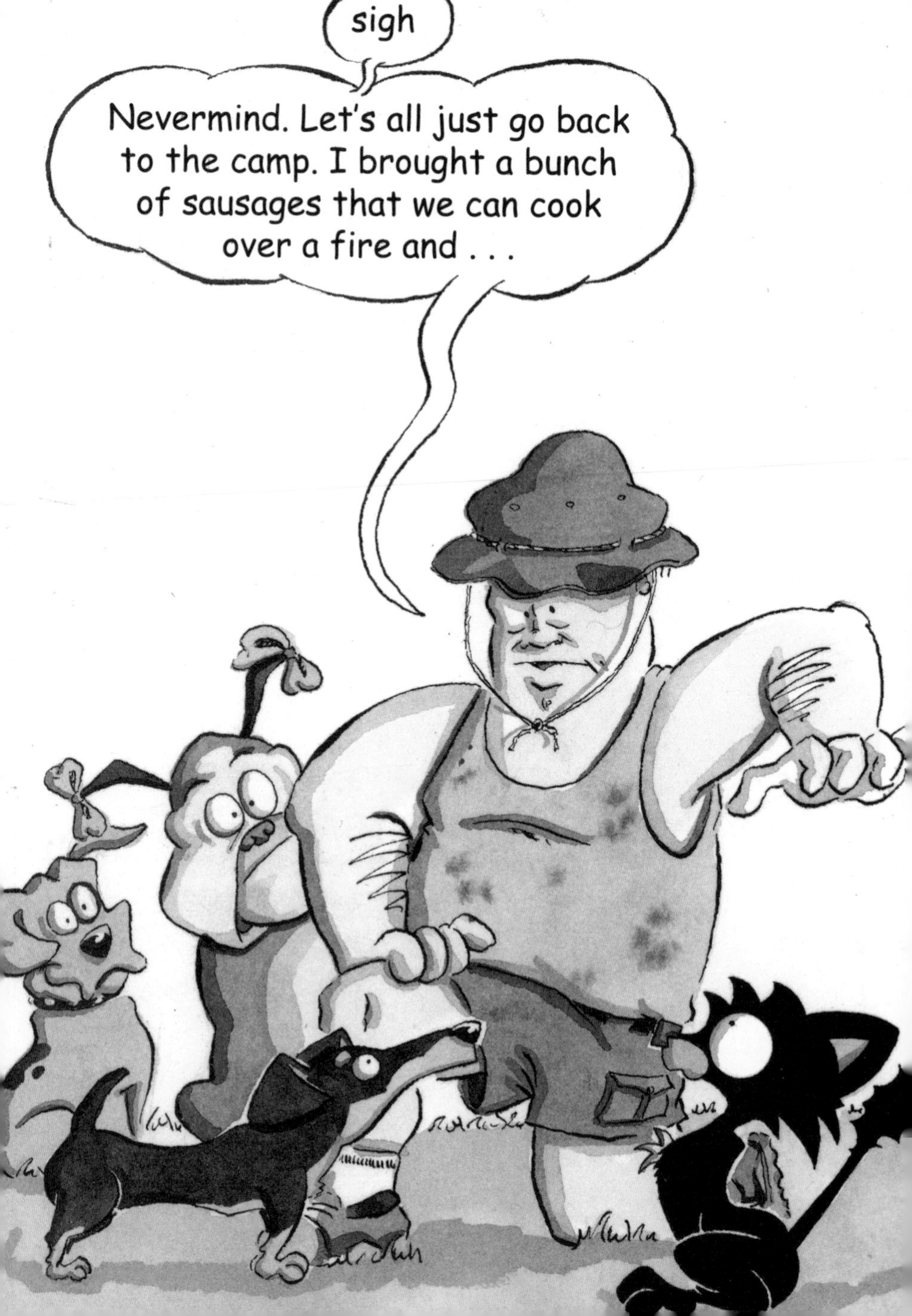
sigh
Nevermind. Let's all just go back to the camp. I brought a bunch of sausages that we can cook over a fire and . . .

•CHAPTER ELEVEN•

HOME AGAIN

WELCOME HOME, PUPPY!
It's great to see you. You look much more like your old self. I think that camp really helped.

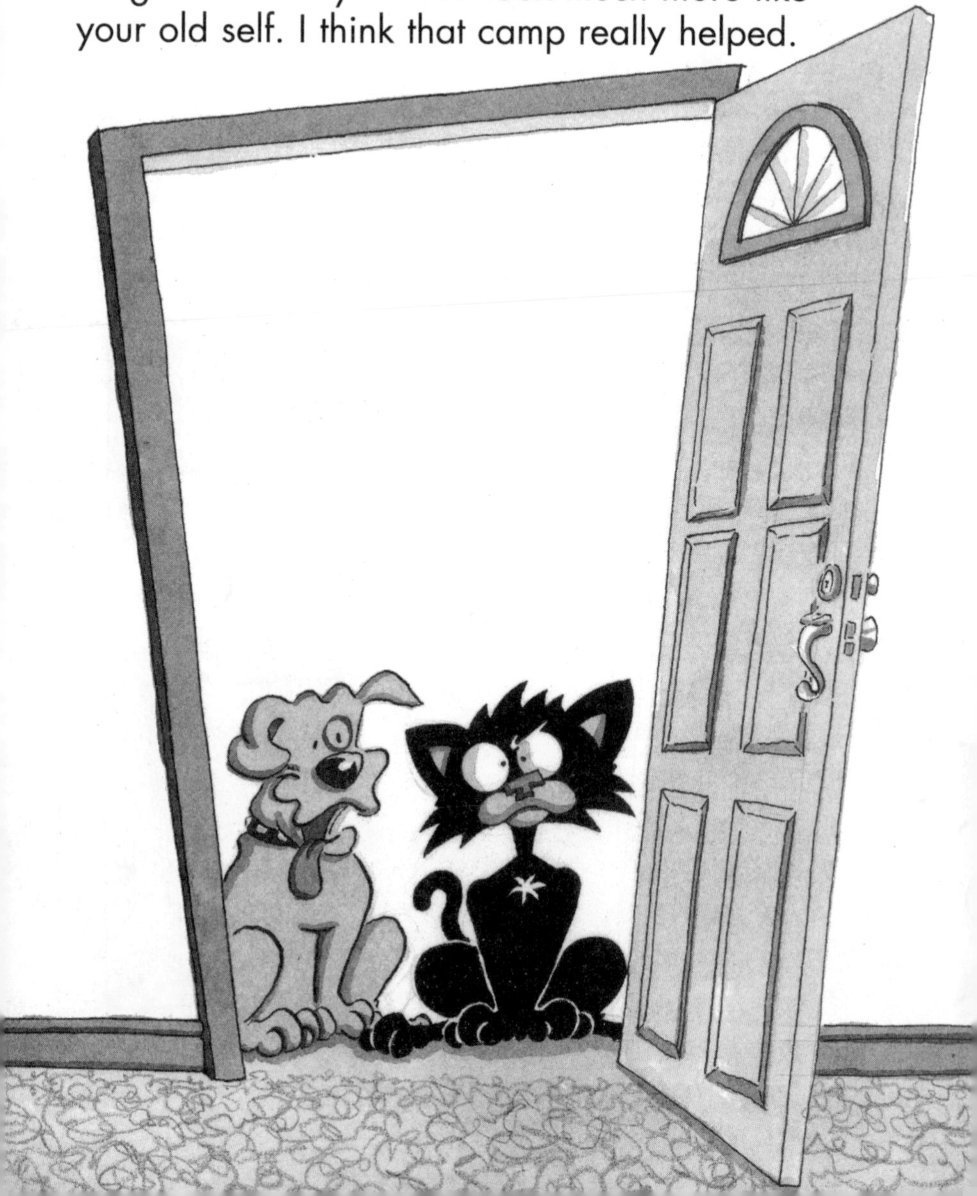

KITTY! Where have YOU been the past couple of days? Did you get lost? And what happened to your brand-new collar? Did you lose it already? Great. Oh well. I suppose it wasn't all that useful if you had it and STILL got lost.

The important thing is that you're both home safe and sound.

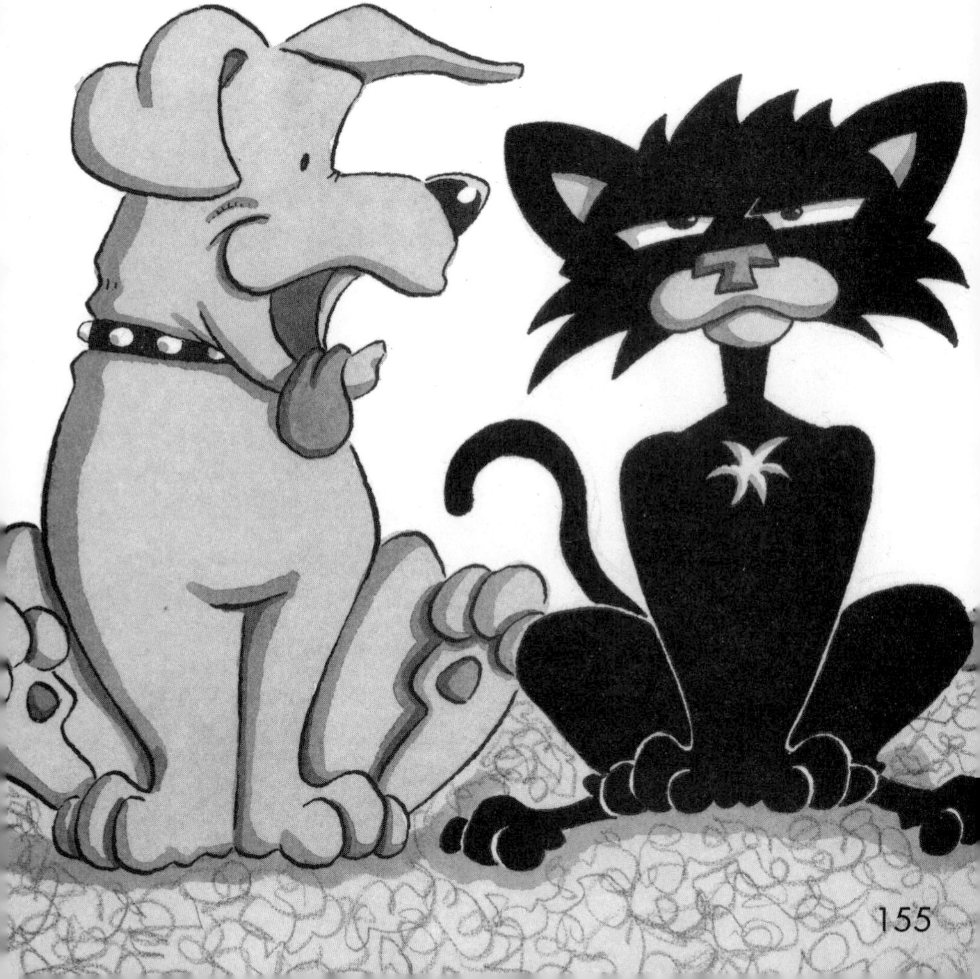

You guys look tired. Why don't you two go lie down and have a nice rest while I put together some food for you.

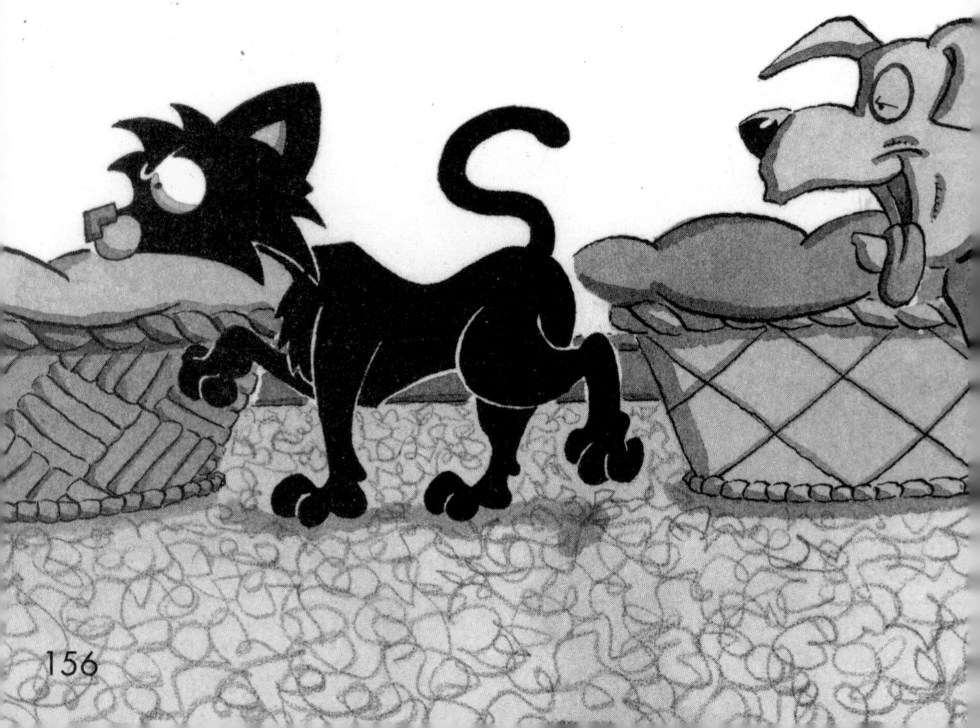

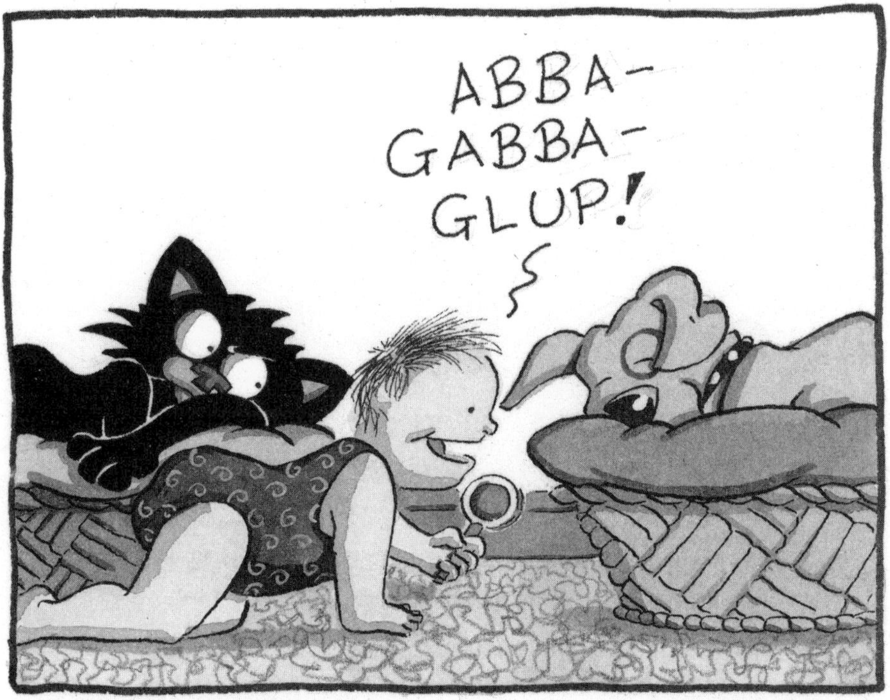
ABBA-
GABBA-
GLUP!

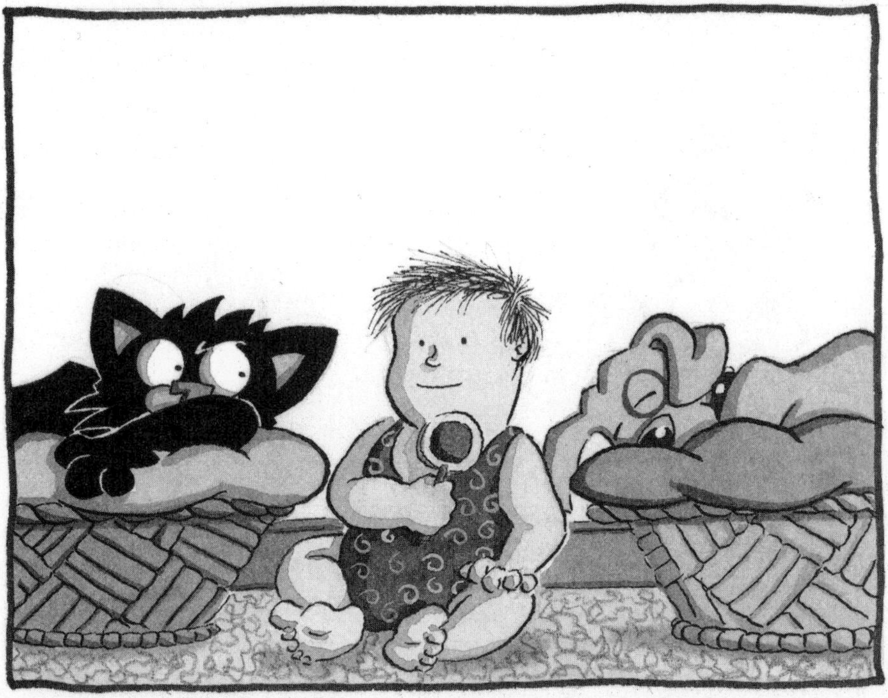

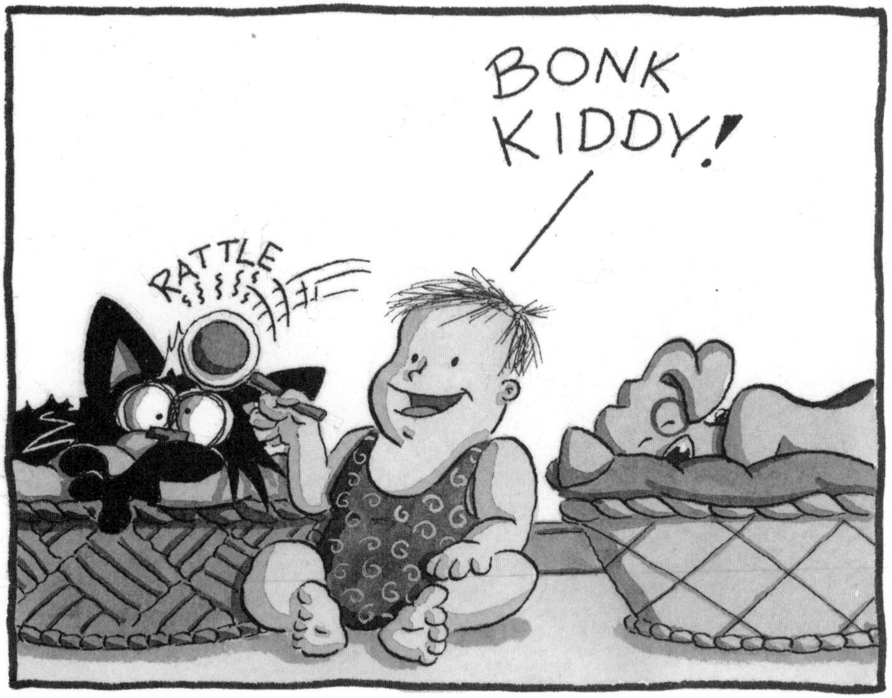
BONK KIDDY!
RATTLE

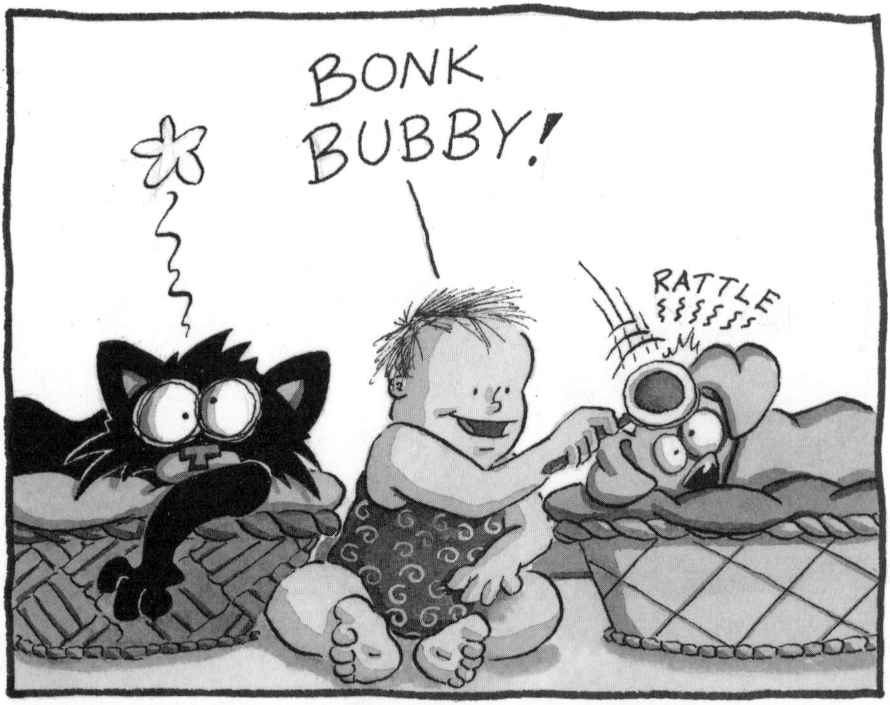
BONK BUBBY!
RATTLE

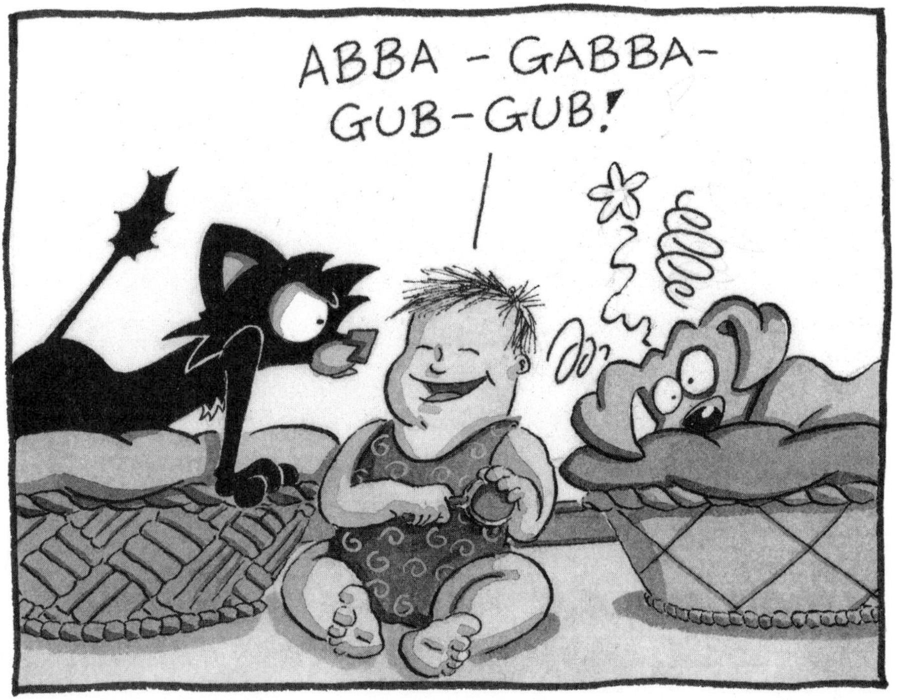
ABBA - GABBA-
GUB-GUB!

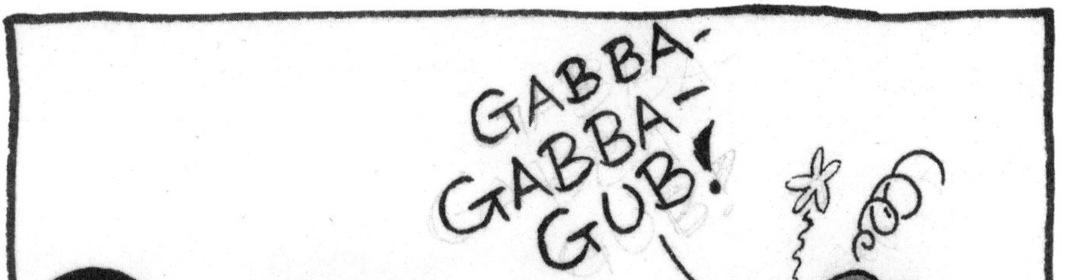
GABBA-
GABBA-
GUB!

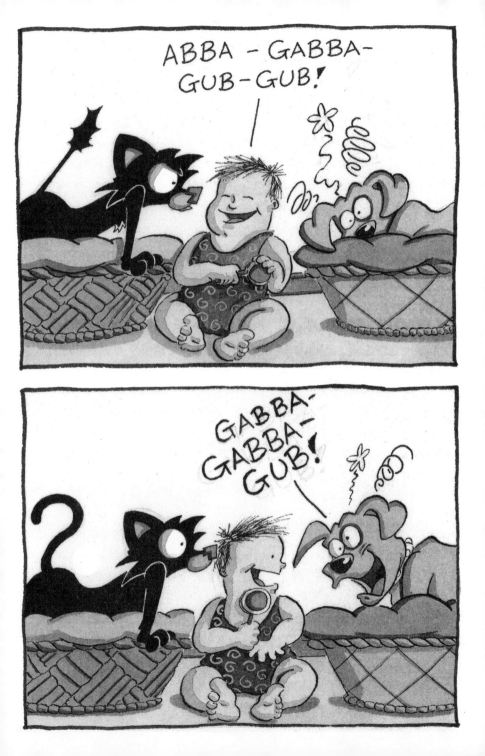